PRAISE FOR
RACHEL WEISS'S
GROUP CHAT

"*Rachel Weiss's Group Chat* hits the sweet spot of modernizing *Pride and Prejudice* in the vein of *Bridget Jones's Diary* and *Clueless*. Hilarious, charming, and as comforting as a warm hug, Appelbaum's debut proves she's a rising powerhouse in the world of contemporary romance."

—Sara Goodman Confino, bestselling author
of *Don't Forget to Write*

"It is a truth universally acknowledged that a book with such a sharp, witty heroine, a swoon-worthy love interest, and laugh-out-loud hijinks must not be missed. Watching Rachel Weiss figure her life out was an absolute delight. Reading this book felt like making a friend."   —Amanda Elliot, author of *Love You a Latke*

"Lauren Appelbaum's charming debut is a laugh-out-loud romp filled with all the best ingredients: sharply drawn female friendships, hilarious social observations, a reluctant appreciation for JDate, and a slow burn, opposites-attract romance between a lovably chaotic heroine and the tech bro next door. It's the perfect pick for readers who crave a good belly laugh with their romance."

—Lindsay Hammeroff, author of *Till There Was You*

"With Rachel Weiss (and her whole *mishpocha*), Appelbaum deftly tackles modern love, second coming-of-age, and zany family antics with heart, humor, and realness. This is a Saturn Return story you'll want to share with the entire group chat!"

—Courtney Preiss, author of *Welcome Home, Caroline Kline*

"With a refreshingly honest and unabashedly flawed protagonist and a hero who can give Mark Darcy a run for his money, *Rachel Weiss's Group Chat* gave me all the *Bridget Jones's Diary* vibes and had me snorting in laughter. A delight from start to finish."

—Meredith Schorr, author of *As Seen on TV*

RACHEL WEISS'S GROUP CHAT

LAUREN APPELBAUM

FOREVER

NEW YORK BOSTON

Forever
Hachette Book Group
1290 Avenue of the Americas, New York, NY 10104
read-forever.com
@readforeverpub

First Edition: September 2024

Forever is an imprint of Grand Central Publishing. The Forever name and logo are registered trademarks of Hachette Book Group, Inc.

The publisher is not responsible for websites (or their content) that are not owned by the publisher.

The Hachette Speakers Bureau provides a wide range of authors for speaking events. To find out more, go to hachettespeakersbureau.com or email HachetteSpeakers@hbgusa.com.

Forever books may be purchased in bulk for business, educational, or promotional use. For information, please contact your local bookseller or the Hachette Book Group Special Markets Department at special.markets@hbgusa.com.

Print book interior design by Marie Mundaca

Library of Congress Cataloging-in-Publication Data has been applied for.

ISBNs: 978-1-5387-5784-0 (trade paperback); 978-1-5387-5785-7 (ebook)

Printed in the United States of America

CW

10 9 8 7 6 5 4 3 2 1

To my daughter, Caroline. May your life be full of friendship, laughter, and library books.

RACHEL
WEISS'S
GROUP
CHAT

CHAPTER 1

"THE HOUSE NEXT DOOR finally sold!"

My mother was in a tizzy. No, tizzy was her normal state. She was in a state most mothers could achieve only by some combination of a Nordstrom liquidation sale and cocaine.

Head pounding, I squinted at my phone. My eyes were too bleary to make out the time, but I was pretty sure it started with a seven. Only my mother would think it appropriate to call at this hour on New Year's Day. Answering the phone: my first mistake of the new year. I blamed my hangover. A muffled groan of protest emanated from the man in my bed. And that man's name was…

It would come back to me.

I turned down my phone's volume and slipped quietly out of bed, planting my feet in my leopard-print slippers.

"Mom," I whispered as I tiptoed to the bathroom. "It's only seven—" But she was barreling on. Mom needed no back-and-forth in conversation; she simply needed a listener with a pulse.

"—thought surely they had priced it too high, but it was finally bought for three-point-five million dollars! By a young man!"

Good Lord, her voice was shrill. Was it normal to be so invested in neighborhood gossip? Somehow I thought not. And yet "normal" had never been a guiding factor in my mother's behavior.

I put the phone on the counter, not bothering to put her on speakerphone as I peed, flushed, and brushed my teeth. I splashed water on my face and rubbed at the black makeup smudged under my eyes. For half a second I considered putting on fresh makeup so I'd look a little more like I had last night when I'd brought home...what's-his-name. *I really thought it would come back to me.* But, on the whole, I couldn't be bothered.

Mom was still in full swing when I picked up the phone again.

"Mom, I have to go," I interrupted. "Sorry, but I was in the middle of something, and I—"

"Come over; we need to discuss this."

"Discuss...what?"

"The house! Next door!"

"You already told me. It sold." I paused, then added, "Yay?"

"There's more," she whispered, in what was clearly meant to be a compelling and mysterious voice.

"Um..." I had been looking forward to a day of rest. You know, a day when I ordered Mexican food, watched trash TV, and only left my couch for bathroom breaks.

"I'll make sandwiches."

"Done." *So what?* As an adult, I'd learned never to say no to food prepared by somebody other than myself.

After hanging up, I crawled back into bed next to the snoring hottie and checked the group chat. All was quiet. Amy, Eva, and Sumira were probably still asleep like normal people with normal mothers. We'd gone hard at our college friend Davis's party the night before. But hey, it was the last New Year of our twenties. We were turning thirty this year. We deserved to go big.

There was no chance of me falling back asleep now, so I opened my Notes app to write some New Year's resolutions. Ten minutes later, I read through my list:

- Smoke one bowl a day or less.
- Ditto coffee: one cup a day.
- Dress for my age. Show less cleavage and midriff. Not saying I need to don linen slacks and sweater sets—*what is a sweater set?*—but I can class it up a little.
- Learn what a sweater set is.
- Try new forms of exercise.
- Be nicer to Mom.
- Be nicer to the nerds at work.
- Finally try Jdate. (Break it to Mom gently so she doesn't expire of happiness on the spot.)
- Comport myself with dignity befitting a woman of my age. For example, starting a conga line while wearing Davis's assless chaps over my jeans with my bra as a hat WILL NOT happen again after last night.
- Oh yeah, DRINK LESS.

It was a good list. Admirable, really. I read through it once more, and then, with a quick flick of my thumb, deleted it. Who was I to try to fix what was already perfect?

The man was now snoring, so I hopped out of bed and began to get dressed. I didn't exactly slam my dresser drawers, but I also didn't try too hard to be quiet—rather hoping he would wake up. I pulled a chunky sweater over my head and watched him for any sign of wakefulness, but he was out cold.

Should I poke him?

I felt bad about the whole not-knowing-his-name thing on top of my desire for him to leave my apartment as soon as possible. Maybe breakfast in bed would soften the blow.

I rummaged around in my fridge and the tiny cabinet that served as my pantry. A trip to Trader Joe's was overdue, to put it mildly. There was nothing here that I could possibly serve to a guest, let alone an attractive half-naked man. Bread: stale. Eggs: nonexistent. Yogurt: mold city. I gagged slightly as I shoved it back in my fridge to deal with later. I really needed to stop buying the family-size tub of yogurt.

Well, at least I had coffee.

A few minutes later, I'd scrounged together something resembling breakfast on a tray.

"Good morning," I said sweetly as I crept back into my room.

He propped himself up on one elbow and gave me a lopsided grin. He had tousled, curly hair and brown skin smattered with freckles. I mentally patted Last Night Rachel on the back. *Nice one.*

"You made breakfast?" His voice was croaky, and slightly awed.

"I did." I slid the tray onto his lap with the coffee facing him. It was the most respectable part of the spread, with a little bowl of sugar and cup of cream next to the steaming mug. His eyes roved over this while he wore a look of amused pleasure on his face. And then he took in the rest of it.

"Is that…ice cream?"

"Yes." I began pointing to the other dishes. "And string cheese. And a pickle!"

He made a face that I couldn't decipher one way or the other and then dug the spoon into the ice cream and took a bite.

I perched on the side of the bed.

"Listen…," I began. He raised an eyebrow.

"Sam," he added, his tone flat.

"Sam," I repeated, a beat too late. *Smooth, Rachel.* I should have made him waffles, poor guy. "I have to head out soon. It was really fun hanging out with you."

"Oh, okay." He looked like he wanted to linger over the coffee, so I busied myself tossing things in my purse.

Ten minutes later, I shouted a cheerful goodbye down the hall of my apartment complex as Sam departed. *Note to self: stop letting the guy sleep over.* The next morning was always so awkward.

Around lunchtime, I arrived at my parents' house and eagerly searched the kitchen for the promised sandwiches. They were in the fridge, piled on a plate wrapped tightly with plastic wrap. I selected a cream cheese and lox one and munched on it as I observed the present state of chaos in the house. My twin sisters were wailing like sixteen-year-old toddlers, Dad was darting about with our older sister on speakerphone trying to calm them, and Mom was nowhere to be found. Apparently the twins had been under the impression that Dad would take them to get their driver's licenses today—the concept of national holidays having never crossed their self-obsessed minds. They believed that since they had been promised their licenses this year, they'd be able to waltz into the licensing office on January first. Jane tried her best eldest-sister peacekeeping over the phone but had the good sense to stay snug in her condo with her cat.

After enduring a good fifteen minutes of screeching, I found Mom tucked up in bed, happy as a clam, with her phone pressed to her ear. She talked for so long and in so much detail about people I'd never heard of, I thought I was losing it and perhaps Mom had a secret family. Finally she put the phone down and pulled the blanket up to her chin. "That was Pamela."

"Who?" Perhaps it came out a touch aggressive.

"The Realtor, darling, the Realtor."

"What Realtor? You're not selling—?"

"No, no, of course not." She patted her curls, which were piled decadently atop her head, and plucked a silver-backed mirror from her nightstand to examine them. "Pamela sold the house next door, silly. We were just discussing the Butkuses."

"The who?" I was sure there was some elaborate joke being played on me. Butkus, I ask you.

"The couple moving in! Oh, come here." Mom patted the bed beside her and held out the edge of her chenille coverlet. With a fair amount of grumbling, I climbed into bed and sat back against the Mount Rainier of throw pillows. "Speak up, speak up, don't grumble."

"The Butkuses?"

"Yes. Ooh." She fluttered her eyelids with relish, as though she had a steaming vat of gossip tea, as the twins would phrase it. *I think. I can never quite grasp their teen talk.* "Ooh, wait till you hear."

"Go ahead, then."

She took a deep breath, then held up one finger and rummaged in her nightstand drawer, from which she extracted a long box of Fran's Chocolates. She was like Mary Poppins—always pulling things out of that bottomless nightstand. She handed me a sea salt caramel and popped one in her own mouth, then continued.

"The Butkuses are a lovely couple about our age. Teachers nearing retirement."

"Teachers?" Confused, I glanced through the curtains, where the edge of the house next door was just visible. It was a sort of nautical, white-brick, Cape Cod house with forest-green shutters and about four thousand square feet—and again, $3.5 million. Sure, back in the 1980s a man like my dad could buy a house in Madison Park on one salary. But oh, how times had changed. Now

RACHEL WEISS'S GROUP CHAT

a couple of hardworking teachers could barely afford a house out in Bothell, let alone this neighborhood.

Mom's eyes positively gleamed. She clasped her hands under her chin. "Their son, Christopher Butkus, thirty-two, bought it for them. And darling..." She was practically weeping with joy. "He's *single*."

"Ah." I made a play for time and reached for another caramel. "And what exactly does Christopher Butkus, thirty-two, do for a living that enables him to buy three-point-five-million-dollar houses for his parents?"

I knew what she was going to say. I knew it. You knew it. Davis's assless chaps knew it.

"Some sort of tech start-up. It's been rather successful." *Of course.*

"Hmm."

"They move in on Monday, darling. I'll invite them all over for a dinner party. You know what you should wear, that green wrap dress from Nordstrom. It sets off your figure, shows a bit of leg. You hear people say, choose whether to show leg or cleavage, but I can't understand why. What's the point of keeping your cards hidden if you've got a winning hand? When I first met your father, I was wearing—"

"Mom!"

She giggled. "Well, anyway, I know you'll look gorgeous. So we should do a Google for Christopher Butkus and see what comes up. I wonder if he's tall."

"Mom," I sputtered through a mouthful of caramel. I considered my words carefully. Telling my mother she was getting ahead of herself was a sure way to get her to speed ahead like a curly-haired bowling ball. I opted for a change of subject. "Do you want to hear my New Year's resolution?"

Clearly I would say anything to shut her up. I took a deep, excited breath and looked her in the eyes. "I'm going to try Jdate."

She let out a bloodcurdling wail—you see where the twins learned it—and flung the box of caramels against the wall. I stared, slack-jawed and glassy-eyed. This did not seem like a cry of delight. Surely this was the same woman who had begged me for the last two and a half years to try something, anything, to find a nice Jewish boy? Had I entered an alternate reality? I pinched myself, then pinched Mom. She screamed louder.

"I thought you'd be happy!"

She shook her head frantically, fluttering her hands in distress as she cried. Finally she raised a trembling finger in the direction of the window. "B-B-B-Butkus!"

"What?" I jumped out of bed. "You want me to give up meeting new people in the hopes that I'll end up with this rich nerd?"

She stopped crying at once, a glowing smile on her face as she nodded.

"No!" I shrieked. "I don't like tech bros, especially ones like him. You know I have to put up with them at work. All they care about is money and algorithms. It's so dull. I can't stand to talk to one for more than thirty seconds. They're all greedy capitalists who couldn't flirt their way out of a North Face jacket. They want robots to take over the world while they relocate their rich-boy club to outer space, where there's plenty of virgin territory for them to pillage and destroy! Meanwhile us mere mortals try to save the dying planet that they ruined with their—"

"Shut up, SHUT UP!" Mom sank back and smashed a pillow against her face. "You're so pretty, Rachel; why can't you be more like Jane? Polite and *quiet*. Jane is going to end up married while you're scaring men off with your politics. Not everything in this world is an apocalyptic corporate conspiracy!"

I pouted for a moment. "I don't want to meet Christopher Butkus."

"Well, I don't want to talk to you anymore. Send your father up."

I turned to leave, hesitated, then scooped up the sea salt caramels from the carpet and put them in my pocket.

I found Dad cowering in the kitchen pantry. He pretended to be searching for something when I opened the door, but I caught him hurriedly stuffing a bookmark into the novel he'd been reading.

"How are the twins?" I asked.

"Fine, fine. I told them I'd take them to Sephora, so."

I cringed. "Did you give them a spending limit?"

"No...I didn't think that would be wise..." He gazed through smudged glasses at the back corner of the pantry, no doubt reliving the trauma of the last hour. I chose not to warn him that he would soon be parted from three or four hundred dollars.

"Mom wants to see you. I'm off."

He nodded, gave me a peck on the head, and left me in the pantry. I saw the appeal at once: it was dark and quiet and smelled like food. I sat on the floor with my back against some cereal boxes, ate my pocket caramels, and plotted out my Jdate profile in my head.

I spent the rest of the day at Jane's, complaining to her while Owen cooked us dinner. I hoped Mom was right about Jane marrying Owen soon. And I did wish I were more like Jane: successful, calm, loved. Probably never worn a bra as a hat in her life.

I shrugged off that train of thought. I learned long ago not to compare myself with my older sister—we're so different. Anyway, I had it all figured out now: I just needed to find a boyfriend immediately so Mom would leave me alone about Christopher Butkus.

CHAPTER 2

JANUARY IS LIKE THE Monday of the year. Time stretches ahead of you with few holidays in sight, only dreary weather as far as the eye can see. Today was one of those Mondays that make you wonder: Is this it? Is this adulthood? My coworkers were all in a postholiday slump, so there was no good gossip to be had. All I had to occupy my brain was actual work—gag.

Working in technical support, you learn quickly that every customer thinks their problem is the most important problem in the world. And there was no shortage of problems today; it was like they'd been hoarding their issues over the holidays. The number of people who'd forgotten their passwords...I slurped my iced coffee and grumbled to myself as I typed off answers to customer tickets.

Eva and Amy were lucky they didn't have to deal with moronic customers. Eva spent her days taking graduate classes at UW for her library science degree. And Amy taught math to gifted students. Although, come to think of it, Eva also worked at a coffee shop to pay the bills. And on second thought, sophomore algebra students couldn't be much fun to teach, based on the way I behaved at fifteen. Sumira, poor thing, was required to take clients out to all kinds of dinners and happy hours. At least my customers were all virtual. Imagine having to watch across the table as a middle-aged client picks his teeth and flicks his eyes across the waitress's bottom. Sumira took it all in stride, though—nothing fazed her.

My phone buzzed. Speak of the gorgeous devil.

Sumira Khan 10:27 AM:
Does anyone want to come to my office postholiday party? It's Friday night. Dress up, get free food and drinks. Should be fun.

Eva Galvez 10:28 AM:
I have a date on Friday. That girl Jennifer from class.

Amy McDonald 10:30 AM:
I'm plotting a date with Ryan.

Eva Galvez 10:31 AM:
Plotting?

Amy McDonald 10:31 AM:
Don't ask.

Sumira Khan 10:32 AM:
Rachel?

Rachel Weiss 10:38 AM:
Yes! I love holiday parties
after the holidays are over.
Let the merriment continue!

With a party for me to look forward to, my mood had considerably improved by the time the day's creepy corporate question popped up on my screen. "How often does your daily work embody the phrase: 'live large, learn lots'?" Honestly, who came up with these? You had to answer the daily questions, otherwise it got marked in your file that you didn't participate in company culture. But the answers were all anonymous, so I made it fun for my own entertainment. Today I typed, "N/A. Prefer to live small and learn as little as possible."

Having accomplished a reasonable day's work before lunch, I rewarded myself by scrolling through predictions for that night's episode of *The Bachelor*. Jane and the girls were coming over to collectively swoon over Jeremy Coltrain, the hottest bachelor in history. I'd learned early in my career never to put in too much effort at work, so my employer's expectations would never get too high. It had served me well so far. I'd never been classified as an overachiever, and I always managed to scrape enough money together to pay my bills. Most of the time, anyway.

By the time Friday rolled around, I was so ready for Sumira's party. The great thing about Sumira being a fancy account executive was all the beautiful people she worked with. It was clearly a company requirement to be drop-dead gorgeous—that couldn't be legal, could it? Anyway, this party was step one in Operation Never Butkus, and I was prepared. So far I had shaved everything, exfoliated everything, done a moisturizing sheet mask, painted my nails, and whitened my teeth. I just needed to get my eyebrows waxed before the party.

I FaceTimed the girls. "Do my nails look okay?"

"What did you do?" Eva appeared to be hunched over the desk in her bedroom.

"It was just a bit tricky holding the nail polish brush steady. I had about six coffees today."

"Six?!"

"I was nervous about the party."

"And I'm sure twelve hundred milligrams of caffeine helped calm you down."

"I feel fine."

"Rachel, what about Jdate?" Amy stirred something in a Le Creuset pot. "I thought that was your plan."

"Yes, it is." I adjusted my fishnets. "But I have to take every opportunity I get, don't I? Life doesn't just throw eligible men in one's path. This is my year of yes. Yes to Jdate, yes to parties, yes to beautiful men knocking down my door."

"I see."

"Who knows, I might even be joining you in Married Town before too long."

Amy snorted bitterly.

"What?"

"Oh, nothing. I'll tell you later. Ryan just got home."

"I have to go too." Sumira's heels were clacking in an echoey parking garage. "I'll pick you up at seven thirty, Rach."

"Perf. Time to get my eyebrows waxed. There's a new place around the corner from my apartment with good prices."

"Have fun tonight," Eva said. "I'm taking Jennifer to the Comedy Underground."

"Good luck! Hope it goes well."

At seven thirty, I examined myself in the mirror one last time. I'd chosen my green wrap dress. Mom had pointed out that it was quite flattering on me, and she was right. Excellent cleavage. If I was trying to meet men that night, there really was no point in hiding the girls away. I turned to examine my derriere in the mirror.

It was also VERY short.

I'd put on some black fishnets to make it a little more modest. Bonus: the fishnets looked excellent with my black velvet block heels.

My eyebrows were still a bit red, but they would be fine shortly.

They were not fine. THEY WERE NOT FINE. Sumira took one look at me and marched me back upstairs to my apartment.

"Ice them." She touched my brow bone gingerly.

"It burns!" I moaned while she taped an ice pack to my head.

"Just give it a second."

"My brain is frozen. My eyebrow makeup is running into my eyes."

Sumira gave me a look and then noticed my nail polish.

"Come here." Ten minutes later she had fixed my manicure

and my makeup. "You look great." She looked in the mirror over my shoulder. Not only were my eyebrows still inflamed, but my entire head was now red from the ice pack. Still, the outfit was working for me. Operation Never Butkus was back on track.

When we arrived, the party was in full flow. It was at the Seattle Art Museum, so there were these very sophisticated— *I think*—sculptures hanging from the ceiling and very artistic (read: flattering) lighting. There was a DJ on one side and a huge table of food and an open bar on the other.

We went straight for the bar, because duh, and on the way I grabbed a plate and filled it with oysters—only ten; I didn't want to seem gluttonous by taking a full dozen—because *free oysters*. After I slurped them down, Sumira handed me the signature holiday cocktail—some sort of bubbly cranberry concoction—and we made the rounds.

Sumira looked breathtaking. She wore a shimmery, drapey black dress and thigh-high stiletto boots. Heads kept turning when she walked by; I felt like I was with a celebrity. The whole thing was dreamy. It was like a movie montage of a glamorous party, drinks and laughter flowing freely. If my eyebrows were still red, I didn't notice. I felt so confident.

Sumira introduced me to her boss, an absolutely charming man who offered me a job on the spot while speaking directly to my breasts. Glancing over his shoulder, I saw that someone was staring at me. Agog, I accidentally stared back for several seconds because I didn't know whether to believe my eyes: this had to be the most beautiful man in Seattle. Chiseled jaw, big, liquid eyes under thick black brows, dark wavy hair cut short at the sides. You know, that haircut that says, *Hello, I am wealthy and hip.* I slowly scanned his body with my eyes—impeccable suit—and received a shock when I saw a strip of bare ankle: he was wearing loafers with no socks. That look was just so insouciant and WASPy, it made me shiver to my core. I blinked and looked away, downing the rest of my drink.

Noting that Sumira's glass was empty too, and that her attentive boss had been replaced by a strapping Pakistani youth who could not have been over the age of twenty-three, I mouthed that I was off to get us more drinks. She nodded and flipped her hair, and I swear I saw the *instant* that poor boy fell in love.

I'd been at the bar for 1.5 seconds when I heard a low voice just behind my ear. Goose bumps exploded down that side of my body.

"Happy holidays."

I glanced demurely over my shoulder. "How very War on Christmas of you."

His lips opened in surprise, and he half laughed. Clearly I had startled him with my cunning political satire.

"I'm kidding." I turned to face him. He didn't hide the quick glance down at my—in truth, superb—cleavage. "Rachel Weiss. I'm here with Sumira Khan." I held out my hand. He took it to his mouth and kissed it.

"Stephen Branson. Senior account exec. Sumira's a great girl."

The casual condescension in his voice took him down several notches in my estimation. I tossed him a dazzling smile and held up the two fresh drinks, indicating that I had other places to be.

"Nice to meet you." I then wove back through the crowd.

When I got back to where I'd left Sumira, she was nowhere to be found. Having no desire to stand there looking like a sad sack who'd misplaced her friend, I downed Sumira's drink—the cranberry fizz really was delicious—and disposed of the evidence on a nearby table. Stephen Branson was sure to come looking for me, and I was still standing alone twiddling my thumbs. There was no one I could foist my conversation upon, surrounded by beautiful sales-type people all engaged in snug chitchat. There was a gleaming dance floor in their midst that was being utterly wasted.

And then, like a gift from God or the DJ, a Beyoncé song came on. I tossed my drink back, straightened my shoulders, and led the charge.

In truth, I had assumed there would be a general swarm toward the dance floor, but apparently I was the only one who could not resist the siren call of Queen Bey. Nevertheless, I persisted. I shimmied and rolled, letting the music carry me away. A peek through my closed eyelids showed that a (small) handful of people had been inspired by my leadership and begun to dance as well. The DJ was, I think, transfixed by my moves, because he transitioned right into another Beyoncé song. I punched the air victoriously and bobbed along to the new beat. And then I felt a hand on my hip.

"May I join you?" Stephen Branson smirked down at me, his eyes glinting naughtily.

The way he asked so politely, and the bad-boy look on his face, sent him soaring back up many, many notches.

"If you must."

And oh, he did not disappoint. Quite nimble on those WASPy ankles, was Stephen Branson. He matched me step for step, roll for roll. He drifted closer, until the front of him molded to the back of me, and I felt his smooth cheek on the side of my face, felt his hot breath, smelled his cologne, and effectively soaked my panties. And then he flipped me around so we were face to face, gripping one hand tightly and clutching me close with the other, one leg grinding between mine. I had become, in an instant, the heroine from *Dirty Dancing: Havana Nights*, all my teen dreams coming true. I stared into his eyes, powerless—surely he was not from Seattle. Men like him didn't *exist* in my world.

When the song ended, he held my hand firmly and dragged me off the dance floor toward a side door. I followed like a sweaty, lust-ridden puppy.

The night air was frigid, and Stephen wrapped me in his jacket. We had stumbled out onto a deserted patio.

"Who *are* you?" Stephen smiled, still panting slightly.

"Rachel Weiss. Poor memory?"

"Trust me, I remember your name. I'm just wondering why I haven't met you before."

"Hmm." I gazed into the darkness. "Probably because I'm very busy and important."

"Of course." He drew a slim vape pen out of his pocket. "Do you mind?"

"Not if you share." *Why? Why am I like this?*

He took a puff and let out a cloud of strawberry-scented vapor, then passed the pen to me. I inhaled the way I did with my weed pipe and sputtered as the sickly-sweet smoke hit the back of my nose and throat. I shoved it back into his hands and hid my coughing attack in my elbow.

He laughed. "First time?"

I gave a noncommittal grunt, still coughing.

He took another puff, then stashed it back in his pocket.

"Are you from around here?" I asked once I was able to breathe again.

"No." He ran a hand through his hair. "I grew up in Chicago. But I moved here for college and I've been here ever since."

"Ah." I remained an expert in the study of Seattle bachelors.

He went on for a bit, telling me about Chicago, his family, and what he'd studied in college. I was beginning to get restless, considering how to break in and suggest a visit to the bar, when he paused for breath and looked at me. He reached for a curl that had fallen into my face and pushed it behind my ear.

"And you are the sexiest girl I've met since I moved here."

Since he moved here? I considered asking him to expand on that point—what sort of Chicagoan vixens was I competing with, exactly? But before I had a chance, Sumira burst through the door, trailed by her besotted young man.

"There you are! I thought you'd been carried off by some—oh, hello, Stephen."

"Enjoying the party?" Stephen asked.

"Definitely much better than last year's," Sumira said. Her fanboy nodded emphatically, and I couldn't help a sardonic look in his direction. He was practically an embryo last year, so of course this year's party was an improvement.

"Shall we go back inside?" I asked. "I could use another drink."

The four of us spent the rest of the evening together, chatting, dancing, and at one point joining a crowd around Sumira's boss that was pelting him with loving insults. Apparently it was a holiday tradition for the employees to rib on the boss, yelling out the things they'd held bottled inside all year. I contributed, shouting merrily, "Fat old perv!" Stephen looked at me in surprise. When I asked him why, he said, "I just noticed your eyebrows are bright red."

The night was a roaring success. And yes, I gave Stephen my number when he asked. He texted me as soon as he got home, so…stay tuned.

Oh, and Sumira went home with the youth. Cradle robber.

The next evening, we gathered for a girls' night at Eva's apartment. As we lounged around the coffee table, which was spread with half-empty wine bottles and a cheese board, Sumira and I recounted our adventures of the previous night.

"I'm glad you two had fun." Eva pinched some cracker crumbs from her sweater and ate them. "My date was a disaster. I've never been so embarrassed in my life."

"What happened?"

Eva groaned like it pained her to recall. "The headliner was looking around for people to razz, and he saw us. He pointed at me and went, 'Hey, I recognize you. We met on Tinder. What, are you experimenting now?' It got a good laugh and then he moved on. But Jennifer was like ice after that."

"It wasn't true, though!" Amy looked concerned. "Your Tinder is set to women only."

"I know. Jennifer believed him, though. We'd just had a conversation about how I hadn't been with a guy since high school, and she said she hadn't either, and it was a whole thing."

"She couldn't laugh it off?" I asked.

"Nope. She barely spoke to me again for the rest of the date. Now I'll just have to live with the embarrassment every time I see her in class."

We clucked sympathetically. Privately I thought perhaps it was for the best. The ability to take a light joke—especially at a *comedy show*—was important in a significant other, I'd always thought.

"I'm sorry, Eva." Amy swirled her glass of rosé. "My date night sucked too."

"How did your date night go wrong? I didn't know that was possible after you were married." Sumira set down her phone and leaned in curiously.

Amy stared into her wine for a moment. "It was nothing. Never mind."

Sumira, Eva, and I exchanged a wide-eyed look. The kind of look that says, "Here we go, ladies. Hold on to your bras, this might be a bumpy ride."

"Spill, Amy." "Tell us everything, right now." "Tell us what happened or so help me, I will start a pillow fight."

"Okay, okay!" Amy set down her glass and sighed, sitting up straighter. "I tried to...but Ryan didn't...and the truth is..." The next part came out very fast. "We haven't had sex in a month."

I may have screamed. Sumira covered her mouth in shock.

"I thought sex was a given when you were married. At least for newlyweds."

"Not helping, Rachel," Sumira said.

"What's going on? Are you going through a fight?" Eva rubbed Amy's shoulder.

Amy shook her head, burying half of her face in one hand like she wanted to disappear. "He just doesn't want to sometimes."

"That lazy little shit." The others glared at me. "What?"

We spent the next half hour alternating between slandering men in general and offering supportive ideas, like couples therapy. Amy seemed, however, even more miserable by the time we said good night.

In bed later, I couldn't stop thinking about it—how was Amy surviving in such a drought?—so I sent a message to Sumira and Eva.

> **Rachel Weiss 10:17 PM:**
> Let's get her some lingerie for
> Valentine's Day.

Sumira Khan 10:19 PM:
Good idea.

Eva Galvez 10:22 PM:
I'm in.

Rachel Weiss 11:56 PM:
Seriously though. POOR
AMY.

CHAPTER 3

IT WAS THE START of a beautiful week. A wintery sun was peeking through the clouds, my curls were bouncing like nobody's business, and Stephen had sent me a naughty good-morning text. And yet by lunchtime, my mood had begun to sour. Customers were especially annoying today, and my manager, Kenneth, was Kennething about all morning. He had a way of talking to me where he tried so hard not to objectify me that his eyes went sort of crossed, and I never knew whether to laugh or cry.

Eva sent an update to the group chat, letting us know that Jennifer had completely iced her out in class and that she was having flashbacks to being bullied and alone in seventh grade. Amy chimed in to say that she hated high schoolers and her husband and everyone except for us. And then my mother began to call me, repeatedly, in the middle of a workday, trying to guilt me into coming over for dinner that night.

By midafternoon she'd recruited Jane to do her dirty work. Jane claimed that it would be a celebratory dinner now that the twins had their driver's licenses. I pointed out that instead of having a dinner party, we should be building an underground shelter and handing out padded helmets to all the neighbors as a precaution. She simply replied that she would be going and bring-ing Owen. So it looked like I was going. I was going to miss *The Bachelor* for this.

As soon as I arrived I could tell something fishy was afoot. Mom and Jane answered the door together, both smiling fiend-ishly. Over their shoulders I could see that the table was set for ten—not seven. Though in my innocence I assumed the twins were having friends over. Mom gave my jeans and sweater a once-over, then touched her nose at Jane as though she were a secret agent in a poorly made movie.

Jane kept smiling in a pained way—always too nice to be a con-vincing liar—and asked me to come upstairs to help her change.

"Help you change?" I took in her cowl-neck dress and tights. "Why do you need to change?"

She cast a panicked look at Mom before the two of them grabbed my arms and frog-marched me up the stairs.

"What's going on?" The foolishly optimistic part of me thought that maybe they had a belated Hanukkah present for me, so I didn't resist. Stupid, stupid Rachel.

They hustled me into Mom and Dad's room, and Mom locked the door behind us.

"Why did you lock the door?" My voice was shrill as it dawned on me that there would be no Hanukkah present.

"Shh," Mom hushed soothingly as Jane rifled through a bag that had been stashed there in advance. She pulled out a black dress, and then she and Mom lunged at me and tugged my sweater over my head.

"Aggghh!" I yelled. "Help! Dad! Arrrgghh!"

We struggled. At one point, in my bra and with my jeans half-way down my bum, I made a run for it—this, at least, counting as my exercise for the day. At the top of the stairs, the twins came out of their rooms to watch placidly as I stumbled, holding my jeans up with one hand and fending off Mom and Jane with the other.

"Nooooo!" I shrieked as they dragged me back toward the bedroom. "Help me!" I held out a pleading hand to the twins. Ollie pointed her phone's camera at me and began filming. Abby waved, straight-faced, as I disappeared around the corner.

In the end, Mom and Jane wrestled me into the black dress of Jane's. Jane's wardrobe is all French chic, minimalistic elegance. In other words, completely wrong for me. I was squeezed into the dress like a sausage, the high neck pinching my armpits and cutting into my windpipe. I felt that if I moved too quickly, my breasts would burst through the fabric.

"Why?" I rasped as Mom slipped her circa-1983 kitten heels onto my feet. "Why are you doing this to me?"

"I'm sorry." Jane swept my hair back into a twist. "Mom convinced me it would be a good idea. But now..." In the mirror, I saw her giving me a highly skeptical once-over.

"It's a surprise, darling!" Mom hadn't even broken a sweat. It was as though she kidnapped and stripped people against their will every afternoon. "A lovely, lovely surprise."

"What—" I began, and then I trailed off—my mind clunking its way toward a horrid realization. Only one thing could make Mom this happy.

The doorbell rang.

"Oh no." My heart dropped. "No, no, no, no..." But Mom had already hurled herself down the stairs.

"Hello!" she trilled from the entryway. "Mr. and Mrs. Butkus, so thrilled. Welcome, welcome. And you must be Christopher!"

I glared at Jane amid the wreckage of my former outfit. *Sorry,* she mouthed. My gaze flicked toward the bedroom window. We were on the second floor, but there was a tree right outside; surely I could climb down.

No sooner had I stood up than Jane flung herself at me and flattened me to the floor with a loud *thunk*.

"I'm really sorry, Rachel." She pinned my shoulders down. "But I want you to find happiness like I have with Owen. Just give this guy a chance. Even if you don't like him, you'll make Mom happy."

"That is the last thing I want to do."

"Please." Jane blinked down at me, looking more like an angel than ever with the ceiling light glowing behind her head.

"Fine. For you. Not for Mom."

Downstairs, I decided to fully commit myself to the evening. I didn't want Mom to accuse me of sulking and try to force me into a second meeting with the Butkuses.

"Hello, hello." I entered grandly, kissing Dad and Owen on the cheek. Then I swept over to the Butkuses, not wanting to leave Mom in charge of the introductions. No doubt she would introduce me as her extremely eligible daughter, dropping unsubtle hints about my spinster status. Mr. and Mrs. Butkus gave every impression of being kindly teacher types, she a short lady with soft gray curls and glasses on a beaded chain, he a reedy gentleman with a sweater vest and a bald patch. My warmth as I introduced myself to them was genuine. I steeled myself to turn toward their son and was annoyed to note immediately that he was not completely foul. He had hair that hovered between blond and brown (untidy—he could use a referral to Stephen Branson's barber), guileless blue eyes, and an unexpected dimple in the center of his chin. He was wearing an unremarkable outfit of jeans, a checkered button-down shirt, and—I couldn't help grinning when I noticed—white socks. He had apparently removed his shoes out of politeness when he came in.

"Hi. I'm Rachel." I offered my hand. He gave it a quick, firm squeeze. His hand was large, warm, and dry. I would absolutely never admit to Mom that this man was—objectively—a hunk. It was a matter of principle; if I admitted it, she would never stop trying to set me up with every single tech bro, doctor, and lawyer who crossed her path.

"I'm Christopher. It's so nice of your parents to invite us over."

Yes, so nice and selfless. I tossed a smirk over his shoulder at Mom, who was giving me a thumbs-up and mouthing, *Tall.*

"They're thrilled to have new neighbors. Will you be living in the new house with your parents?"

"Um, no." He looked a bit puzzled. "I live in Fremont."

Hmm. I had assumed he would live in a penthouse downtown. He must've bought himself one of those hideously modern Fremont town houses. How inconvenient. I hoped I wouldn't run into him around my neighborhood.

"So, Rachel, what do you do?"

Oh God. I glanced around to see if any alcohol was forthcoming. Mom, Jane, and Owen were crowded around Christopher's parents, the twins were sprawled on the couch snickering at a video, and Dad had retreated to the kitchen.

"I'm in technical support," I told him, sweetly, yet in a quelling manner. I knew he was moments away from offering me condescending professional advice, or worse, expounding on his own boring career. "If you'll excuse me, I'm going to see if my dad needs help with the food."

In the kitchen, I found Dad backed against the wall beside the refrigerator, eating dry cereal from a box.

"Hi, Dad." I reached into the fridge, drawing out a bottle of white. I unscrewed the cap and poured myself a generous glass, which I drank in two gulps. "Wine?"

"Whiskey, I think." He stowed the cereal back in the pantry.

I poured him a healthy measure of whiskey and we drank in silence.

"Should we bring drinks out to the others?"

"Mm." He nodded. "And your mother mentioned something about cheese cubes."

Armed with alcohol, cheese, and toothpicks, we rejoined the cocktail hour. I kept my distance from Christopher, not wanting to encourage any dull tech talk.

We migrated to the dining room, where Mom bodychecked me into the seat across from Christopher like a scrappy defensive tackle in the body of a Jewish mother. Jane helped her serve dinner, a lurid green chicken curry spooned over clumpy white rice. The twins complained loudly about the food. I tried to give them a big-sisterly *Shut up, I mean it* look, but they glared back at me, contracting their solid black, painted-on eyebrows. I'm afraid they won the showdown. Teens really are scary these days. After everyone had taken a few bites, Dad silently left the table and returned a moment later, tossing a loaf of sliced bread in a plastic bag and a tub of butter onto the table. The twins lunged for the bread, arguing over the butter. I'm no fan of Mom's cooking, but my face burned with embarrassment for her. The Butkuses carried on eating as though they hadn't noticed a thing.

"So, Rachel," Christopher began, "your mom tells me you—"

"Has Jane told you about her work?" I interrupted. "It's very interesting."

"No." He smiled down the table at Jane. "What do you do, Jane?" I stifled a surprised grin; his genuine earnestness was kind of charming.

Jane explained about her career as a researcher for the local news channel as Owen grinned fondly, holding her hand on the tablecloth.

"Would you like to be in front of the camera someday, or are you happy behind the scenes?" Christopher took a sip of wine. Grudgingly I appreciated the way he actually listened to my sister and seemed to find her as fascinating as I did.

"I wouldn't mind being on-screen." Jane blushed. "Maybe if they asked me. But I do love my job right now."

"That's wonderful. It's so important to love what you do."

I scoffed—couldn't help it. Every head turned toward me.

"Food go down the wrong way?" Mom asked hopefully.

"It's easy for you to say that." I smiled broadly at Christopher.

"Say what?" He really was innocent—how he'd gotten to be a multimillionaire without someone swindling him out of his money, I didn't know.

"'It's so important to love what you do.'" I kept my voice light. "When money's not an issue, sure, do what you love. Become an art teacher in a nudist colony. But most of us—ninety-nine percent of us—can't afford to be so selective, waiting around for our dream job. We need to pay the bills."

"Of course." He set down his fork, looking troubled. "I didn't mean...Just meant that if you can make a career out of something you love, then it's—"

"As long as you understand that it's a very privileged thing to say."

"I see what you mean." He looked down at his plate, his brow furrowed. Mom glared at me across the table.

"Jane is one of the lucky ones," I continued. "I consider myself lucky too—I have a roof over my head and a support system—but do I *love* working for a company that exists to make money for its shareholders? Of course not. Capitalism is a scourge on society. It's what's keeping the general populace from doing something that might benefit society instead of just feeding the vicious cycle of consumer—"

"And now that you have some work experience under your belt, what's keeping you there?" Christopher interrupted. "We're not all slaves to the capitalist market, even if it feels that way. Have you considered how you might do some good in the world if that's so important to you?"

"Me?" I was fuming, my vision turning red. *How dare he?* "Have *I* ever considered...? Perhaps the man buying a three-million-dollar house in this skewed economy should consider—"

"Of course," Mom interrupted so loudly everyone turned to her, "your parents have had long, lovely careers in teaching." She turned to the Butkuses. "Tell us about that!"

Mr. Butkus expounded on the joys and perils of teaching social studies to a generation of middle schoolers. Jane gave me a pitying look. I refilled my wineglass and shrugged, trying to let Christopher's words wash over me. He was just retaliating because learning is uncomfortable. *Someone* had to teach these privileged techies about the real world.

Dessert was a perfectly adequate store-bought chocolate cake and coffee. Christopher didn't try to ask me any more questions. He and his parents left shortly after nine, and I took that as my cue to change back into my own clothes and say good night. After what she'd put me through, I didn't feel like helping Mom clean up.

I wanted to be smoking a bowl in my pajamas as soon as possible, so the bus was out of the question. I called an Uber and waited for it behind a bush in the yard. The Butkuses were still talking over in their yard, and I didn't want them to see me.

"...polite to go...new neighbors," I could hear Christopher saying. "...might avoid them...seem like the kind of people who want something."

"...was perfectly nice," came his mother's voice.

"...even so...really the sort of people you want to be friends with?"

My face burned at Christopher's words. In my mind's eye, I saw tonight's dinner from their point of view: desperate Mom, avoidant Dad, twins acting like they'd been raised by hyenas, and me being my loudmouthed self. I don't get embarrassed easily, but oh God.

They were still talking when my Uber arrived. There was no avoiding it: they would see me. I stomped out from behind the bushes. The Butkuses were startled into silence as they watched me go, surely trying to guess how much I'd heard. I slammed the car door behind me without saying goodbye.

Mom had gotten her wish—Christopher Butkus and me in the same room together. And now I hoped to never see him again.

CHAPTER 4

TWO FULL WEEKS PASSED with no more calls from my mother. Finally some peace.

I was relaxing on my couch with my feet up, scrolling on my phone with a trashy reality show playing on TV, when the group chat pinged. It was Amy, informing us that she'd had sex.

I typed back quickly.

Rachel Weiss 9:19 PM:
Hallelujah!

Sumira Khan 9:20 PM:
Me too.

Eva Galvez 9:22 PM:
Me three.

Rachel Weiss 9:23 PM:
WHAT? Who are you all

having sex with? And why am I not?

Sumira Khan 9:30 PM:
Why haven't you slept with Stephen yet?

Rachel Weiss 9:31 PM:
We've only been out a few times and I'm trying to be... you know, I can't really remember my reasoning anymore.

I switched over to Instagram and pulled up Stephen's profile. I'd browsed through it plenty of times before, but that didn't stop me from being struck by the glamour of it. He had tons of high-quality photos and looked fantastic in all of them. His fabulous life was full of concerts, vacations, boats...Ooh, maybe he would be my ticket to finally getting invited on a boat! Eva had sneered something about him being an influencer when I showed her his profile, but...

I got a notification that I had a new follower, and my heart skipped. But it wasn't Stephen. Nor was it Colin Firth or Barack Obama, as one might hope.

It was Christopher Butkus.

Ew.

Why now? Why was he following me two weeks after our regrettable meeting? Had he been thinking about me? Had he typed my name into the search bar? This was so weird.

I went to his profile, which was ridiculously sparse. He truly was old and sad. He had five—yes, five—photos, including one of a work party and one of him giving a TED Talk. He *was* only two years older than me, said a mean little voice in my head. And it wasn't like my Instagram profile was much better. My online presence consisted mostly of blurry karaoke pictures and heavily filtered pictures of my sister's cat.

Stephen wasn't following me; why? I had followed him after our second date, a perfectly reasonable amount of time to wait, I'd thought. Perhaps I just wasn't enough of a content curator for him. Perhaps it had never even crossed his mind to look me up.

I was feeling this strange, foreign weight in my chest. Like some sort of...doubt, or self-consciousness. I did not like it, and I would *not* accept it. I was, and always had been, a goddess. The type of goddess who took care of herself and did healthy things like...yoga. *Hot* yoga.

A quick search on my fitness app and two minutes later, I'd signed up for a hot yoga class the next day. It would help me feel calm and centered. Plus, I had a date with Stephen the next night, and now I would have that healthy exercise glow when I saw him.

I went to bed feeling confident once more, and rather proud of myself for silencing that self-doubt. Rachel Weiss, hot yoga goddess.

Saturday morning I strolled into the yoga room in a skintight, neon-yellow getup. Bless the creator of the bike short—absolutely the best way to show off one's natural curves while still being clothed.

I smiled at my fellow yogis as I stretched luxuriously on my mat to warm up. It was so lovely in here—white curtains, dim lighting, gentle music. And that soothing humid heat, so pleasant compared to the frigid February rain outside. The teacher, a short but alarmingly muscular girl, beamed at us from the front of the room.

"Welcome. You have found yourself here today for a reason. Each of you made the decision to show up for yourself. Close your eyes, take a deep breath, and say thank you. When things get hard, when you feel tired, remember this feeling and thank yourself again."

Wow. Just wow. It was like she reached into my soul and saw me. I beamed back at her.

"Okay. Let's get started in child's pose."

I opened my eyes to find myself in my bed. My whole body felt hot and dry, like an overgrilled hot dog. *Oh my God. What time is it?* My hand flopped around on my nightstand until it found my phone. Two twenty-five p.m. My yoga class had started at 10:30 a.m. *How?*

The last thing I recalled was going into downward dog. Yes, it was coming back to me. The teacher had kept spouting these yoga words that apparently meant something to everyone else because they all knew what to do. I could barely see past the sweat pouring into my eyes, but I did my best to copy the poses. We went into downward dog; I checked the clock on the wall and saw that we still had half an hour left. Then the music changed from gentle wind instruments to something with a pumping beat. I was really feeling it. I threw myself into the moves with the fervor of an exercise convert. The flow got faster and faster and culminated in something called...eagle pose? I was a vertical pretzel, my heart pounding painfully, my spandex soaked through. I remembered wondering how I was going to unpretzel myself. And then I woke up here—buck naked. Lordy. Had I contracted heat stroke and heaved my flaming-red body through the streets of Fremont for all to see? I could only hope that wasn't the case. I checked my phone for clues. Nothing, aside from a message from Amy asking how the yoga class had gone.

I typed a reply as fast as my dehydrated fingers would allow.

> **Rachel Weiss 2:29 PM:**
> I HATE YOU ALL. WHY
> DIDN'T YOU WARN ME?

Sumira replied with, in my view, unnecessary snark.

> **Sumira Khan 2:30 PM:**
> Warn you about what? That
> hot yoga is hot?

> **Rachel Weiss 2:31 PM:**
> I'm lucky to be alive.

> **Eva Galvez 2:33 PM:**
> What happened?

As I told them my tale of highly public woe, I gulped down water from the bottle on my nightstand. The hydration made me feel alive again.

> **Eva Galvez 2:40 PM:**
> I'm glad you're okay.

Sumira Khan 2:40 PM:
You can never go back to that yoga studio, lol.

Amy McDonald 2:41 PM:
Are you going to be all right for your date with Stephen tonight?

Rachel Weiss 2:42 PM:
Oh yes. In fact, I think tonight might be his lucky night.

By eight o'clock, I was back to my usual level of perfection, though still a bit dehydrated. My curls were bouncy, my winged eyeliner was on point, my crop top and high-waisted jeans were on. I even had the yoga glow! My skin was sort of shimmering with health, as though my little blood cells were all working hard and…whatever it is blood cells do. Perhaps the hot yoga wasn't such a terrible idea.

I got to the Backdoor exactly on time, but Stephen wasn't there yet. I ordered a gin and tonic and got a table facing the door. After a few minutes, I became uncomfortably aware of my aloneness, so I messaged the group chat, asking Amy how she was doing. She admitted to being holed up in the bedroom watching a Katherine Heigl movie while Ryan and his friends played *Assassin's Creed*. Then she added,

> **Amy McDonald 8:22 PM:**
> Is Stephen not there yet?
> 20 minutes late?

I stashed my phone back in my purse and slurped the rest of my gin and tonic. I was halfway off my stool, about to order another drink, when he arrived. And damn it if his swagger, his leather jacket, and his smirk didn't make me forget just how long he'd made me wait.

"How was he?" Sumira asked in an excited whisper. We were at Bellefleur, shopping for lingerie for Amy. I plucked a fire engine–red teddy off the rack and considered it.

"Pretty decent." Sumira and Eva just looked at me, so I added, "Bit small."

Sumira burst out laughing, then covered her mouth at a look from the saleswoman. "Oh, I can't wait to see him at work, knowing that about him."

I replaced the teddy on the rack and examined a black lace bra. "I also threw up on his bath mat."

Sumira wrinkled her nose and Eva gagged.

"How did he react?" Eva asked.

"He was pretty grossed out. He stayed in bed and told me where the cleaning supplies were. But, you know, he was drunk too, so I don't blame him."

"Are you going to sleep with him again?"

"Yeah, of course. It's only likely to get better, right?"

"If you say so." Eva held up a padded leopard-print bra. Sumira shook her head at it.

"My tits would look amazing in this." I held up a navy-blue lace camisole.

Eva grinned. "Are you going to wear it for Stephen?"

"I'm not sure. He didn't really stop to look at me the other night. My clothes just sort of flew off and then we were at it."

"What a heartwarming image. I'm getting this." Sumira was referring to a black garter set with a price tag of nearly two hundred dollars.

"Please tell me it's not for the youth from your office. It would be the end of him."

"It's for my future husband."

"What future husband?" Eva looked confused.

"I don't know yet, but I'll know him when I see him. And he'll know he needs to marry me when he sees me in this."

"Brains and beauty. You amaze me."

Once we were all clutching purchases for ourselves, we completed our actual mission of finding the perfect lingerie for Amy. We settled on a red, lacy matching set—demure yet devilishly sexy. Under the pretense of a girls' night at her place— Ryan was at a friend's playing *Warhammer*—we surprised her with the V-Day gift. She loved it and said she couldn't wait to show Ryan on the fourteenth. Ryan was going to eat her up, I just knew it.

And I was glad one of us was looking forward to Valentine's Day. So far Stephen hadn't mentioned a thing about it. Not that I would expect him to, but you know. When you're boinking someone new in the first half of February, things get dicey.

Tuesday morning, I soared into work (a little late) on an iced coffee high. I grinned at my computer screen in my cubicle and stretched my fingers: the daily corporate question was practically made for me.

"How much of your time is spent thinking about the customer and their needs?"

My answer: "Literally all the time. I cannot stop thinking about the customer. 24/7. I even dream about them. Completely obsessed! My therapist says it's fine, and that it just shows I'm really, really dedicated to my job."

How I loved the thought of brightening the day of some poor soul in another cubicle somewhere far away, in one of our other offices. Imagine sifting through earnest answers to horrid questions all day. Really, I just did it to make someone, somewhere, laugh. It was a solid momentary distraction. The truth was, I was becoming obsessed with something else entirely. That something was a man with a cheeky grin who was supremely average in bed. Even the second time.

Yes, Stephen had booty called me and we'd done it again. No, he hadn't noticed the lingerie. And no, he had not mentioned Valentine's Day, which was now two days away.

Not that it bothered me. I wasn't the Hallmark holiday type, really.

So I'd been known to wear head-to-toe green on St. Patrick's Day. Bunny ears on Easter. Spangled miniskirts on July Fourth. So what? Valentine's Day was just a silly, little…

I swiveled myself away from my desk and texted the group chat.

Rachel Weiss 3:39 PM:
No word from Stephen yet. Getting a little anxious to be honest.

Sumira Khan 3:41 PM:
Some men get weird about Valentine's Day. Especially when you've only been dating for a little while.

Amy McDonald 3:42 PM:
Maybe he'll surprise you last minute.

Eva Galvez 3:59 PM:
I've already accepted that my latest Tinder hookup has ghosted me. I have a date at the Wildrose on Valentine's. Big old lesbian dance party. I hope you're not getting ghosted, Rachel. You're probably not though.

Rachel Weiss 4:08 PM:
Oh my god, AM I getting ghosted?

Eva Galvez 4:09 PM:
Sorry. Shouldn't have mentioned it.

Rachel Weiss 11:18 PM:
Stephen is still not following me on Instagram!

CHAPTER 5

I WAS NEVER LEAVING my apartment again. Leave it to me to have one of the top five most mortifying experiences of my life while my best friends were off having romantic Valentine's Day evenings like true adult women.

Amy was having dinner at Copine with her husband. Eva was at a dance party. Sumira had deigned to let the youth—Ajay—take her out. (I told her not to toy with his young heart, but alas.) And I? I had decided to embrace my status as a nearly-thirty spinster. My vagina, and my heart, were closed for business. Love and fuckboys were all behind me.

So naturally I decided to do a self-care night. Face mask, mani-cure, solo dance party, the works. I biked over to PCC for supplies.

There were happy couples everywhere. Strolling down the sidewalk holding hands in their scarves and coats. Inside steamy, candlelit restaurants. Groping each other outside of bars. One man started shout-singing at me as I rode past—some pervy song about a girl on a bicycle. So at least I had that going for me.

I slouched through the store, tossing the necessary items into my basket—a bottle of red, a frozen pizza, a box of brownie mix, microwave popcorn, and a bag of cookies. They were having a little wine tasting—clever marketing, perfect for singles with nowhere to go like myself—so I got in line. I was patiently, if a little sadly, staring into space while waiting for my turn to have a free minuscule paper cup of rosé, when I heard my name.

"Rachel?"

I jumped. It was a deep man's voice, and even if it took me a second to recognize it, every fiber of my being recoiled at the thought of a man I knew seeing me like this.

"I thought that was you." It was Christopher Butkus, approaching with a smile. He was also trailed by an offensively beautiful girl of ambiguous racial identity—all tan skin, Bambi eyes, and blinding white teeth. I saw her eyes flick from my bike helmet (which I was still wearing, thinking it preferable to squashed helmet-head curls) over my bare face to my basket of sad snacks.

"Oh, Christopher. Didn't see you there. Hello."

"This is Xio. Xio, Rachel. How are you?" He was making intense, unfaltering eye contact. Had he done that the first time we met too? Was he one of those people? I felt like a deer caught in his headlights.

"Fine, fine." I tried to inject some airiness into my voice. I noticed the two of them were not holding hands. "Happy Valentine's Day."

Xio smiled dazzlingly and inched closer to Christopher. I peered behind them to check how close I was to my wine sample. The line seemed to have stalled. Of course, lonely singles drinking free wine were apt to make small talk.

"You too. Do you have any plans or—well…" Christopher trailed off, seeming to notice my state of disarray and the contents of my basket.

I laughed and mumbled something about friends waiting for me at my apartment. Xio wrinkled her brow pityingly.

"So you live around here too?" Christopher was being very friendly; perhaps he knew I'd overheard him trash-talking my family and wanted to make amends.

"Um, yes, just over..." I pointed a vague finger over my shoulder.

"Cool! We're neighbors then. Just like our parents. Y'know, it's funny, I thought I saw you the other day...Do you run?"

"Run?" I glanced at Xio's toned physique and considered lying. "Um, no?"

"Huh. I could've sworn it was you. You were wearing neon yellow and you looked a bit...overheated." Christopher chuckled. "I almost stopped you to offer you some water."

My nostrils flared with a sudden rush of understanding. He must have seen me during my hot-yoga-induced blackout. Right. Of course he did.

"Hmm..." I feigned confusion. "Oh, my line's moving, so I'll just...good to see you, Christopher. Xio..."

I turned away from them and stepped up to the wine tasting table. The PCC employee was a grandmotherly type, and she handed me my small paper cup with a gentle expression, looking for all the world like a nurse handing out medications to terminal patients. I drank my half mouthful of rosé, then asked if I could have another.

"Of course, dear, here you are," Her voice was so kind I almost wanted to cry. "And you have a little something right there." She gestured to my forehead, and I wiped at it with dread. "That's better," she said. There was a crusty green smear of face mask on my fingertips.

There was only one register open, and Christopher and Xio were in line, clutching bags of chips, a tub of the expensive guacamole, and a twelve-pack of beer. Christopher gestured that

I should go before them, insisting on this awkward gallantry until I accepted.

With a silent nod of thanks, I stepped in front of them and placed my items on the conveyor belt with all the dignity I could muster, knowing as I did that I was wearing my old yoga pants with a penny-size hole in the center of one butt cheek.

After making a sizable dent in the bottle of wine, I found Xio on Instagram. She had over five thousand followers and a lot of photos of her posing leggily on the edges of canyons, waterfalls, and mountaintops. How did she find the time to keep up her beauty routine *and* have an avid interest in nature? I couldn't even remember the last time I had been on a hike.

Why did I care? I despised hiking and being outside in general. She could keep her Girl Scout badges *and* Christopher Butkus. I had a fresh batch of brownies with my name on it.

On Saturday, Amy somewhat urgently requested a Valentine's Day debrief, so we met at a coffee shop near Eva's apartment. We swirled and sipped our cold brews, sharing a giant piece of coffee cake as Amy got straight to the point.

"I know your hearts were in the right place, and the lingerie is really pretty, but it backfired so badly."

"How did it backfire?" My surprise was written on my face, my straw halfway to my mouth.

"Ryan and I had a really nice time at Copine. We were both a little tipsy when we got home, and he went straight for his Xbox.

I told him I had a surprise for him in the bedroom and basically forced him to get up, so he was already annoyed with me for making him leave his game. When he saw me in the lingerie, I could tell he liked it, but all he said was, 'Wow, you look great, babe,' gave me a kiss, and tried to leave the room. I grabbed his arm and asked if he wanted to. I even had lit candles. But he claimed he wasn't in the mood, and I immediately burst into tears."

"Oh, Amy…" Eva sighed.

Sumira looked pale, her face reflecting my own shock.

"I told him I knew he wasn't attracted to me and I didn't know what to do about it and that if even this didn't work then I must be the most hideous, unlovable woman in the world. And then he started yelling that I was beautiful and *he* was the fat, ugly one, and me dressing up like a Victoria's Secret model only made him feel a million times worse. He told me I was the most gorgeous woman he had ever seen and he had no idea why I'd married him, that he knew he would never be enough for me."

"Oh no." I covered my mouth with one hand.

"I had no idea he felt that way. I had never heard him say anything about being self-conscious before. I tried to tell him I love him, that I find him attractive, and that I just want us to have more sex, and then he sort of roared in frustration and left the house."

"Where did he go?" Sumira asked.

"He texted me later that he'd gone to Peter's to play video games and that he loved me and was sorry. But I feel like shit."

"But…Victoria's Secret model…that's something." I tried to sound encouraging.

"Yeah. I feel like a shitty, sexy Victoria's Secret model. I feel guilty for being so gorgeous."

"NEVER apologize for that, you beautiful beast," Sumira said.

"I just wish I knew how to make Ryan feel better." Amy gazed miserably at the crumbs of our coffee cake.

"I guess we should've gotten you a vibrator instead." I received a kick under the table from Eva.

That night I received an unexpected but not unwanted text. It was Stephen, asking me to hang out.

I was relieved. Honestly, I was not a fan of all that ghosting business. And let's face it, I was too young to be a spinster.

We spent a perfectly adequate hour in his bed—was he getting better? And then I filled him in on the Amy gossip, making her out to be a sexy, frustrated teacher (which is exactly what she is), and Stephen agreed that Ryan was a loser. I had sort of been hoping for a bit of advice from a man's perspective.

That night I lay awake, my mind doing that stupid spiraling thing it does sometimes. What *was* the deal with Stephen ghosting me over Valentine's Day? Logically I didn't care that much because we had just started dating. But there was a part of me that was stung by it. And—it was almost hard to admit it to myself—his conversation left something to be desired. After sex, he tended to respond in monosyllables before reaching for his phone and then, a few minutes later, falling asleep. It's not that I wanted long, soul-baring conversations as he held me in his arms and gazed into my eyes. But a *smidgen* more eye contact might be nice.

Against my better judgment, I had agreed to spend my Friday evening with my mother at her (insistent) request.

When I arrived at the house, she had already nearly worked herself into hysterical tears. Dad was sitting with her at the kitchen table, sort of patting her head and pointing out things he thought she'd like in the Restoration Hardware catalog.

"Ooh, look, dearest, a weathered teak outdoor patio set. What do you think about that, hmm? The whole family could gather around the firepit"—he glanced out the back door, where frigid rain dripped invitingly in the seasonal five p.m. darkness—"in a few months' time."

Mom rocked back in her chair, moaning and counting something silently on her fingers. Whatever she was tallying seemed to displease her, because she let out a small shriek and muttered, "Hopeless...oh no..."

"Or look!" Dad flipped the page and motioned to me to sit down. "A rococo chandelier! For over the dining table, yes?"

Mom was distracted for a moment, peering down at the chandelier with bright interest. As I took the seat across from her, she seemed to remember herself and shook her head, saying, "No, it won't help...Won't help at all..."

"Mom?" I ventured, clutching my purse protectively in front of my chest. She's been known to throw things, and that Restoration Hardware catalog was heavier than a brick. "Is everything okay?"

"Should have listened to me." She blinked up at the ceiling, dabbing at her mascara with her pinkie. "If she had stayed with Robbie Steinberg..."

"Ah." I was slowly catching on. Robbie Steinberg was Jane's boyfriend before Owen. He'd been pathetically obsessed with her. He made her life very dull. Even girls like Jane need a bit of excitement.

"But Mom, she didn't love Robbie Steinberg."

"...could have been married with three children by now."

"Three—?" I spluttered.

Dad was rubbing circles on Mom's back, shaking his head in apparent agreement that it was a real shame Jane had let Robbie Steinberg get away.

"Jane is thirty-three years old." Mom's voice became choked with tears. "And she has been dating Owen Foster for twenty-one months. That is nearly TWO YEARS." At this she crumpled forward and sobbed onto the image of the rococo chandelier. "It's hopeless. All her potential w-w-wasted."

I tried to catch Dad's eye to share a sardonic look—after all, Jane had a successful career and a full life—but his eyes filled with tears too, as though he'd just realized his eldest daughter was, in fact, a failure.

"Look." I crossed the kitchen and filled the kettle. "Most people date for years before they get engaged. Two years isn't long at all."

"NEARLY two years," Mom screamed. "Don't exaggerate, Rachel, for God's sake!"

"Sorry!" I wiped at my shirt with a dish towel—I had splashed water from the kettle down my front when Mom screamed. "I just meant it's a perfectly normal amount of time. He probably *will* propose. Don't worry."

"Probably. Probably?" Mom's voice had gone cold and calculating. It was a chilling transition. She fixed me with an intent gaze. I backed into the counter beside the stove. The water warming was the only sound, hissing in the sudden, eerie silence.

"W-where are the twins?" I asked, finally noticing the absence of chaotic teen energy.

"Out driving with friends," Mom said. I shivered deep in my soul.

The kettle whistled, and I bustled around making tea, hoping the other shoe wouldn't drop but knowing that it would. I handed

Mom and Dad their steaming mugs and sat down again, noting with dread that Mom's expression had changed to one of alert politeness. It was the sort of expression she wore when she was about to ask a neighbor not to leave their dog's poo on the median in front of their houses. *It is communal property, after all.* Gracious, wide-eyed smile.

It was this smile that she turned on me now. I hastily gulped down some Earl Grey, scalding my tongue.

"What is Jane doing tonight?" she asked.

"I don't know…"

"Perhaps you should go have dinner with her. At her condo."

"Um…what if Owen's there? He lives there too."

"That won't stop you taking a peek around. It might even make it easier. You could just get him alone and *ask* him, instead of snooping."

"Snooping? Ask him…what?"

"Oh, Rachel." She gave me a fond look, her head tilted, as though I were an idiot child she had a soft spot for.

Twenty minutes later, I was ringing the bell at Jane's Green Lake condo. She answered, looking bemused, wrapped in a soft cream-colored cardigan with leggings and fluffy slippers. Her orange cat twined around her ankles, glaring at me.

"Hi!" Jane ushered me in at once. "Everything okay?"

"Everything is great!" I hung my coat and scarf on a hook by the door. "Just felt like hanging out with my favorite sister."

"Okay, well…Owen, look who's here!" Jane called over her shoulder. "We were just making dinner."

"Smells delicious."

"It's risotto." Jane's face brightened. "Would you like to join us?"

"Ooh, yes please."

"Hey, Rachel." Owen appeared, wearing an apron and with a

dish towel draped over one shoulder. He gave me a big hug. This made me feel terribly guilty about my secret mission.

Owen went back to cooking, and Jane and I settled on the couch with two glasses of red wine. She filled me in on the latest gossip from work—news stations have alarmingly good gossip—and my mind drifted toward her red-haired beau. Owen really was delightful. If I could choose the perfect man for Jane, I don't think I could find a better one. Okay, perhaps I'd give Owen bigger biceps and slightly better fashion sense, but really, those are small complaints.

The way they'd met was worthy of a romantic comedy. Jane was a new cat owner, and she had taken Linus—the cat currently purring on her lap and gazing at me, threateningly and unblinkingly—to the vet in a fit of worry after he'd thrown up a hairball. The vet was good looking and charming and made a corny joke asking where Linus got his hair done (because his own hair was the same color). He was perfectly professional, telling her to brush Linus once a day and to call him if anything else worried her. Two days later, she received a voicemail from him, apologizing for his lack of professionalism and saying that he hadn't been able to stop thinking about her. He asked if she would like to join him for dinner on Saturday—and said that regardless of her answer, he was thinking of Linus and hoped he was feeling better. Their relationship proceeded without a hiccup from that second meeting. Jane had asked Owen to move into her condo about a year before, and here we were.

I knew Jane wanted to get married—she was my sister, so of course I knew. Growing up, she'd had simple dreams: she wanted to find her prince, have a big white wedding, and have two children—a girl and a boy. And if anyone deserved to have her dreams come true, it was Jane. She had never done anything wrong in her entire life. She was kind, she was curious about other people, she had recurring donations set up for about a dozen charities. I had friends with older sisters who had made their lives hell. I couldn't relate. Jane was my best friend growing up, someone to giggle with as we played make-believe games about fairies and gnomes. And when she wasn't being a playmate, she was like a mother to me. My first day of kindergarten, she held me while I cried after our mom dropped us off. When I got my first period, she showed me how pads worked and how to heat up the hot-water bottle. As an adult, she's someone I can talk to about anything and everything. So yes, I'd agreed to help Mom with her reconnaissance mission, because I also had a vested interest in making sure Jane got her happily ever after. Also, if I hadn't agreed, Mom probably would have made herself sick and posted up in bed for the next week. I couldn't do that to Dad.

Jane got up to check on dinner, and I excused myself to the bathroom. I bypassed the powder room off the kitchen and went instead to the primary bathroom. With the door locked behind me, I poked around on Owen's side of the vanity, looking behind cologne bottles and shaving accessories. I tried the linen closet, looking behind towels and rolls of toilet paper. There didn't seem to be a little jewelry box hidden anywhere. But on the highest shelf—too high for me to reach—was a box of what appeared to be odds and ends. I stood on the edge of the tub, bending sideways to reach for the box. I just had it by the tips of my fingers, but it was heavier than I'd expected and crashed loudly to the floor, scattering bottles of sunscreen and shampoo. I wanted to believe Jane and Owen might not have heard, but I was not such a foolish optimist.

"Rachel?" Jane called after a pause. "Everything okay?"

"Yes!" I scrambled to toss everything back in the box.

Having replaced everything and assured myself there was no engagement ring, I went back to the kitchen. Owen was ladling risotto into three bowls, eyeing me suspiciously as I entered.

I beamed at him. "Anything I can do to help?"

"Hmm. Could you grate that parmesan cheese? And honey, can you take these to the table?"

Jane took the bowls of risotto. I grabbed the block of parmesan and began to grate, but stopped when I noticed Owen an inch away from my elbow.

"You were looking in the wrong place." He wore an impish smile.

"What?"

"Come with me."

I put the cheese down and followed him to the bedroom, where Owen beckoned me over to the dresser. He opened a drawer, drew out a pair of socks, and unrolled it. I watched, dumbfounded, as he revealed a green velvet box.

"See?" He opened it. Inside was the most beautiful ring I've ever seen. A thin gold band set with an elegant emerald-cut diamond. Absolutely perfect for Jane.

"Oh my God," I breathed. I looked up at him sharply. "Wait, how did you know what I was looking for?"

"Beth put you up to it, didn't she?" He closed the box and replaced it carefully in his sock.

"As a matter of fact, yes, she did. But how…?"

"Your mom has been pestering me with questions the last few months. Asking what my plans are, if I'm ever going to marry Jane…"

I dropped my face into my hands. Of course she had. Mom had all the subtlety of a…well, of a desperate Jewish mother with four unwed daughters.

"That's so embarrassing."

"No, it's not." Owen laughed while gently moving my hands away from my face. "I love Jane. Your mom is part of who Jane is—you all are. If she hadn't had a mom like Beth, Jane might not be so sweet-tempered."

I narrowed my eyes; if Jane had grown up to be sweet—the opposite of Mom—what did that make me?

"And anyway," Owen continued, "I don't want her to worry. So can you tell her I have a ring? And if she asks..." We both knew there was no *if*. "Tell her it'll be soon."

Later, as we ate risotto and salad, I was uncharacteristically quiet. Jane was going to marry her prince. There was going to be a *wedding*, at last. There hadn't been a wedding in our family since my dad's creepy cousin Collin had married a nineteen-year-old Ukrainian girl nearly ten years earlier. (And even more mind-boggling: they seem to be very happy together.)

I was so, so happy for Jane—and somewhat alarmed to find that happiness tinged with sadness on my own behalf. I was not desperate to be married: I was *only* twenty-nine, for God's sake. But the thought of having someone as a buffer between me and the world, someone who made life's annoyances a little less important, someone to curl up to at night...it was a lovely thought.

Looking at the pair of them, with Linus perched self-importantly on the chair in between them (still staring at me—why?), I decided that maybe I should try harder. If Stephen couldn't be bothered to invest more time in me than the occasional booty call, then perhaps it was time for Jdate after all.

CHAPTER 6

THE GIRLS AND I were sprawled across my small living room, scrolling on our phones as the credits for *The Bachelor* rolled on the TV.

"Maybe instead of Jdate I should go on *The Bachelor*," I mused.

"You don't really want to go on *The Bachelor*." Amy didn't bother looking up. "You just want to get it on with Jeremy Coltrain."

"Hmm, you may have a point."

Eva nodded thoughtfully. "I don't even like men, but there's just something about Jeremy."

"That southern drawl." Sumira tossed her head back against the couch cushions. "Sexy as hell."

I was deep down a Jeremy rabbit hole on my phone. "Did you know Jeremy was a vegan for a full year because of the environment? He wrote a whole Medium article about it. Very interesting statistics. We should all stop eating beef immediately."

"He truly is the perfect man."

"Aren't you supposed to be making your dating profile?" Eva asked.

"Right you are."

I opened Jdate and got to work. Did I drink? Um...let's say

socially. Did I want kids? Sure, someday. I'd be a *cool* mom. Could I insert a *Mean Girls* meme into my profile? I spent the next several minutes trying to figure out how to upload a GIF. Finally I acknowledged that I was procrastinating, and I hit publish on my profile. The girls were quiet, save for the occasional low chuckle as they scrolled past something amusing.

Swiping through Seattle's eligible Jewish bachelors was immediately underwhelming. Some of them seemed sweet and earnest. Many of them were bald. And one of them sent me a message that read, "Hey gorgeous...want to have my Jewish babies?"

I screamed and threw my phone across the room.

"What's up?" Eva glanced up from her phone.

"There is something wrong with men."

"Well, yeah."

"Coming from a lesbian, that is not entirely helpful."

"Is it Jdate?" Amy and Sumira were giving me their full attention now. "What happened?"

"Let me see." Sumira darted across the room and picked up my phone.

My three friends huddled together, swiping through the dating app and making various noises of dismay, curiosity, and disgust.

"Ooh, what about this one?" Amy read aloud, "Thirty-two, lives in Seattle, works in a medical lab, loves dogs..." She held out my phone to show me his photo. He was blandly good looking and, it had to be said, not bald.

I let out a low growl.

"What? He seems nice!"

"He seems...abstract." I folded my arms and leaned back against the couch.

"What does that mean?"

"All these guys, they're just..." I struggled to find the words.

"They're just pictures and words. There's nothing real or compelling or, you know." *There's no whiff of cologne that makes me lose my mind*, I added privately. *There's no eye contact or knowing smirks.*

"Yeah, that's kind of how dating apps work. You've used Tinder. You know this." Sumira tilted her head at me, as though I were being difficult on purpose.

"Right." There was a realization forming that I wasn't quite comfortable with. "I think it's Stephen. I know I should take a step back and try meeting some other guys. But I can't stop wondering why he hasn't texted me in three days."

Sumira let out a long breath and put down her phone. "I told you he's a fuckboy, didn't I?"

"Maybe he's busy?" Amy suggested.

"It's just…" I sat up straight and brushed potato chip crumbs from my shirt. "I'm Rachel freaking Weiss, right?"

My three best friends eyed me warily. They might or might not have become numb to my inspirational-speech voice over the years.

"And I, Rachel Renée Weiss, do not obsess over men. They come to *me*, they blow up my phone, they cry over me and occasionally stalk me when I dump them. That is the natural order of things."

Sumira and Eva gave noncommittal shrugs while Amy nodded earnestly.

"Stephen Branson wields some mystical power that has upset Mother Nature's delicate balance." I tossed my hands up in exasperation. "It's like, I don't even know if he's *the* guy for me, but I can't get past the way he makes me feel. No one has ever played me hot and cold like this. I don't like it. But I feel like I need to conquer it."

"Ahh." Sumira looked as if she'd realized something. "Rach, I'm sorry, but I think you've been dicknotized."

We all looked at her.

"It's like hypnotized. But with a dick."

We raised our eyebrows at each other and then, without a word, Eva and Amy went back to their phones.

I pondered Sumira's words. "But how did he manage to dick-notize me with such a modestly sized one?"

Ping. I nearly dropped my phone in surprise. How was that for timing?

"He just texted me."

"What did he say?" Eva and Amy clustered around me to peer at the message while Sumira looked on, her perfectly threaded brows arched with curiosity.

I read aloud. "'Just thinking about you. Wondering how you and the girls are doing.'"

"He asked about us?" Sumira sounded intrigued and bemused.

Ping. "'And by girls I mean those ripe, juicy—'"

"Okay!" Eva threw out her hands to stop me. "We get it."

I burst out laughing. It took a minute before I could compose myself, gasping and wiping away tears of mirth. His timing. His raunch. The way he unknowingly trolled my besties for a second there. Man, he was good.

"You know what?" I smiled. "I'm going all in. No Jdate. Just Stephen."

"Really?" Eva looked skeptical.

"Really. He better gird his loins. Mama's coming for him."

And on that decisive note, I texted him back. *Tongue emoji. Sweat emoji. Peach emoji.*

His response came almost at once.

> **Stephen Branson 8:32 PM:**
> My place tonight?

A week in, I was still feeling confident about my decision. After putting all my eggs in his basket, I was determined not to over-think every little interaction. I no longer worried about coming on too strong. We hung out three times in one week. He seemed, for the moment, as invested in our budding relationship as I was. It felt good.

But by the next week? I was back to remembering why I'd been hesitant in the first place. It seemed like every day he took a little longer to text me back. The cycle had returned: boning, waiting by the phone, and spiraling anxiety. When had I ever been the sort of girl to wait by the phone? I enjoyed being in the same room with him, but when we were apart, I didn't like the way I felt. I felt needy. And I hated feeling needy. It made me want to text him every night to see what he was up to, which, of course, would be too much.

But tonight I was forced to put him out of my mind, because I was the one who was busy. I had a fancy sustainability dinner to go to. Much to my chagrin, I'd earned the title of sustainability ambassador at work. All because I'd hidden the paper coffee cups in the kitchen and replaced them with mugs from Goodwill. In a corporate work environment, one must be careful about showing any kind of initiative. Managers eat that stuff up. Yet it often only gets you elected for more work disguised as exciting projects—or in this case, even worse: a work event. My manager lived for writing recommendations to higher-ups, filling out kudos reports, giving out stickers that read "I did a great job today!" (What a strange man. It really was tiring having a manager who was so eager to see the good in everything.) And it was due to Kenneth that I would be sitting at a banquet table listening to smug capitalist hypocrites congratulate themselves all night.

I arrived at the banquet hall alone. I was sure there were plenty of people from my company there, since we were the ones hosting it, but I saw no one I knew. I was seated at a table near the back with seven strangers from companies with names like Insiqlo and Polecat.

They were all a little on the meek side—engineering types—so I took one for the team and started a robust conversation.

"Hi, tablemates! Rachel Weiss." I jabbed a finger at my name tag. "So nice to meet you, Katelyn, Dan, Edgar..." I inclined my head at each of them as I read their names, smiling warmly. Their little faces broke into relieved grins. Edgar in particular looked like he couldn't believe his luck in being seated next to an extrovert. Truth be told, he also seemed delighted by my choice of attire. While the others were wearing drab button-downs and khakis—even poor Katelyn—I wore my beloved green wrap dress with black tights and booties. A pineapple charm necklace drew attention to the oodles of cleavage spilling from the dress's low neckline.

"So," I said as people took their seats at the tables around us and waiters began filling wineglasses. "What did you all do to get invited to this shindig?"

"Well," Katelyn began timidly, shaking her head no at the waiter's proffered options of red or white. Poor Katelyn. I indicated to the waiter that I would have the white, including Katelyn's portion. "I led a company-wide initiative to go carbon neutral by 2024. We decided to go off the grid…wind and solar…and reduce garbage and recycling waste to zero. We actually ended up beating our goal and going carbon neutral quite a bit earlier than expected…but it is a pretty small company, so…"

I stared at her open-mouthed, my wineglass halfway to my lips. Dan asked her an interested question, which I completely missed as I was suddenly feeling intensely inferior. But I gathered myself, took a bracing sip of wine, and practiced my active listening as the rest of my tablemates told us their accomplishments.

Note to self: Ride bike more. Try zero-waste lifestyle. Use hair dryer less. Who was I kidding? My diffuser gave me life. *Try guided meditation aimed at banishing impostor syndrome. I wonder if that would work if I actually* am *an impostor.*

"And what about you, Rachel?" Trey turned to me after explaining his project to transform a local landfill into a park.

"Me?" I beamed at them, my mind working hard; how could I spin "I bought some mugs at Goodwill" into something big and impressive? And then I was saved by a woman tapping at the microphone onstage. "Oops, looks like they're starting."

"Hello, hello, everyone!" The conversation rumbled to a halt as everyone turned their attention to the pretty blonde in a truly excellent floral dress. As a fellow woman in tech and wearer of excellent dresses, I found myself eager to know who she was—an environmental consultant or even a CEO perhaps? Had she once used meditation to cure impostor syndrome? But after a gushing introduction, she handed the microphone over to a lanky, bald nerd in a black suit—my company's CEO. Ugh. I should have known. What I wouldn't give to hear more speeches from women at events like this.

I turned my attention sulkily to my wine as Mr. Wonderful

droned on about how proud he was of everyone here today rep-
resenting local companies doing great things. Thankfully, a distraction arrived in the form of dinner. Several steaming dishes
were placed on our table; it was family style, each dish carefully
labeled. I glanced at the options: beef ragout, chicken parmesan,
shredded pork and beans, and three-cheese zucchini casserole. I
rolled my eyes, but no one else at the table seemed to notice the
irony. With a sigh, I helped myself to some ragout and casserole,
tuning out the sound of my CEO's self-congratulatory spiel about
how hard his company worked to leave a smaller footprint—*I've
seen no evidence of this*—and how much he personally loves the
planet. *Doubt it.* I noticed he did not see fit to mention that most
of his own money was going toward a penis-shaped rocket that
was decidedly not carbon neutral and would serve as his personal
escape vehicle when the rest of us burst into flames.

I snagged a passing waiter and held out my empty wineglass
for a refill as a spokesperson for another company was introduced
next. This one was, if possible, even balder. I could tell it was
going to be a long night.

Several speeches later, it was time for Q&A with the people who
had spoken, all currently seated onstage. Audience members stood
one by one and asked sycophantic questions, like whether the tech
sector could be considered a leader in sustainability, their voices
dripping with desperation at the chance to address this panel of
visionaries. Poor Katelyn surprised me by asking a question with
a bit of backbone: whether any of their companies would consider
joining a pact to go carbon neutral within five years. My CEO gave
a patronizing chuckle and tap-danced his way around what was,
essentially, a *Hell no*. Katelyn was trembling when she sat down.
I think it was this that made me stand up, or perhaps the way the

smug millionaires had been making my blood simmer all evening, or maybe it was just all the wine I'd had.

"Yes, you in the green dress," floral maxi dress called out.

The traveling Q&A microphone was handed to me.

"Hi." My voice lingered sweetly on the word. "Thank you so much for this fabulous event." My CEO gave a hearty "You're welcome," eyeing me appreciatively.

"The food was delicious, but I couldn't help but notice it wasn't exactly on theme." A prickly silence followed; I could tell they weren't sure where I was going with this. "Beef, chicken, pork, and dairy." I ticked each one off on my fingers. "Beef alone produces nearly thirty pounds of carbon dioxide per pound of food. That's three thousand pounds of CO_2 for the amount of beef in this room alone, and the other options aren't far behind in emissions." I paused, looking around. Edgar was gazing down at the crumbs on his plate, aghast. "That's a bit ironic for a sustainability event, don't you think?"

"Thank you, Miss…," my CEO began.

"Rachel Weiss."

"Thanks, Miss Weiss, but people gotta eat." He laughed and added, "Am I right?" as the crowd laughed with him.

"People can *eat* plant-based foods." My smile felt forced now. Floral dress woman was watching the panel closely, frowning.

"Listen." Mr. Wonderful leaned forward, his elbows on his knees. *Ugh.* "I appreciate the point you're making. But let me ask. Are *you* a vegan?"

There were titters throughout the room.

"No, I am not. But I feel guilty about eating animal products. Isn't that the unspoken agreement we've all made? To feel guilty about it?"

People laughed. One person clapped. And then I noticed Katelyn's downcast eyes and empty plate.

"Was there even one vegan dinner option?" Floral dress woman looked like she might cry. "Wait. This is a room of smart people who care about the planet. Raise your hand if you *are* vegan."

At least a dozen arms shot up in the air. A round of applause followed.

"With all due respect," I continued, "I think we could have shown *true* leadership in this area if the dinner had been mostly plant-based."

Whoops and cheers followed my words. *I could get used to this.*

It took a while for the noise to die down this time, but when it did, my CEO said, "That should be a personal choice. We wouldn't serve a roomful of people alternative food that they didn't consent to."

I could barely get a word in with my microphone as people began tossing back retorts, but I finally yelled, "Why should you have to consent to a vegetable? A lentil doesn't offend me, sir!"

That was the end. People were on their feet, laughing, jeering, shouting exuberantly at the panel. The mic was grabbed from my hands, my CEO walked off the stage, and the blond woman declared that the Q&A session was over. Edgar was clasping my shoulder and shaking me with fierce pride. Katelyn gave me a watery-eyed smile and a thumbs-up. A horde of startlingly loud people (by Seattle standards) was surging toward our table, and suddenly I was being congratulated as if I'd just won the World Cup.

"—marvelous—"

"—well said—"

"—so refreshing—"

I finally managed to extricate myself with a queenly wave and smile, making it clear to my adoring fans that I was just headed to the bar. The bartender was an impassive twentysomething who treated me the same as anyone else, which was a bit of a letdown. But there were still plenty of people on this side of the room vying for my attention, albeit in a more civilized manner. I sipped my chilled white, inclining my head graciously when addressed.

"Rachel, was it?" I found myself face-to-face with floral dress. "Hi, I'm Amber Crowley."

"So nice to meet you. Great job tonight." I shook her hand.

"Thank you so much. Anyway, I just wanted to say that you really made me think. I helped organize this event and a vegan option didn't even occur to me. Trust me, I won't be making that mistake again. And also," she added in an undertone, "it was kind of amazing to see those old farts taken off guard."

"Someone had to do it." I smiled modestly.

"Oh, I'd also started thinking…" Her eyes flicked toward someone in the crowd behind me. "Do you know Pageant? They do really great work."

"No, I'm not familiar with them." Was I going to be offered a new job out of all this? How exciting. "What do they do?"

"I'm surprised you haven't heard of them. They have apps and programs that help people and businesses make more sustainable choices. It tells you the carbon footprint and monetary cost of different choices you make and offers suggestions for alternatives. You talking about plant-based eating made me think of it."

"That sounds great. Pageant, was it?"

"Yes. In fact, you should really speak to the guy who started it." Amber glanced around. "There he is!" *Oh God*, I thought, patting my hair and feeling my teeth for lipstick. She threw out an arm and plucked a man out of the crowd.

Christopher Butkus appeared before me, his face slightly flushed, grinning as though he'd just been laughing at a joke when he got pulled away.

"Hi, Amber—oh, Rachel, hi! Great question tonight." He rumbled with laughter.

"Hello, Christopher." So Christopher Butkus's company was actually one that was trying to do a bit of good in the world. I'll admit, I had assumed it was one of those excruciatingly dull software companies that help other companies manage their time better or some other variation of "make more money."

"You already know each other? Then I'm *really* surprised you hadn't heard of Pageant, Rachel. I'll leave you two to talk." Amber slipped off with a wave of her fingers.

I gazed at Christopher for a moment. At least I looked better than I had the last time he'd seen me. I looked better than he did tonight, really. He was wearing a faded blazer over a T-shirt and jeans. What was *wrong* with the millionaires of today? I supposed I should be glad he wasn't wearing a hoodie. If I could dress him, the man had the potential to actually look like a million bucks. Wait, why was I thinking about dressing him? My brain really had a mind of its own.

"So, how's—" he began, just as I said, "So why Pageant?"

"Pageant?" he repeated. "Uh, well…" He stalled and took a sip of the whiskey he was holding. "'The cloud-capped towers, the gorgeous palaces, the solemn temples, the great globe itself—yea, all which it inherit—shall dissolve, and, like this insubstantial pageant faded, leave not a rack behind. We are such stuff as dreams are made on, and our little life is rounded with a sleep.'"

I stared. He blushed.

"Did you just quote Shakespeare at me?" I was slightly in awe.

"Well, it—it's why I chose the name Pageant."

"I see." I took a measured sip of wine. "Nerd."

"Hey!" He boomed with laughter again. It was a nice sound, even if he was sartorially challenged.

"I enjoyed *The Tempest*, actually." Two can play at the nerd game.

He raised his eyebrows.

"English major," I said, and he grinned.

"You know, I'm surprised at you." He wagged a playful finger at me. "When we first met, I got this vibe from you, like..."

I pulled a face. Where was he going with this? I already knew his first impression of me was not, shall we say, flattering.

"Like you weren't exactly crazy about your job."

"My job?" I wasn't sure what I'd expected him to say, but that wasn't it.

"You kind of smeared the whole tech industry. I got the feeling you weren't exactly career focused. No offense!" He shifted his tumbler from hand to hand. "But just now...I mean, you clearly have a spark of passion. I think you might be a force to be reckoned with. At least, if you put your mind to it."

"Oh, I'm a force all right." My tone was casual, but my mind was tumbling. He'd gotten nonserious, noncareer-focused vibes from me? *Is that what I am?* And tonight I'd shown a spark? *I mean, I'm nothing but spark!* But did that mean he thought I had career potential? Or...wait, why did I even care what he saw in me?

I took a gulp of wine and promptly coughed as it went down wrong, dribbling a splash down my chin. *There. That will teach him to see my potential.* I subtly turned my head away to wipe my chin with my hand.

"So I was wondering." His lips quirked in amusement. Oh no, was he going to ask me what I had done to get invited here tonight? I couldn't bear to tell him about the Goodwill mugs. "Who's the guy?"

"What?" This conversation was giving me whiplash.

"Who's the guy? When I saw you on Valentine's Day, it seemed like, you know..."

Like I was a sad sack waiting for a guy to call me? *Honestly! How rude.*

"And you think I should tell you his name, as if you know every guy in Seattle?" I silently cursed myself for giving away the fact that there was, in fact, a guy.

He gave me an annoying know-it-all look.

"If you must know, because you are apparently an extremely nosy person, it's a guy I met at my friend's office holiday party. We had only gone out a few times, so it's not like I was expecting anything on Valentine's Day. I actually prefer to have a nice self-care night sometimes, you know, some alone time. It's an introvert thing." I lifted my chin in a dignified way.

He stared at me with his mouth open. "You are so *not* an introvert!"

"You don't know that," I pouted.

"Come on, it's obvious. Like it's also obvious that you're a Sagittarius."

"What the—" How the heck did he know that? If he was one of those people obsessed with astrology, I would be leaving this conversation at once.

He threw back his head and laughed. "It's on your Instagram profile."

"Oh my God." He was messing with me! And he had broken that unspoken twenty-first-century rule where you don't tell people information you've gleaned from stalking them online.

"And you're a—" I sized him up. "What? Virgo?"

"Not telling."

"That's no fun. Tell me."

"Nope. You'll have to figure it out. Now what's the deal with the guy? Are you still talking to him?"

He really was very interested in hearing about the guy I might or might not be seeing. I had to admit, his interest was flattering. I was never one to turn down an opportunity to flirt, and Christopher was surprisingly easy to flirt with. Something I would never be admitting to my mom, ever.

"As a matter of fact, yes."

"And how's that going?"

"Fine, thank you." I paused, considering it. "We hang out once a week or so."

"Ah. And you want it to be more?"

"Well...I mean, I wouldn't mind." What was happening? How was he breaking into my defenses?

"Hmm. Can I see your last text conversation?"

"No, you may not!" I cried, offended. *The audacity of this guy.*

"Okay, okay. Without any *context*, it's hard for me to give advice."

"I didn't even ask you for—!" I considered him for a moment. He was so not my type—not much fashion sense, certainly not the *Dirty Dancing: Havana Nights* type, probably had never partied on a boat in his life—but he was objectively handsome and clearly had no trouble dating gorgeous women. Plus, he apparently had more depth than I had given him credit for. I felt a new, inexplicable kinship with him after learning about Pageant. Before I knew what I was doing, I found myself handing him my phone, the conversation with Stephen open on the screen. "Fine. But no scrolling back."

Christopher snorted. "'Hot guy from holiday party'? That's his name?"

I'd forgotten that little detail.

"I hate to think what you'd label me as if you had my number." He began reading the messages.

Probably something like "Tech bro who insulted my family after we served you a lovely dinner in our home." My smile turned brittle at the memory.

"No scrolling," I warned as his finger hovered over the screen.

"All right." He handed it back to me. "So, you asked him if he was free at all this weekend, and he said he'd check and get back to you. Then a few hours later you said"—Christopher's mouth twitched—"if you don't answer for a while it's because you're at a dinner full of sweaty nerds in bad suits patting themselves on the back for doing the bare minimum."

I had thought that was sort of funny. But Stephen hadn't even responded.

"No response," Christopher added unnecessarily.

"Correct."

"I would say you should let him sweat a little bit. Stop texting him, at least until he texts you first."

I rolled my eyes. "Are you saying play hard to get?"

"I suppose, yeah. If you stop popping up in his daily life with easy little messages, he'll be forced to give more thought to how he interacts with you."

"And what if he doesn't? What if he just forgets I exist?"

"Trust me, he won't." And I swear to God, Christopher Butkus's eyes roved from my face downward, until he seemed to catch himself, swilling down the last of his whiskey. The exposed skin of my chest and neck erupted in goose bumps. *Not now, girls,*

I mentally chided my ovaries. *This is not the time or the place—or the man.*

"So...stop texting him. That is your great advice."

"And it wouldn't hurt to show off the times you're having fun without him. Like now, for instance. You could add this party to your Instagram story."

I wrinkled my nose. "He doesn't follow me on Instagram."

Christopher sucked in his breath. He didn't say anything, but I could tell he thought it was a bad sign too.

"Okay, then maybe just post it instead. He can see that at any time in case he searches for you when you stop texting him." He was doing it again! Broadcasting the fact that he knew my profile was public. "Here, I'll take one of you now." He reached for my phone.

"What? Really?"

"Yeah, come on, you look great."

"Flattery will get you everywhere." I posed with my wineglass at a jaunty angle.

"Turn toward me a little bit...Perfect." Christopher snapped a photo and returned my phone.

"Thanks." I glanced at it and felt an instant lurch of surprise. I'd expected to see a glazed smile as I posed in front of a dull, work event backdrop—but I was glowing. There was a glimmer in my eye and a healthy flush in my cheeks. Like the photographer brought out this merriment in me. I looked up at him, my lips parting to say—I wasn't sure what.

"We could take a—" Christopher began, but we were interrupted by a young woman with chic bangs.

"Rachel Weiss? I finally found you! I'm a reporter for the *Seattle Times*, doing a story on this event. Do you mind if I take your picture and ask you a few questions?"

Christopher mouthed, *Bye* with a warm smile before drifting away into the crowd.

When the reporter had finished jotting down her notes, I glanced around for Christopher. I was exhilarated from the evening and more than a little surprised at how much I'd enjoyed talking to him. And then I spotted him engaged in a cliquish conversation with none other than my company's CEO and a few of his henchmen. From across the room, Christopher blended in with the rest of the nerd bosses. And the sight of them conversing and laughing so easily—the fact that Christopher *was* one of them—scrambled my brain. I'd forgotten, during our brief conversation, that there was a reason I'd disliked him in the first place. Okay, so it turned out that his company existed to try to improve the world. He was still part of that privileged white male club. After years of working in tech, the contempt I felt for my company's CEO and everyone like him was so ingrained, it was like a visceral reaction. For a moment, I tried to shake it off, but then I thought—why should I? I was dating Stephen. I didn't have to like Christopher.

I left without saying goodbye.

Before lunch the next day, I received a company-wide email stating, rather sternly, that all Q&A questions for future company-sponsored events would be screened in advance.

Huh.

Who says you can't make a lasting impact as a mere technical support representative?

CHAPTER 7

"WHAT KIND OF MOTHER sees her daughter's picture in the *Seattle Times* and calls to scream at her?" I paused to sip my mimosa. The four of us, along with most of the population of Seattle, were enjoying a Sunday brunch at Portage Bay.

"Does she ask me anything about the event or congratulate me on my keen and penetrating mind? No. She wanted to know how I could make such a scene in front of Christopher. The only part of the article that mattered to her was the bit that said, 'Other notable attendees included Pageant CEO Christopher Butkus.'" I stabbed my fork into my *migas*.

"Maybe you should tell her about Stephen." Amy had a mouthful of French toast. "That would calm her down, wouldn't it?"

"It might. Or it might send her into a tailspin of despair. She seems quite obsessed with Christopher for some reason."

"Some reason…" Sumira made the universal sign for *cash* with one hand.

"You know, you're right. I wonder if my parents forgot to start a 401(k) and now the future of their retirement rests on my marriage prospects. That would explain a lot."

We chewed for a moment as the server refilled our coffee mugs.

"You know Christopher's strategy?" Eva began thoughtfully. I had filled the group chat in on everything Christopher had said after the sustainability dinner. "Playing hard to get. Do you think it's effective? It sounds like a cliché, but if it works, I'll try it. Clearly I'm doing something wrong. Maybe I come on too strong."

"Um," Amy started before I could reply. She wore an embarrassed grin. "It worked for me."

"What?"

"After Rachel told us about Christopher's advice, I tried it on Ryan." She laughed. "I literally just ignored him. I acted happy and busy but I didn't seek him out or try to initiate sex or anything. And he *did*."

"He did?"

She nodded. "Clearly Christopher is onto something. I mean, he's a guy, so I guess he gets it."

Eva looked to me for confirmation.

"Yeah. I'm shocked to say that it worked on Stephen too. I didn't text him for a couple days and now he's a Chatty Cathy. He actually invited me to a wedding."

"Really? Wow. When is it?"

"Next month."

"That's short notice for a wedding." Sumira tilted her head back to drain her mimosa.

"Let me have this, okay? I love weddings. Free food, free booze, open dance floor…not to mention love in the air."

Eva buried her face in her hands. "Don't become a romantic now; I can't handle it."

Amy, Sumira, and I exchanged sympathetic glances.

"No word from Erica, then?"

"Erica? I haven't heard from her in over a month. No, I met a girl named Sherry at the Wildrose on Valentine's Day, but she's ghosting me."

"Women should know better than to ghost other women." Amy tutted.

I polished off my food, dabbed my mouth with my napkin, and announced, "We're going out. Let us be your wingwomen, Eva."

"Yes!" Amy clapped. "I could really use a night out. I'll leave my wedding ring at home and pretend to be single. For wing-woman purposes."

"Amy!" Eva looked scandalized.

"I'm kidding!" Amy rolled her eyes before mumbling under her breath, "Sort of."

Amy and Eva's dilemmas aside, love was in the air as spring approached. On my lunch break, I was browsing for a dress to wear as Stephen's wedding date when Jane called me.

"Are you in a public place?" she asked.

"Why?" I shiftily glanced around the Nordstrom dress department. "You're making me nervous. What's wrong?"

"I'm going to text you a picture and it might make you scream."

"Did you injure yourself? Because, as you remember from the time you shut your thumb in your car door, I can't handle gore." I had a feeling I knew what was coming, and it wasn't a picture of a thumb injury.

"No. Shush and look at my text."

It was a photo of her manicured hand wearing a gleaming, emerald-cut engagement ring. I shrieked, paying no mind to the shoppers and salespeople nearby.

"He asked you? You're engaged? Tell me everything!"

"He took me to see *Pride and Prejudice* at the Seattle Rep last night, and when the lights went down after the first half, he got down on one knee, so when the lights came back up for intermission I was like, 'Where are you?' until I looked down and saw him kneeling in the aisle, holding the ring. He said, 'Jane, will you be my bride?' and I said, 'Yes!' and everyone started clapping! We're going to have a New Year's wedding!"

"Oh, Jane. I'm so happy for you. You deserve all of it. The perfect proposal, the perfect husband. Everything."

"Thanks, Rach. You know, none of this would have happened without you."

I inhaled sharply, feeling a tad emotional.

"What you said to me when I was dating Robbie," Jane continued. "No one else was brave enough to say anything like that to me. But you were."

"I had to try, you know? If you'd wanted to stay with Robbie, I would've shut up about it. But it felt like I had to say something."

"'Are you sure he's enough for you?'" Jane quoted my own words back to me, her voice thickening with emotion now. "'Funny enough? *Fun* enough? Because if he is, I'm happy for you. But I don't think he is.' You called out something that I felt deep down but was trying to repress. And if you hadn't had the guts to say that to me—even though I was hurt at the time—I would never have met Owen. My life would have turned out so different. I love you, Rach."

And now I was wiping away tears in the middle of Nordstrom.

"I love you too. And I love Owen. I'm so happy for both of you."

"Okay, I have to call Mom."

"She might die of happiness."

"I know."

I stashed my phone back in my purse and found my attention drawn to the far corner of the dress department. The wedding dresses. Before I knew what I was doing, I had crossed the floor and told the salesgirl, beaming, "My sister just got engaged." She smiled indulgently at me as I caressed creamy silks and petal-pink tulle. I oohed over a few chic, elegant dresses that would look spectacular on Jane. And then I stopped, my heart swelling, to gaze at a different sort of gown. It was a lacy column dress with a long train and a gently plunging neckline. It was like my childhood princess dreams had married my adolescent fashion dreams and given birth to this confection. Instantly I was off, picturing myself walking down a grassy aisle, holding a simple bouquet of pale pink peonies, a veil blowing around my face in a gentle breeze, and—*what?*

Why was I doing this? Since when was I a woman who stared longingly at bridal gowns? So I liked princesses and fashion; I had never pictured my wedding day. I didn't even know if I wanted an outdoor wedding, or a veil.

Rachel Weiss, get a grip on yourself.

Besides, who was I going to walk down that aisle toward? Stephen Branson? I'd have to see how things went as his plus-one before I started picturing myself as his bride.

Before I knew it, we were halfway through April. The gray clouds cleared long enough for us to catch a glimpse of sunrays and blue skies. On Saturday afternoon, Stephen picked me up from my apartment like a true gentleman in his VW Golf.

I'd spent all day getting ready: I did a face mask and a hair mask, whitened my teeth, painted my fingernails and toenails a bridal-blush pink, and did full body exfoliation, depilation, and hydration. I wore a short and sweet dress with a tropical floral pattern and cutouts at the waist. That, plus strappy nude sandals and my white blazer, made me feel, frankly, smokin' hot. I could tell Stephen approved. He wolf-whistled as I climbed into his car. He wore a navy suit with—*oh Lord*—bare ankles peeking tantalizingly out of his loafers. I could tell it was going to be a good night when he kissed me so enthusiastically in the car that I had to wipe my lipstick off both our faces.

The wedding was at a sweet little Woodinville winery. There was a white canopy and twinkly lights overhead and in all the bushes. The aisle was a brick path lined with rustic wine barrels topped with white hydrangeas. The bride and groom were both college friends of Stephen's. I was quite excited to meet his friends. The first order of business was the ceremony. It was one of those blessedly short Unitarian ceremonies and went off without a hiccup. All of a sudden, it was time for the cocktail hour, when they were serving a vodka cocktail hilariously dubbed the "Marry Me."

Stephen guided me around with his hand on the small of my back, introducing me to various friends. He was so charismatic and (there's no other word for it) sexy, I could tell people were quite dazzled by him. His friends would blink in surprise and exchange looks with each other when Stephen graced them with his presence. I curled my hand into the crook of his arm and almost felt guilty about our effervescence as a couple; I didn't want to show up the bride and groom.

Shortly after I snagged my second Marry Me from a passing server, the happy couple made their grand reentrance. The DJ announced them and, as everyone cheered, I shouted, "Mazel tov!"

Stephen shot me a naughty grin and pulled me over to the grass, where he gathered me close to him and began to rock back and forth in an intimate slow dance, even though it wasn't time for dancing yet. We revolved slowly on the spot to the jazzy cocktail hour music, earning wistful and approving gazes from some of the older guests. I looked up at the strong, jutting line of his jaw, nestled above my head, and felt a catch in my chest. My heart leaped as though it could tell that this moment was something to remember.

He planted a lingering kiss on my hair, and then I felt the ruffle of his breath as he whispered, "For fuck's sake."

"What?" I asked, leaning back.

"Just saw someone." His voice was gruff. He tried to laugh it off. "You know how it is at these things. You never know what ghosts from the past will show up."

"Ooh, is it an ex-girlfriend?" I was intrigued. I craned my neck around but couldn't make out a specific face among the crowd.

"No, nothing like that." Stephen pulled me against him with a playful show of possessiveness.

"Good. We wouldn't want a catfight to spoil this beautiful evening."

He laughed, showing off his shiny white teeth and the curve of his Adam's apple. (Good God, he was an attractive man.) "Come on, let's get another drink."

"Marry Me?"

"What?" He stopped dead, his hand trailing out of mine.

"I only meant, did you want a Marry Me cocktail?" I blinked innocently.

Color flooded back into his face and he laughed again. "Sure, why not."

I have to admit, I'd thought it would be a cute joke (since the name of the cocktail practically begged for it), but Stephen's reaction was less than flattering.

"Two Marry Mes, please." I sashayed up to the bar ahead of Stephen.

I had only just registered that there was a familiar profile in my peripheral vision when I heard Stephen grumble behind me, "Actually, I'll wait back at the—"

The man beside me turned to look at us.

"—table."

"Rachel," Christopher Butkus began in surprise, and then he stopped. His eyes fell on Stephen, and he blanched as though someone had thrown water in his face.

"Hi, Christopher." I looked from him over my shoulder toward Stephen—but he had disappeared. "Um. Fancy meeting you here."

Christopher was still staring off toward wherever Stephen had gone; he wrenched his gaze back toward me with apparent difficulty.

"How—how do you know Jake and Vanessa?" he asked.

"I don't, but my boyfriend went to college with them." I took a guilty sip of my cocktail; I hadn't yet confirmed the whole boyfriend thing with Stephen.

"*That's* your—that's the guy?" Christopher asked with a touch of alarm. I was simultaneously annoyed and pleased at the intimacy in the question, the reminder that we'd had a (weirdly) open conversation the last time we'd met.

"Stephen?" I was puzzled. "Yes…" And then, as Christopher blinked in confusion and visibly tried to shake off whatever was bothering him, it all clicked. Christopher *liked* me. He liked me, and he was appalled to see me with a guy who was so clearly more attractive than him.

I stifled a giggle and placed a comforting hand on his arm.

"Look, Christopher, I really appreciated your advice last time. It was sweet of you. And"—I thought I'd throw him a bone—"I think it actually helped. So you can feel good about that."

The poor man. How had I not seen it before? He seemed to be getting even more worked up, no doubt with regret that he had helped me nab a different guy. I slid Stephen's untouched Marry Me toward him in sympathy. He accepted it and drank half of it down.

"There you are." A woman appeared at Christopher's shoulder. "I was wondering what was taking you so long."

"Hey, babe." Christopher's face softened. "I got caught up talking to a friend."

My drink seemed to freeze in my throat. The woman twining her arm through Christopher's was the most stunning woman I'd ever seen in real life. She had a thin ski-slope nose, demure rosebud lips, and those jutting collarbones I'd always thought were photoshopped in. Her hair was perfectly straight and shiny, the color of honey, and she wore a chic, shapeless silk dress that hung off her body in a revoltingly effortless way. Suddenly I felt hideous, scantily clad and overdressed at the same time, my floral cutout dress screaming where hers whispered, my curly chignon trying way too hard, and my giant Julia Roberts mouth deafeningly loud even when I wasn't speaking.

I wanted to melt into the floor and disappear.

"Rachel, this is my date, Andrea. Andrea, Rachel," Christopher said.

"So nice to meet you. Your dress is to die for. And I'm just so happy this guy was able to find a date!" I gave Christopher a playful punch on the arm—*why?*

Andrea gave Christopher a *Who is this crazy lady?* look, squinting her makeup-less eyes. (Makeup-less? God, was she really not wearing *any* eye makeup?)

Andrea's appearance as Xio's replacement cemented how very wrong I'd been. Christopher didn't *like* me. He was more of a fuckboy than Stephen was, dating gorgeous women and replacing them just a few weeks later.

"Well, I should get Stephen another Marry Me since you've finished his." I laughed and noticed that Andrea seemed pouty. This gave me a surge of confidence: I might not be a five-foot-ten supermodel type, but at least I was fun.

"Don't worry about it, Rach," came Stephen's voice in my ear. I spun around, and he wrapped his hands around my waist. "Let's get a couple tequila shots instead."

Christopher made a grimace of distaste. Stephen seemed to notice because he scoffed and rolled his eyes before placing our order at the bar.

"So, I take it you two, um...," I started, then faltered. Their expressions did not look at all receptive to friendly small talk. I glanced at Andrea, intending to share a *What's up with these guys?* look, but she had taken out her phone and was swiping at it intently. She didn't look *quite* as beautiful with her neck craned at a ninety-degree angle.

"Small world." Christopher addressed his words to Stephen. "I know your girlfriend. Congratulations, by the way. I know it's not easy for you to settle down. Rachel's a good one."

My eyes darted between them. I was confused. Christopher's tone did not sound sarcastic, but it also didn't quite fit with his ostensibly friendly words.

Stephen didn't flinch at the G-word. He arched his eyebrow at me almost imperceptibly and collected our tequila shots. "Thanks. I know she's a good one, or she wouldn't be my girl. See you."

He led the way through the crowd, over to our dinner table. He handed me a shot glass and clinked his against it.

"Cheers!" I followed suit, and we thumped our empty glasses down on the table.

"What a lucky guy I am." Stephen leaned toward me with a devilish smile. "I have the hottest girlfriend at this wedding."

"Look. I know we haven't really discussed—"

Stephen stopped me. "No, it's okay. I like it."

"You do?" This was the easiest Define the Relationship talk I'd ever had.

"Yeah." And he draped his arm over the back of my chair, as if he wanted the whole wedding to look at us and see a couple.

We talked and giggled our way through dinner. Honestly, I hadn't realized how much fun he was before tonight. He was as much of an exuberant extrovert as I was, and he had our table-mates conversing with such gusto, it became apparent that our table was the life of the party. He was so amusing that Annette—fiftysomething former aunt of the bride by marriage, now divorced—screamed with laughter, and people at the other tables looked around in apparent jealousy. When dinner ended and people began to disperse, heading to the bar or the dance floor, Stephen pointed out various people he knew and told me all the college gossip about them.

At one point, he flagged down a couple more tequila shots, and we whooped and high-fived each other after tossing them back. I leaned in for a kiss and he scooped me into his lap instead, making me shriek until he kissed me to quiet me down. I was having such a good time—and was so tipsy—I don't know what compelled me to open my eyes as Stephen's mouth moved down to kiss my neck. Perhaps I felt someone looking at me. At the other end of the white tent, Christopher sat rigidly at his table, staring at me with a stony expression. Was he judging me for having a bit of fun? It was a wedding, for God's sake! I noticed Andrea was sitting next to him, her neck now resembling that of an ancient turtle as she jabbed at her phone. I pointed at Andrea and mouthed, very clearly, to Christopher: *Kiss your girlfriend.* He looked both startled and offended. I mouthed it again, as obviously as possible. Christopher narrowed his eyes at me. Stephen looked up.

"Did you say something?" he asked—and then his gaze followed mine. He stood up so suddenly I slid onto the floor.

"Ow, what?" I straightened up, rubbing my hip.

"What are you..." He turned his back to Christopher and spoke as quietly as possible. "How do you know him?"

"Christopher? Our parents are neighbors."

"Jesus," he muttered.

"Why? What's going on with you two?"

"Nothing."

"Then why have you been huffing and ignoring each other all night like old lovers?" I asked.

"Like—what?" Stephen mouthed wordlessly for a moment, then grabbed my hand. "Come on."

"Where are we going?" I hurried after him gleefully.

He pulled me into a bush full of fairy lights.

"Here?" I breathed as a branch jabbed into my thigh. "Well, okay, but you better hurry up before this bush gets there first."

"What?" Stephen looked appalled. "I'm not—I wouldn't try—not here!"

I felt myself pull an Andrea-like pout; that was the second time tonight he hadn't gotten my joke.

"Why have you dragged me in here?"

"To tell you about..." Stephen looked nervously over his shoulder. "About Christopher Butkus."

I stopped fidgeting with the bush at once. *Yes!* This would be the best gossip I would hear all night, I knew it.

"Go on."

"It's not a fun story." He sounded stern. I nodded and adjusted my expression to one of somber respect.

"We were friends in college. Best friends, actually."

"You were?" I tried to picture it, but they were so different: tall, fair, innocent-looking Christopher and the smaller, darker, naughtier Stephen.

"Yep. We met in our frat."

Ugh. So Christopher was a frat guy on top of everything else? Gross.

Wait, what was I saying? That meant my boyfriend was a frat guy too. Yet somehow it wasn't as surprising for Stephen.

"We did everything together," Stephen went on. "Took the same classes. Our senior year, we were partners for our final project. Everyone was supposed to come up with a business idea." Stephen swallowed hard and dropped his eyes; I could tell this memory really upset him. "One night, we were brainstorming, and I came up with this idea..." He paused, letting it sink in. He couldn't be going where I thought he was going with this, could he? "And we ended up using it for the project. And then, a few years after graduation, imagine my surprise when..." He stopped and looked around; we both gazed into the distance at Christopher, who was under the tent, dancing with Andrea.

"When what?" I prompted, breathless.

"When I heard that he had turned my idea into a real company and gotten filthy rich from it."

"Oh my God." My stomach lurched; it was so horrible. "He didn't even ask you first?"

Stephen shook his head. "Nope. Just took my idea and ran with it. And now look at him. Worth millions. Must be nice."

"Stephen, I'm so sorry. That's *awful*."

He looked down at me, his face glowing with saintly martyrdom. "You know what? It's okay. I've got a great job. Plenty of money. And, oh yeah…" He gripped my hips and kissed me. "A hot girlfriend. It just, ah, it can be weird to see him. Because of everything that happened."

"Of course. We won't say another word to him tonight. Now let's go dance."

Whether Christopher and Andrea left soon after or not, I had no idea. I didn't spare him another thought for the rest of the evening. Stephen and I whirled around the dance floor and, when there was a lull in the energy under the tent, I got the DJ to play "Hava Nagila" and started up a rip-roaring hora. I even got people to hoist the bride and groom up in chairs; they'll remember that moment for the rest of their lives, bless their Unitarian hearts.

Shortly after the hora, Stephen brought his sweat-slicked face close to mine (how does he look so good sweaty?) and proposed that we find a room in the hotel. An hour of pretty good drunk sex ensued. I could *swear* he was getting better.

Who would have thought? I had a boyfriend (who actually consented to being my boyfriend)—hoorah!—and another reason to hate Christopher Butkus. I decided not to tell Mom the sordid details about her beloved Butkus—for her health.

CHAPTER 8

THE NEXT WEEKEND, AMY and I were at Eva's apartment, getting ready to go out. Eva had decided her birthday was the perfect time to take us up on our offer to be her wingwomen.

"I've swiped through so many people on Tinder that it's now showing me Portland lesbians." She dusted bronzer onto her cheekbones.

"Portland? Boo, hiss."

"I know, right?"

"Aw, I love getting dressed up together!" Amy wrapped a lock of hair around a curling iron. The room filled with the smell of sizzling hairspray. "These days I spend every weekend in sweats watching Netflix on my iPad. This is like old times."

I grunted in agreement as I struggled into my Spanx. "How did we do this every weekend in college? I feel like a bewigged, lipsticked baboon."

Eva glanced over her shoulder at me. "Your curls *are* doing the most tonight. Is it humid or something?"

I gave her a look. She'd just had her hair done, and her fresh balayage combined with the bronzer made her look like she'd just stepped off a tropical island. I was truly blessed with gorgeous friends.

"By the way, why couldn't Sumira make it?" I asked.

"She just said she was busy."

"Hmm." I perched against Eva's bed, troubled by a sudden thought. "Do you guys think everything's okay with her? Has she been kind of distant lately?"

"I figured she was living her glamorous life." Amy fluffed the roots of her hair.

"You don't think she's..." I paused. I didn't even want to say the words. "Drifting apart? Outgrowing the group chat?"

"No way!" Eva cried. "Impossible."

"I think we need some shots." Amy bustled off to the kitchen and returned with three shot glasses full of tequila and a fistful of lime wedges. We clinked. "To Eva! Happy birthday!"

"I can't believe my girl's turning thirty!" I whooped and we tossed the tequila back.

"Capitol Hill, here we come, baby!"

Here is the thing about going out at the advanced age of twenty-nine and, in Eva's case, thirty. You're so confident and mature that nothing can faze you. The awkward little things that once would have killed your vibe (such as the bartender pretending not to see you, or having to pick your Spanx wedgie five times an hour) just roll off your back; with a hardened shield of age and wisdom, you become unstoppable.

The ladies of the Wildrose had no chance. It was over when we walked in. They've got all sorts there, and by all sorts I mean lesbians in flannel, butch lesbians, and butch lesbians in flannel. So naturally, when the three of us walked in wearing short skirts and lipstick, we had them right where we wanted them.

To be truthful, Amy seemed a bit disappointed that there were so few men for her to flirt with. Although I thought it was rather clever: since she was so eager to flirt but less eager, I assumed, to commit adultery, why not flirt with women? That way there would be much less risk of an oopsie, as Amy was staunchly heterosexual.

We approached the bar and, indeed, were pointedly ignored by the bartender—buzz cut with neck tattoo—who carried on her conversation with a voluptuous drag queen for a good five minutes before addressing us. I assumed this was our punishment for not adhering to the dress code.

Vodka sodas in hand, we ventured to the perimeter of the dance floor. A charming sort of industrial screech rock was playing, the musical assault captained by a petite blond DJ wearing grandfatherly wire-rimmed spectacles.

"She's cute," I yelled in Eva's ear, pointing to the DJ.

Eva smiled vaguely, scoping out the room. "Not really my type."

"What is your type?"

"Oh, you know."

I did not. Amy and I shared a wry look. Eva had dated across the spectrum of womankind: the armpit-bush farmers market hippie; the skateboarding dog walker who'd turned out to have a cocaine problem; the corporate, stiletto-wearing Barbie; the Polynesian opera singer three times Eva's size; and many in between.

"What about her?" Amy nodded toward one of the flannel-wearers. Eva shrugged and sipped her drink.

"First things first." I downed my drink and approached the DJ. I wiggled in front of her, trying to get her attention. Wiggled, smiled, wiggled, pouted. When it was clear she was not going to acknowledge me, I leaned over her table.

"I can't really dance to this." I gave her sad baby eyes.

She slipped her headphones off one ear.

"What?"

"Can you play something we can dance to?" I pouted some more and surreptitiously squeezed my boobs together with my arms.

She pressed her lips together as though it physically hurt her to contemplate bending her art to such a base request.

"Please?" I glanced over my shoulder. "My friend over there is going through a bit of a heartbreak." Constant romantic frustration is a kind of heartbreak, right? "We're trying to cheer her up. Plus, it's her birthday." The DJ's eyes flitted toward Eva and Amy.

"What could you"—she gave a dejected sigh, as though she'd suffered a humiliating defeat—"dance to?"

"She loves Robyn!" I beamed.

With a curt nod, she jutted her jaw and waved me away. As I rejoined Amy and Eva, the music shifted, the screeches dying off and the beat pumping louder; I could tell she was doing some fancy hocus-pocus to transition the song. The energy in the bar shifted with it, growing still and then rising as though everyone scented the change on the wind.

Eva looked at me askance. "What did you—" And then the first notes of a remixed "Call Your Girlfriend" played, and Eva squealed.

The dance floor filled quickly. I glanced at the DJ to see if she would acknowledge my brilliance, but she was chewing on a Red Vine and appeared wholly unconcerned with the general state of euphoria the song had inspired.

Eva was having the time of her life. All eyes were on her. Amy and I were living it up too, but there was something to be said for gaydar. Several suitors vied for Eva's hand; she danced with a hefty flannel with an undercut while Robyn played, then a denim-clad ginger, and then a tiny woman with box braids during a Lady Gaga song.

After the Lady Gaga song ended, Eva dragged us over to the bar, panting and smiling.

"I liked her," she said, as Amy waved down the bartender.

"Yes, Lady Gaga *is* very popular," I said kindly, thinking Eva really needed to get out more.

She swatted my arm. "No, the last girl I danced with, idiot."

"Ooh." Amy and I both swiveled around to scope out the mark. She was wearing an itty-bitty crop top and high-waisted jeans and was now dancing with the ginger.

"Go dance with her again."

"I can't just cut in." Eva wrinkled her brow as I handed her a fresh vodka soda.

"Why not?"

"That's awkward."

We all slurped our drinks thoughtfully and watched as Ginger ground her way closer to Eva's crush.

"Cringe." Amy shook her head.

"She looks like she likes it, though." Eva looked put out.

We watched as Ginger leaned in and whispered something that made the other girl laugh.

"You're much hotter than the ginger," I pointed out. "She'll probably be so grateful if you go dance with her again."

"Rachel, I'm not…" Eva paused, and I was startled to hear a catch in her voice. "I'm not like you. I can't just wag my butt in someone's face and get them to like me."

Wag my butt…? I had to think about that for a moment. I liked to think I had more class—that I enticed people with my candor and wit rather than my backside. I had been joking about feeling like a baboon earlier, but perhaps that was truly how my friends saw me: as a sort of sexy Jewish red-bottomed baboon. I tried to catch Amy's eye, but she looked away pointedly, sucking on her straw.

"But you're perfectly—" I stopped, noticing that Eva's face had grown blotchy; she really was upset. "Come on." I grabbed her hand and led the way to the bathroom.

In the bathroom's fluorescent light, it became apparent that Eva was on the verge of a breakdown. She gulped, groping for a paper towel as she blinked back tears. Amy and I crowded around her.

"What's going on?" Amy asked gently.

"I can't do this." Eva's voice trembled.

"Do what?" I was confused. "Drink? Dance? Have fun?"

"I can't DATE," she exploded. Amy jumped, splashing vodka on herself.

"What do you mean? Of course you can! Don't you want to find someone?"

Eva looked at me like I had sprouted a luscious beard from each nostril. Her eyes were red and her mascara had smeared (which, if I'm being honest, gave her a sex-kittenish look).

"Are you as stupid as you are gorgeous? Of course I want to find someone, Rachel!"

"Well, then?" I glanced at Amy for help, but she was dabbing paper towels on her arm where she'd spilled.

"No one wants to find *me*! There's something wrong with me."

"Don't say that!" Amy and I shouted over one another.

"You take that back! You're a perfect human being."

Eva pressed the paper towel to her face and sagged against the (filthy) sink.

"It's true." Her words were muffled. "Everyone I've asked out this year has said no."

"What? Who—?" I'd wanted to say, *Who are these Tinder girls who rejected you and where can I find them to beat them up?* but Amy interjected.

"That's not true. What about Erica? And the other girl?"

Eva cast a dark look over the both of us.

"If they go out with me, have sex with me, and *then* ghost me, it's even *worse* than saying no in the first place."

I blinked. Her words had rendered me speechless. My mind grappled with competing thoughts: *There is no way anyone in their right mind could dislike my best friend; I must shout down her harmful self-talk at once; Is it possible she has a point?* But—no! It was too much for my brain to handle, the reality of the beautiful human standing before me and the indisputable fact that she had been rejected. *Multiple times.*

I mouthed silently, looking to Amy for help. Her lips were pursed, her brow creased, and I could tell she was undergoing the same painful internal dilemma as me.

"It just...It makes no..." I trailed off, thinking of my own problems with Stephen—dicknotized—and Amy's inexplicable problems with Ryan. I got the sudden feeling that I was facing a difficult question in a field in which I was not, as I had thought, an expert.

"Everyone in the world is insane except us," Amy whispered, and I nodded my agreement. The fact that we were four flawless women and the world was not throwing itself at our feet was just—well, perhaps Sumira was different. In fact, maybe she would be able to offer us some—

"Christopher," Eva croaked, straightening herself up with an air of resolve.

"What?" I was aghast.

"Let's ask Christopher what to do."

I felt my eyes widen in shock as I held out my hands defensively.

"Look, Eva, I don't think that's really—"

"She's right." Amy stepped forward so she was shoulder to

shoulder with Eva, the two of them facing me down like bullies in a schoolyard. "We have no idea what we're doing. But Christopher does. His advice helped me; it got Ryan to initiate sex, for God's sake. Only a couple times, but still." She set her mouth in a hard line, and I was distracted for a moment by my poor, sweet Amy who clearly hadn't had sex in at least a week, and who could be more deserving than her? But I would have to come back to that thought.

"Do it. Ask him." Eva's tears had subsided and her cheeks were turning pink; she was shifting from distraught to excited, and there was no way I could say no to her now.

I let out a long-suffering sigh my mother would have been proud of.

"I don't have his number."

"Instagram," Amy said instantly. "You know he uses it."

I sucked on my teeth, putting off the dreaded moment a little longer.

"DO IT!" Eva shouted, and I jumped so badly I dropped my phone.

"Aw, gross!" I picked it up gingerly. Amy dampened a paper towel and wiped at my phone impatiently, with the air of a teacher who has dealt with a lot of gross things.

"Come on, that girl could leave any minute."

Realizing Amy was right, I opened Instagram and found Christopher Butkus quickly.

"Dear Christopher," I began.

"Come on!" Amy jiggled her foot. "Just get to the point. Ask him for advice to help Eva get a girl."

I started the message again. "Hey, Christopher, remember when you gave me advice about"—I stopped and decided not to mention Stephen's name, in case it caused Christopher to toss his phone in rage—"a guy? Wondering if you could help my friend. She's having bad luck with the ladies. Keeps getting rejected, ignored, and ghosted. She's hot so that's not the problem."

I sent it—and then decided to add some more details.

"We're at a club and there's a cute girl here. But my friend is scared because she's been burned too many times. Thoughts?"

"Okay. Well, that's out there now. Should we go back to the bar and—" I was going to say that we should carry on with our night because there was no telling when he would respond, but then I glanced back at the conversation and gasped. "He's typing back now."

Amy and Eva crowded around me, and we peered down at my phone.

"People are all the same," he wrote, and the three of us intoned his words aloud. "We like a bit of competition. We like to think something is our idea. We like to feel like luck is on our side."

Eva looked up at me, puzzled.

"Can you be more specific?" I typed. "What should she do?"

"Have fun in front of the girl in question. Maybe talk about other girls where she can hear you. Get her to approach you."

"What does he—" Amy began, but something clicked in my brain.

"I got it!" I typed a quick thank-you, then slipped my phone back in my purse.

Back in the club, I told Amy to follow my lead.

"Eva," I said, "I'm going to find someone for you to dance with, and you have to do it. It's just a dance, nothing more has to come of it with the person, okay?"

Eva nodded.

I scoped the crowd and found an edgy-looking woman with tattoos and long blue hair dancing with a group of friends. I pointed her out, and to my surprise, Eva didn't ask anything further. She slithered through the crowd and danced right up to the blue-haired girl, smiling and confident. The girl looked delighted and turned her back on her friends to dance with Eva.

Next, I fished in my purse and pulled out a ten-dollar bill.

"Excuse me." I approached a woman in a leather jacket sitting at the bar. After I had explained my request, she snorted and nodded with a grin as she pocketed the ten.

I dragged Amy onto the dance floor, where we started to dance right next to Eva's crush and her latest partner. I gave a thumbs-up over Amy's head, and the woman in the leather jacket gave me a salute. I felt like I was in a spy movie.

Leather jacket woman danced over to the short girl with box braids and shouted, "'Scuse me; I was wondering if you could introduce me to that girl? I saw you dancing with her earlier."

"What?" Eva's crush looked confused.

"That girl." Leather jacket woman pointed over the crowd to where Eva was dancing. I mentally patted myself on the back for the excellent choice of decoy dance partner; dancing with the blue-haired girl, Eva looked untouchably cool. "D'you know her? Can you introduce me?"

"Um..." On her tiptoes, she peered at Eva, and her next words were tinged with regret. "Not really, sorry."

I waited a beat, and as the woman in the leather jacket gave a convincingly dejected shrug and walked away, I said, "I actually do!"

The girl with the braids looked at me.

"Oh, I guess she didn't hear." I turned back to Amy.

"Sorry, what did you say?" Box braid girl's partner was starting to look irritated.

"I was just saying I do know that girl over there," I shouted. "She's my friend."

"Oh!" She smiled and it lit up her face. "Um." She gave a slightly apologetic look as her partner rolled her eyes and slunk away into the crowd. "What's her name?"

"Eva!" I continued to dance with Amy unconcernedly.

I could practically feel the tension in the air as the girl stood on her tiptoes to look at Eva again. Amy grinned and gripped my hand.

"I think I danced with her earlier," the girl said.

"Yeah, she's danced with a lot of people tonight."

"Do you know if she's single?"

"Sorry, it's really loud in here. Do you want me to just introduce you to her?"

"That would be cool!" she shouted. "Thanks!"

I led the way across the dance floor and over to Eva. She did an excellent job of not noticing us.

"Hey, Eva, this is…," I began.

"Jasmine!"

"Eva, this is Jasmine. We were just dancing over there; she's really cool."

I winked at Jasmine, and she pressed her hands together, mouthing, *Thank you.*

"I think Christopher might be a genius," I told Amy a few minutes later as Eva and Jasmine leaned their heads together at the bar, deep in conversation.

"I think you might be a genius," Amy said. "It was your idea."

"Christopher led me there."

"Well, maybe you make a good team." I snorted skeptically.

"I wonder…" Amy sounded thoughtful. "I wonder, if you were the one married to Ryan, if you'd have the same problems that I have."

"What?" I set my empty glass down on the bar. "What are you

RACHEL WEISS'S GROUP CHAT

talking about? Ryan said himself that he's the problem, not you. He called you a Victoria's Secret model, remember?"

Amy gave a little shrug and looked away.

"It just seems like it would be easier if I had your confidence," she said quietly.

"Ames…" I didn't know what to say. This night was supposed to be about my friends—helping Eva find someone and getting Amy out on the town—but they kept stroking my ego.

I didn't hate it, of course. Us red-bottomed types enjoy a compliment as much as anyone—possibly more.

"I'll just try to be more like you." Amy's voice was stronger as she grinned at me. "You know I've looked up to you ever since we met freshman year. Any tips?"

"Just…If you see something you want, just go for it. Don't sit there wondering whether you deserve it or whether you'll fail. You always fail if you don't try. And don't let Ryan's—or anyone's—reaction to you impact the way you feel about yourself." I thought about it for a moment and continued, "Have you ever tried daily affirmations? Every morning, you stand in front of the mirror and tell yourself something good, like 'I am whole, I am safe, I am loved.'"

"Do you do that every morning?" Amy asked.

"Yep."

"What do you say to yourself?"

"Me?" I waggled my eyebrows at her. "I say, 'I am smart, I am successful, I am sexy as hell.'"

Amy burst out laughing.

"It's true."

"How did I get such amazing friends?" Amy bumped her hip into mine.

"Back at ya." I planted a kiss on her hair.

Eva and Jasmine joined us, and we decided to have a round of shots and then head over to Havana for a change of scenery. After the infusion of tequila to my bloodstream and all the compliments that had been showered on me, I was feeling pretty fantastic, like I was floating down a red carpet, or like I was one of those fembots from *Austin Powers* with superhuman breasts. I wanted to shower everyone with love—including myself. Which is why I sent a secret text as we clattered down the sidewalk toward Havana.

Inside, the dance floor was packed and the gilded bar swarmed with people, every plush red booth full. We managed to squeeze our way up to the bar to order four mojitos. We were just plotting how best to carve out a spot in which to drink our cocktails when Stephen appeared at my shoulder. My stomach did a flip-flop at the smell of his cologne and the sight of him in a gray T-shirt and high-end black jeans. There was truly something about the cut of his jaw, the pout of his lips, and the haughtiness of his hairstyle that made me feel like my insides were melting.

"Hey." He was panting slightly as he put his hand on the small of my back and kissed my lips.

"That was fast."

"I was out with some friends nearby, but I'd much rather be with you." He tipped his mouth to my ear. "You look amazing."

Goose bumps exploded down my arms and legs. Figuring it would be impolite to jump on him then and there, I pulled away from him and turned to the girls.

"This is Stephen. Stephen, these are my friends, Amy, Eva, and Jasmine."

Eva looked like she was close to laughter; she said hello and raised her eyebrows at me. Her eyes flicked sideways as she tried to catch Amy's eye, but Amy was staring at Stephen as though he were made of diamonds.

I elbowed her and whispered, "I know, right?" She didn't

respond but seemed to catch herself staring and hastily gulped down half of her mojito.

A new song started, and Jasmine led Eva by the hand onto the dance floor; Eva waved her fingers at us as she went, very pleased with herself. I have to admit, I was pleased too. I felt a sense of pride that I'd had a hand in creating the adorable couple now grinding before me.

A half second later, my pride was replaced with panic when I realized that by inviting Stephen, I had made Amy the fifth wheel. I cast my mind about for a topic of conversation that would be engaging enough to withstand the allure of the dance floor and the pumping music. But before I could say a word, a tall, dark-haired man with a Hispanic accent held out a hand to Amy and asked if she'd like to dance.

As she whirled away with the handsome stranger, her strawberry-blond tresses flying, Stephen asked, "Which friend is that again?"

"That's Amy."

"Ah." His lips curled. "The sexually frustrated teacher."

It was then that I noticed with a lurch that Amy's left hand was bare, her wedding ring nowhere in sight.

Stephen and I danced through two sweaty songs, and then he declared that he was in need of liquor. While we waited for our turn at the bar, catching our breath, we heard someone say Stephen's name.

We both looked around to see a guy in a bright orange polo shirt with a couple of friends.

"Stephen Branson, is that really you?"

"Brett." Stephen wasn't looking altogether thrilled to see the bro in front of us. "How's it going, man?"

"I haven't seen this dude in so long," Brett told me as he clasped

Stephen's hand. I grimaced, not seeing a need to reply to this pronouncement. "How's business?" he asked Stephen with a slight laugh in his voice.

For some reason, Stephen's face hardened. "Going great, actually. Good to see you, man." He turned his shoulder toward me, effectively shutting out Brett, who didn't seem to mind.

"Who was—" I began, but then I stopped. Brett and his friends had moved a few feet down the bar, but he was talking animatedly and gesturing toward Stephen. A moment later, they exploded in bro-y laughter.

Hard lines appeared around Stephen's nose; he looked like he'd just smelled something foul as he stared down into his whiskey.

"Stephen, who was that guy?"

"Some idiot I knew in college."

"Oh." I wondered if Brett had been alluding to the fact that Stephen had had his business idea stolen from under him; that would explain Stephen's reaction. "What a jerk."

Stephen worked a muscle in his jaw and glared back at Brett. He muttered darkly under his breath.

"What?" I asked.

"Nothing. Let's go." And he pulled me back onto the dance floor.

After a while, Stephen seemed to shake off the dark mood that seeing Brett had inspired. I was relieved, because it was hard enough to be charming when he was in a normal mood, given how jittery I always felt in his presence; with him pissed off and scowling, it was nearly impossible for me to make it fun. But after a particularly sexy Latin song, a smile crept back onto his face. I noticed the girls were back at the bar—Amy's dance partner hadn't stuck around—so we joined them.

Eva and I exchanged thrilled looks behind Jasmine's back at the fact that Jasmine was *still there*. We were going on two hours since they'd been introduced and she seemed to be thoroughly enjoying Eva's presence. When Stephen went to the bathroom, I took the opportunity to chat with them, making sure to slip in some anecdotes that made Eva look good. Jasmine ate it all up. Stephen returned and struck up a conversation with Amy, who still looked starstruck. (I didn't hate the fact that I was dating a guy who had that effect on people.) Glancing over at them, I felt a rush of warmth: Stephen was truly making an effort to get to know my friends. Maybe it would be time to introduce him to my family soon—okay, maybe just Jane; I didn't think Mom could handle it. After all, no matter how handsome he was, he was no Butkus.

As Jasmine told an amusing story about her sister's dog, Amy glanced over her shoulder at us. I waved happily. She shifted to one side and I noticed the bright orange of Brett's shirt nearby; Stephen noticed it too. I saw him pull a face and then shake it off, no doubt attempting to maintain a friendly demeanor for Amy. And then all thought of the weirdness with Brett vanished from my mind when the first notes of an ABBA song blared.

Eva and I shrieked, and—to her everlasting credit—so did Jasmine. We hustled onto the dance floor along with most of Havana's female population. A mad attempt at disco ensued. A few songs and a bathroom break later, I realized Stephen had disappeared. I found the girls at a table and asked them where he had gone.

"Not sure," Amy said. "I think he left."

"Oh." I was slightly crestfallen. "He was a bit upset earlier. He probably just went home."

I had been looking forward to ending up at home *with* him—he smelled *so* good—but given how tired and sweaty I was, I wasn't too disappointed.

"I think I'm going to head out." Amy's eyes were on her phone.

"Really? Are you sure?" Eva sounded disappointed.

Amy nodded, her lips pressed together. "I'm tired."

We hugged her goodbye, and she slipped off through the still-crowded dance floor.

"Did she seem weird to you?" Eva asked.

"Probably just tired, like she said." I didn't add that I thought being the fifth wheel had bothered her more than she'd let on. I felt a guilty pang, wishing I had spent more time talking to her about Ryan and everything.

The three of us ended the night with burgers and shakes from Dick's, and then I excused myself, leaving Eva alone with Jasmine. On the bus home, I took out my phone to see if Stephen had sent me any messages. He hadn't. I had seven texts from Mom asking if I'd started planning Jane's bachelorette party yet, which I ignored. And I had one new Instagram message. For some reason that I could not account for, my heart sped up as I opened it.

It was from Christopher. "How did your friend do? I hope everything worked out." With a smiley face.

Something welled up in me—something sad, quite incongruous with the thoughtful message I'd just read. And as my thumb flicked from Instagram over to my text messages with Stephen, I realized that Christopher's kindness made a harsh juxtaposition with Stephen's silence.

I typed out a message to Stephen: "You disappeared! Are you okay? It was fun dancing with you tonight. Xoxo."

He didn't respond.

CHAPTER 9

STEPHEN EVENTUALLY CALLED ME back. He apologized for leaving without saying goodbye that night, but I still had this feeling that something was up. He was being squirrelly about making plans to hang out. But tonight was Jane and Owen's engagement party, so I was too busy to dwell on Stephen.

The party was a relatively small affair—*not*. Mom had invited every person with any possible link to our family, Jane, or Owen. All of her friends. All of Jane's friends. Our rabbi. Owen's third cousin once removed, the only family he had in town. Jane's first grade teacher—ninety-three now, so I don't think she knew exactly why she was there. Jane's boss. The Butkuses sent their regrets.

Jane was glowing. We'd gone shopping the previous weekend, and she'd gotten the most angelic dress: a silver midi with spaghetti straps and a slit up one thigh. Her hair was down, sleek and freshly highlighted, and she was wearing a shimmery pink lip gloss with the rest of her makeup minimal and flawless. No jewelry other than her gorgeous new ring, which people asked to see about a thousand times. My sister is goals, as the kids these days would say.

And Owen—well, of course he was perfect. He was so friendly and smiley, the most charming groom-to-be.

I felt a bit gaudy next to Jane in my navy maxi dress and red lipstick, but no one was paying me any attention, so I didn't mind. As expected, I spent most of the party taking Mom's orders: refilling snack bowls, picking up plates and napkins, and making sure everyone's champagne was topped up. Mom was swanning around as though the party were for her. She was so serene and blissful, no one would have guessed that she's actually a desperate maniac. A few hours into the party, she beckoned me into a corner.

"Is it time to bring out the cupcakes?" I wiped a sweaty curl off my forehead.

"No, no." Her voice was breathy and mysterious, her eyes darting around to make sure no one was listening. "Rachel, I need you to do me a favor."

"Oh my God, you *do* need money. How bad is it?" It had to be pretty damn bad if she was asking her middle daughter, who currently had $207 in the bank. (*What?* Payday was two weeks ago.)

"What?" Mom snapped, sounding offended. "This isn't about money. Look…" She pulled me deeper into the corner so we were sort of huddled behind a chair. Her hand drifted up to pat her curls nervously. "I need you to recommend the twins for an internship at your work."

"Excu—*cough*—what?" I choked, having chosen the wrong moment to swallow some champagne. My eyes watered.

"The twins…your *sisters*…I am asking you to recommend them for an internship."

"In…what?" I asked, glancing over at the twins, who were skulking behind Jane's friend Kailey, who was holding her baby on one hip. They were pulling faces in an apparent attempt to make the baby cry. When they succeeded, Kailey looked around to comfort him and the twins scurried away, snorting with laughter.

"In, you know"—Mom waved a vague hand—"computer engineering."

"What?! Mom, they can't…They're not…"

"They're not what? Smart enough?" Mom asked, her face set in a forbidding expression.

Of course they're not smart enough, I thought. They had migrated to the snack table, where Abby was now filming Ollie as she, apparently, endeavored to find out how many olives she could fit in her mouth at once. No doubt the live footage was being broadcast to their little friends on TikTok or something.

"It's a really competitive company."

"*You* work there," Mom pointed out.

"Yes, but even *I'm* not an engineer." My teeth clenched. "They would need really good grades and test scores to even be considered for an internship."

"They have all that." She sounded breezy.

"They do?"

"Yes, of course, of course. The SAT…Flying colors…"

"Really? What was their score?"

"Fifteen-seventy and fifteen-eighty, if I'm remembering correctly." Mom sniffed.

"Are you? Remembering correctly?" I was astounded. We both turned to look at them; Abby was using two fingers to pry a mush of olives out of Ollie's mouth, both of them crying with laughter.

"Yes, I am. They're really quite bright. So anyway." Mom sounded businesslike. "I'll send you all the materials on Monday."

"I doubt that I have much say over anything."

"You're an employee. You can refer them. That's worth something. I've researched it."

"Do *they* want an engineering internship?" I asked skeptically.

"Oh, they don't care, as long as it's something that will look good on their college applications."

"All right." I figured it couldn't hurt to try. The worst thing that could happen was that they didn't get the internship. "Email me their info and I'll do it on Monday."

"Thank you, darling." She pecked me on the cheek. I couldn't help being a little pleased that I'd had an entire conversation with Mom without her bringing up Christopher Butkus.

"Incidentally." Mom hurried to keep up with me as I strode off to rejoin the party. "*Did* you manage to get a word with Christopher Butkus at that environmentalist event?"

How I manage to maintain such naivete at my advanced age, I don't know.

"How is that 'incidentally,' Mom?"

"But did you?" she hissed at my elbow, nodding and smiling at her guests as we passed them. "Because it would be such a shame if you wasted that opportunity. Just because his parents live next door doesn't mean he'll always be around—he's a busy man, Rachel. You're not likely to get lucky again, seeing him serendipitously like that."

"If only that were true." I sighed.

"What?" We came to a halt in the kitchen.

"Yes, Mother, I exchanged a few words with him. But I wouldn't want to get *too* close to him. My *boyfriend* might not like it."

Mom's hands flew to her face in shock, sending her champagne glass hurtling toward the floor. (I caught it; years of dealing with Mom's tantrums had honed my reflexes.) She let out a high-pitched warble, apparently unable to form words.

"Did I just hear you say 'boyfriend'?" Jane asked, beaming. She had wandered into the kitchen with an empty water pitcher.

"Yes, Jane." I threw my shoulders back with pride. "I've been seeing a lovely young man named Stephen Branson."

"No, no, no," Mom moaned to herself. It was as though a window had opened into her brain, and I could see a neon billboard flashing: *Stephen Branson ≠ Christopher Butkus.*

"Yes, yes, yes." I smiled in Mom's face. "I think you'll adore him. I know I do."

Mom had gone pale, her coral lipstick and black mascara standing out against her shocked white face. She looked from me to Jane, as though hoping Jane would tell her it was all a joke.

Jane looked pointedly away from her, her face radiating joy. "Rachel, I'm *so* excited for you. All I want in the world is for you to be happy. I wish everyone could be as happy as I am tonight."

As though magnetically attracted to his betrothed, Owen drifted into the kitchen and put his arms around her waist. They nuzzled each other. If anyone else had done that in my presence, it would have made me queasy, but watching Jane and Owen, I felt all soft and melty inside.

"Thanks for being so happy for me, Mom." I took the empty water pitcher from Jane and refilled it at the sink. "It really means a lot."

We left Mom in the kitchen, where she stood at the window gazing toward the Butkuses' house, doing her best impression of a war widow watching the ghosts of dreams past, forever just out of reach.

I skulked off to the bathroom to check my phone and let out a surprised snort of laughter. Mom's dream son-in-law had replied to my latest Instagram story—a selfie of me all dolled up—saying, "Another sustainability banquet?" With a winky face!

I typed a quick reply: "Aren't you nosy? It's my sister's engagement party."

"Congrats to Jane and Owen! Where was my invite?"

I grinned. It *was* rather classy of him to remember both of their names. I started typing something about how his parents had, in fact, been invited—and then deleted it. It felt awkward to point out that his parents had declined. Someone knocked on the bathroom door then, so I shot off a quick tongue-sticking-out emoji before stashing my phone in my purse. It did not escape my notice that I had a smile plastered on my face for the next ten minutes. I told myself it was because of the joyous occasion, nothing more.

Later that week, whatever happiness I'd felt at the party had melted away, and I was missing my besties. We hadn't heard from Sumira in a while, but it was Ramadan and she'd warned us that she might be quiet on the group chat because she was going to be hangry all month. I might not have thought much about it, except it occurred to me that Amy had been unusually quiet too. I'd thought she'd had fun when we went out for Eva's birthday. Maybe things with Ryan weren't going well and she was too embarrassed to tell us about it.

I had to keep my spirits up somehow. Beginning with the daily question at work: "How do you feel about your manager, in general?"

I smirked as I typed off a brisk reply. "I have never FELT my manager in any way and I resent the implication that there is any feeling going on between us whatsoever. Kenneth is a gentleman." I couldn't help the little snort of mirth that escaped me. My cubicle-mate, Sheryl, glanced at me curiously, but I immersed myself in my unread emails.

Huh. At the top of my inbox—usually full of automated

support ticket emails—was an email addressed specifically to me from someone named Jennie.

"Hi Rachel, this is Jennie from HR. I've put a meeting on your calendar for today; please let me know if the time isn't convenient for you..."

Who the hell was this Jennie? Why did I have a meeting with HR?

Oh no. What did I do?

For the next hour, as time ticked closer to the meeting with Jennie, I mentally catalogued all the things I might have done to get myself fired. There were a lot. For example, there was the time I went to a waxing appointment in the middle of the day (unfortunately missing a team meeting I'd forgotten about). The few (dozen) times I'd shown up late to work with Starbucks in hand. The time I slept with Scott from IT. The time I told Sheryl a joke about Scott's girth that he may or may not have overheard.

Oh, please don't let me get sued for sexual harassment. Again.

(Kidding.)

As I walked to Jennie's office, I had to pass Kenneth's desk. He looked up at me with this expression like I was walking to the guillotine and he was the one who had turned me in. I narrowed my eyes at him. *Kenneth*. What had I ever done to him?

Well, it was official. I was an idiot with a capital *I*. The responses to those daily questions from my corporate overlords were not, in fact, anonymous. I couldn't get Kenneth's puckered little face out of my head. He'd been reading my answers all along! And, apparently, saying things like "I dream of one day throwing off the shackles of capitalism and bending the city of Seattle to my will

as my true self, supervillainess Gull Girl" in response to "How
do you dream big?" was enough to get me referred to a shrink.

I, Rachel Idiot Weiss, had been referred to a psychologist
by HR.

At least I still had my job. For now.

You know, I could try to make a joke out of it. My job was truly
terrible, and it didn't pay that well. But I *did* need it. Everyone
knows how expensive rent is. I had no car because who could
afford that? Paying a hundred bucks a month for public transit
was hard enough. I was still paying off debt to my parents from
when they lent me my first month's rent and security deposit.
And I had credit card debt from ill-advised shopping and that trip
to Cancún. And medical debt from the time I went to the ER with
a broken toe from playing soccer in my Toms. Even with all that,
I knew I was lucky, because my parents had been able to pay for
my college. I hated this job, but I also needed it.

Sure, I could find another job if I needed to, but I had no savings. I would have to find another job, like, immediately. For
some reason, Christopher Butkus's words floated through my
mind: *You might be a force to be reckoned with. If you put your mind
to it.* I didn't know about a force to be reckoned with, but deep
down I knew that I had the potential to be good at my job, to be
an actual professional. And clearly my MO of making a joke out
of everything was proving dangerous. So that was it. No more
messing around. No more funny business at work.

I could now cross "attend an employer-mandated shrink session"
off my bucket list. They'd referred me to someone who wasn't
affiliated with the company, so maybe it was actually just like

normal, non-employer-mandated therapy. But she started with the old, "So, I hear you've had some trouble at work."

"Not exactly." I was grumpy.

"Would you like to tell me about it?" It was like all the therapy sessions I've ever seen on TV: she was a nondescript woman with a gentle smile and a notepad, and there was an abundance of pillows and tissue boxes around me. It was the only time I'd been in the spotlight and felt uncomfortable about it.

"Um." I gave a nervous laugh. "We have to answer these stupid questions every day, and I like to give funny answers. You know, to entertain myself. I thought they were anonymous."

She paused; I wondered if she counted to ten in her head before speaking.

"Why do you feel the questions are stupid?"

"Well." I could feel my soapbox nudging itself under my feet like a friendly pup. "I think it's an invasion of privacy to be constantly surveying us about our state of mind, our work environments, and our attitude toward our jobs. Working for a huge corporation, you *know* you're just a cog in a machine, and it can feel dehumanizing when they're constantly collecting metrics about you. They monitor how many hours I work every day, how many phone calls and tickets I answer, how many smiley faces the customers give me. It feels insulting to have to answer those prissy questions every damn day."

She paused again; she must have counted to twenty this time.

"Do you like your job?"

I squinted at her. "Do you report back to my employer about what I say?"

She shook her head. "Rachel, everything that you or I say in these sessions is strictly confidential. I will never tell anyone what you say in my office."

"Okay, then, no. There's not much to like about my job other than the paycheck and benefits."

"What would you do if money weren't an object?"

I scoffed. "I can't afford to think like that."

Another ten seconds.

"What about your parents? What sort of careers have they had?"

I felt like I was getting whiplash from how quickly she pivoted to my parents.

"My dad is an aerospace engineer. My mom is a professional Jewish mother."

"What does that mean?"

"She was a stay-at-home mom. Now she volunteers and has her clubs—knitting club and book club—and tries to marry off her daughters."

"You have sisters?"

"Three. One older, two younger."

"Tell me about them."

"Jane, my older sister, is...well, perfect, really." I heard my voice grow soft and happy. "She's really smart, so beautiful that she doesn't even have to try, and just the kindest person I've ever met."

"That's a glowing recommendation. What about your younger sisters?"

"They're..." I let out a harsh laugh as I pondered how to explain the twins. "They're sixteen. They're sort of...nutty." I nodded, satisfied that I'd thought up a nice way to say *feral*. "They don't take anything seriously. They're just, you know, teenagers in the worst way. Completely ridiculous."

Twenty very long seconds.

"Do you see yourself in them?"

I was so shocked, my first impulse was to throw a box of tissues at her. But I refrained and breathed in through my nose, trying to collect myself to prevent myself from hissing, *Absolutely fucking not.*

"Me...in the twins?" I pretended to give it some thought. "Not really, no."

She waited for so long the silence was deafening.

The twins were just so *silly*. They did whatever they wanted, whenever they wanted. They didn't care what anyone thought of them. It was like they were the stars of their own personal show and *oh my God*.

"They are just like me," I whispered, horrified.

I could have sworn I saw a satisfied smirk flit across the therapist's face.

"But how...? But I'm not...I thought we were nothing alike. I mean, I don't even really like them."

"Oftentimes, we are quick to criticize others for qualities we dislike in ourselves."

I was not ready for that wisdom mic drop. I had to sit and think about that for a good long while. If she started asking if I was like Mom, I would have to leave. (Spoiler alert: the answer was probably yes, but I would never be thinking about that again, ever.)

Finally she said, "Since your work is what brought you here, would you like to talk more about your career?"

I shrugged.

"What did you study in school?"

"I was an English major."

"And why did you choose that?"

"I like books."

"Did you have any careers in mind when you chose your major?"

"Not really. I never was much of a planner."

She smiled. "That's perfectly okay." That was when I realized how mean I was to myself sometimes. When I'd said, "I'm not a planner," what I'd really meant was *I am lazy and irresponsible*. I blinked for a moment, trying to reorient myself around the idea that some of my "flaws" might actually be "perfectly okay."

"Um. Yeah, so I just sort of fell into tech support because I needed a job, and that's what people do here, right?" I gave a little laugh. "Work in tech?"

"Some people. What did you want to be when you were a child?"

"President, of course."

She smiled more broadly this time. "Not every child wants to be president."

"Oh. Well, I definitely did. I ran my own campaigns and everything. I even shot a commercial when I was eight. My mom probably still has the VHS."

"Do you still have an interest in politics?"

"I don't think it was an interest in politics when I was a kid so much as just wanting to be the center of the universe. But yes, I still do."

She paused for so long I thought maybe the appointment was over and she was waiting for me to see myself out.

"Yeah, I mean…," I continued. "I follow politics. I like to complain about how horrible everything is and daydream about how I would fix things."

"That's another thing not everyone does."

"Hm."

"Just remember that there is a whole world out there outside of technical support."

It was my turn to smile; this was the first cheerful thing she'd said all hour.

"Rachel, our time is up for today. Would you like to make another appointment?"

I hesitated. "My insurance covers this, right?"

She nodded.

"Okay, sign me up."

And that was how Rachel, formerly a self-destructive sex goddess, became Rachel, responsible woman who sees a therapist and Takes Care of Herself (and was, hopefully, still a sex goddess).

Friday morning I sent a message to the group chat saying, "Is it just me or is our chat a little quiet these days?"

I was riding a Friday iced coffee high, avoiding my work responsibilities, as one does. And, in the spirit of honesty, I had sent a text to Stephen a half hour earlier and gotten no response. It was something along the lines of "TGIF," and if that seems like I was fishing for him to ask me to hang out over the weekend, that's because I was. But alas, no fish were biting. So I thought trading some gossip with the girls would make me feel better. I grinned when my phone lit up immediately with Eva's reply.

> **Eva Galvez 11:01 AM:**
> It has been quiet! I've been spending a lot of time with Jasmine. ☺ How are you three?

Rachel Weiss 11:03 AM:
I've been seeing more of my therapist than Stephen. He's still doing this hot-and-cold thing. It's starting to bother me a bit.

Eva Galvez 11:07 AM:
I'm sorry, Rach.

I stared at my phone for another minute or two to see if any more sympathy was forthcoming. To see if Amy and Sumira would say anything at all. They did not. I swiped back to my text messages with Stephen. No response. No typing bubbles.

My caffeine buzz withered in my veins.

I chewed my lip and jiggled my foot anxiously. I just wanted a quick dopamine hit of incoming messages; was that so much to ask for? So I took a silly selfie with my coffee and posted it with the caption, "How much iced coffee is too much iced coffee on a Friday?"

Less than two minutes later, my phone buzzed.

Christopher Butkus 11:15 AM:
Depends. How badly are your hands shaking?

I snort-laughed. Dopamine hit acquired.

CHAPTER 10

THE MONTH OF JUNE wasn't off to the best start. I'd spent the last week moping around, stewing in loneliness. I was happy that my friends were happy—Eva with her new girl, Amy with her husband, Sumira with...who could say?—but couldn't they show a little care for me in my time of need? I mean, sure, I was ostensibly coupled up as well, but my so-called boyfriend had been doing less than the bare minimum. We'd hooked up once in the last two weeks and it had seemed like his mind was elsewhere. Which, as you can imagine, was not at all flattering. Anyway, I had been through all the trashy reality shows Netflix had to offer, and the cashier at PCC had started giving me side-eye when I checked out with my solitary bottle of wine and bag of cookies each night.

On a Monday morning, I was two and a half coffees in when I received a cryptic meeting request from Kenneth's boss, Mike. Why was it that I'd gone my entire career with nary a cryptic meeting request, and now I was getting one monthly?

When I got to his office, Jennie from HR was there too. I thought for sure I was getting fired, but I had no idea why. Jennie gave me a pitying look, like, *Poor thing, you're stupid enough to give joke answers to your daily questions and now you're getting fired too?* I wanted to toss my coffee at her. (I was onto my fourth now; I was nervous and needed the liquid comfort.)

Mike, a powerful-looking man with a thick head of graying hair and a very square jaw, gestured to a chair on one side of his office. I sat down, suddenly self-conscious about my knees, not knowing which direction to point them. I settled on tucking them to one side; my hands shook as I clutched my coffee cup on my lap.

Jennie didn't sit but instead stood like a security guard beside the door. I took this as a bad sign. Mike heaved a sigh so laden with disappointment and foreboding that I couldn't take it anymore.

"Is everything okay?" My voice came out aggressively chipper.

"Actually, Rachel," Mike rumbled, "no. There's something we need to discuss."

The combination of caffeine and dread was so potent my teeth began to chatter; I felt like I was actually going to faint.

"W-what's wrong? Have I done something?"

Jennie's lip curled in disgust. She was clutching a folder against her chest, and I wanted to rip it from her arms and scream, *What's in the folder, Jennie?!*

"We took a look at the referral you submitted for your sisters," Mike said.

This was such a surprise that I forgot my nerves. "What?" I'd almost forgotten about the whole referral business. "If they didn't qualify for a summer internship, it's okay. They can just get a job scooping ice cream or something. They'll be fine." I was getting rather heated, annoyed that they had made me think I was getting fired, raising my blood pressure to unprecedented levels in the process, when it was really just about my mom's harebrained scheme. I had known the twins weren't qualified for an engineering internship. There was no need for all this drama.

"It's not that they didn't qualify." Mike's deep voice was cautious.

I froze. Was he, perhaps, about to tell me that the twins were off-the-charts brilliant and they wanted to bring them in at once? My brain sped off, imagining the twins being interviewed on the local news, answering the newscaster's questions with grunts and eye rolls.

"Our company, along with other companies and schools in the area, has been working with law enforcement on an ongoing investigation."

I felt my jaw slacken. Why was he telling me this, and what could this possibly have to do with my sisters?

Mike stood and began to pace, gazing at the carpet with his hands clasped behind his back.

"When we see test scores above a certain threshold, we engage our law enforcement liaison to make sure everything is kosher." He swallowed and shot me an uncomfortable look. (I swear, people at this company had no idea how to talk to a Jewish person. Or a woman, for that matter. I must've been a total enigma to most of them.) He continued. "Given your sisters' ostensibly excellent test scores, we followed this protocol."

I was catching on now. All warmth seemed to leave my body. I set my coffee cup on Mike's desk, barely able to breathe.

He stopped pacing and looked at me gravely. "Due to the combination of their test scores, the location where they sat the exam, and the proctor who administered it, your sisters will be under further investigation for fraud."

"I..." My mind buzzed, a desolate wasteland of disconnected thoughts blowing through like tumbleweeds.

"I'm afraid I can't say anything more since it is an ongoing investigation." Mike peered at me with something bordering on kindness. I must have looked like someone had just slapped me with a cold fish.

"F-fraud? But…how would they have…?" My voice petered out as I thought of the twins' total ineptitude at anything outside of TikTok and drawing on their eyebrows, and then my mom's face billowed into my thoughts, one minute desperate and sobbing, the next minute hard and determined.

I dropped my face into my hands.

"I suggest you don't say anything more about it here because of the investigation." He paused. "I just wanted to tell you the reason we won't be offering your sisters an internship."

I gave a weak laugh. They were *never* going to get an internship. But now, because Mom had forced me to submit their applications, they *were* going to be under investigation for a crime.

"Was there anything else?" I asked stiffly.

Mike shook his head. Jennie stepped aside to let me through. Without looking at either of them, I shuffled out of the office.

That night I paced back and forth in my parents' living room, my mom on the couch watching me.

"This is bad, Mom. You could be charged with a federal crime."

"I still have no idea what you're talking about." Mom selected a biscuit from the tray on the coffee table.

"I've explained it to you three times. I know you know what I'm talking about."

She crunched into her biscuit and chewed thoughtfully for a long while. "I hired them a tutor."

I groaned in frustration. "It was more than a tutor and you know it."

"No, I don't. I don't know what you're talking about."

I glared down at her. "Yes, you—" I stopped and sighed; she looked up at me, eyes wide, mouth chewing primly, looking like an innocent dairy cow. "Jesus Christ, Mom. Where are the twins, anyway?"

"I had your father take them shopping. I didn't want them to hear this."

"Why not? They're implicated in this too."

Mom waved an airy hand. "Hearing that they're being accused of cheating on the SATs? It would hurt their confidence."

"Hurt their—?!" I stared, disbelief clashing with fury inside me. Had my mother turned into a completely different person in the thirteen years between my birth and the twins'? The idea that she had ever worried about *my* confidence was laughable. Let's see, there was the time when I was six and she had my hair cut like Brittany Murphy's in *Clueless*—adorable on Brittany; hideous on chubby six-year-old me. There was the year she took me to countless tween modeling auditions. (Surprise: no one wanted to sign a twelve-year-old with ginormous breasts and unmanageable hair.) And the summer when she insisted I try out for the role of Titania in the community theater's *A Midsummer Night's Dream*, and instead I got cast as Puck, spending the whole summer prancing around the stage as a horny clown.

"Rachel." Mom brushed biscuit crumbs from her hands. "I don't want to talk about this anymore. If we're going to be questioned by some...policeman, I don't want you involved. You know nothing. The twins and your father know nothing. I know that I hired a tutor. That's it."

"But this is serious."

"Yes, it appears so. Which is why this discussion is over."

I deflated a little. She really wasn't going to discuss this with me? I felt unexpectedly disappointed in her. My mother had never been a paragon of morality, but the idea that she would fake the twins' SAT scores…it was just wrong. We already had so much privilege as a family—did she not see that? The twins would be just fine, even with abysmal test scores.

She patted the couch cushion beside her. I sat down and she offered me a biscuit.

"Thanks." I bit into it thoughtfully. "Mom, I don't think you understand. It's not right to—"

"Hush now." She pushed my hair back from my face. "Why don't you tell me about this so-called boyfriend of yours?"

I choked on a mouthful of dry cookie. With some deft maneuvering, I brought the conversation around to Jane's upcoming bridal appointments. Her wedding was just over six months away now, but part of me wished we could stretch out the planning phase for several years. There's nothing more effective in distracting Mom than wedding planning.

Mom promised to keep me updated about anything involving the investigation, and I, in turn, promised not to tell the twins about it.

"I suppose I can ask your father to get them an internship at his company."

"Mother!" I cried, horrified at the thought of yet another company reporting the twins to law enforcement.

"Oh, yes, I'd better not." After a moment of quiet contemplation she said, "Then I think I can get them an interview with the temple's summer camp. No test scores needed to be a camp counselor."

I held my tongue, deciding it was wise to pick my battles and trying not to imagine the consequences of leaving the twins in charge of small children.

My year had started off so promising. How had it all gone to shit six months in?

Now, on top of my ever-increasing loneliness, my mom was involved in some sort of criminal fraud conspiracy. And despite my geriatric age of nearly thirty, I had an alarming zit on my chin. How was that fair, I ask you? The combination of pubescent blemishes and elderly complaints, such as the lines forming around my mouth and the way my ankles cracked in the morning, was frankly depressing.

It was a Friday evening and I was alone in my apartment, examining my features in the mirror above the sofa. So far I'd counted thirteen gray hairs. *Thirteen.* Even worse: the lines around my mouth stayed put no matter how much I relaxed my face.

I flopped back onto the couch and called the girls. Surely they were all busy doing Friday-night things, but we had a sort of understanding about answering out-of-the-blue phone calls.

Eva answered first, and I could hear the low murmur of TV and Jasmine's voice saying hi in the background. Sumira answered too, with no hint to her whereabouts. Amy declined. *Odd.*

With no preamble, I said, "I have finally seen the light regarding Botox. Of course it's worth injecting neurotoxins into your body in exchange for smooth, elastic skin."

"Don't do Botox; that's silly," Eva said.

"Why not?" Sumira asked. "I've done it."

"Sumira Khan, you've been holding out on us!" I perked up, wondering if this was exactly the sort of pampering treatment I needed.

"You never asked."

"We divulge a lot of information that is not explicitly asked for," I pointed out.

"Like the time you gave us the blow-by-blow of your gyno appointment?"

"That is a good example, yes."

"When did you do it?" Eva asked. "What does it feel like?"

"I've done it twice over the last year. It doesn't feel like anything. I got it around my forehead and between my eyebrows. It just freezes your face for a while. The movement of your muscles is what causes wrinkles over time, so Botox prevents you from using those muscles."

"And we never noticed? How much did it cost?" I asked eagerly.

"A little under three hundred."

"US dollars?" I deflated at once. "More than half my life's savings. So much for that plan."

"Wait." Sumira sounded concerned. "You don't even have a separate savings account? I always thought you were just telling us your checking balance."

I got an uncomfortable twinge in my stomach. "Does everyone have a so-called savings account except for me?"

"Um, I think so," Eva said.

"Great. Fantastic. I'll just add that to my list of failings. Oh, I haven't even told you about my dentist appointment the other day. I swear there's a conspiracy happening."

Sumira interrupted. "As much as I would love to hear this story, I have to go. Talk to you guys later."

"Go on," Eva encouraged me. "Did the dentist sexually harass you?"

"No, Dr. Melinda Chung did not sexually harass me. Do you think I would go to a male doctor of any kind? Unlikely. Anyway, there was a new dental hygienist, Sam, who was all up in my business. She kept saying things like, 'At your age, this kind of plaque buildup can be really dangerous.' 'At your age, you're looking at bone deterioration.' 'At your age, you might want to invest in a Water Pik.' I swear to God."

"That is so rude."

"And then she called Dr. Chung over to take a look at something. So Dr. Chung poked around in my mouth and made all these concerned noises. 'Cavities aside,' she said, 'I'm not liking the look of these back molars. Do you grind your teeth at night?' I was like, 'Just at night? I wish!' When she didn't laugh, I said if she met my mother she'd understand."

"What's wrong with your back molars?" Eva asked, because that's the kind of caring friend she is.

"That's the good part. Dr. Chung goes, 'I'm going to have you wear a night guard and use some enamel strengthener daily. Otherwise you're looking at dentures in a few years' time.' I swear Sam had to swallow a shit-eating grin. Why does Sam hate me?"

"*Dentures?*" Eva yelped.

"As if it wasn't hard enough to find a man, now I'll be able to entice them by going to bed with the retainer of a thirteen-year-old and, soon, the fake teeth of a ninety-year-old."

"Technically you do have a man already, right?"

"Right, my delightful boyfriend who can't be bothered to text me, let alone see me. It's for the best. My dentures would only scare him away."

"When are you going to get your cavities filled?"

"I haven't decided yet. Letting my teeth rot and fall out would only add to my crone mystique."

There was a pause. I heard Jasmine say she was going to make more popcorn.

"Hey." Eva's voice was gentle. "Is everything okay with you and Stephen?"

"Honestly? I don't think so. We've only hung out a couple times since that night we went out with you."

"It's been over a month since then."

"I know."

"Has he told you anything that might explain why?"

"Nope. It sort of feels like if I didn't keep trying, he would be content to just fade away without having to go through an actual breakup."

"Like Nolan Thompson in seventh grade, remember?"

"Oh, Nolan. He asked me out. We went to the movies. I fantasized all through social studies about holding his hand. And then?"

"Nothing."

"Never spoke to me again. I should look him up. Technically we're married now. Common law or something, right? We've been dating for sixteen years, after all."

"So you think Stephen would pull a Nolan Thompson?"

"It sort of feels that way." I paused. "Not that I would let him. I've learned my lesson. Damn you, Nolan. Never even got to hold your hand."

"Are you going to talk to him?"

"Nah. I'm pretty sure he's married with a bunch of kids now."

"Not Nolan. Stephen."

"Yeah. I guess I should."

"Okay. I'm here for you if you need me."

We hung up, and I stared into the gathering darkness outside my window. I felt an emptiness in the center of my chest. Wrinkles and gray hairs aside, I didn't feel like myself. I felt forgotten and forgettable. Fragile and bruised. For once in my life I didn't feel strong enough to meet whatever storm was coming my way.

CHAPTER 11

I'D GATHERED MY COURAGE and invited Stephen to the Fremont Solstice Parade. He took four hours to respond but finally deigned to say, "Sure." So here I was, waiting for him at Fremont Coffee. The place was swarming with people. It took me twenty minutes to get an iced latte. And of course Stephen was late, so I spent half an hour on the front porch between a drooling English mastiff and a four-year-old who stared avidly at me as she devoured a cookie the size of her head. Why was I so nervous waiting for a guy I'd been dating for nearly six months?

By the time he arrived, my mood was sour. It was never a good sign when someone was this late and didn't even bother to text or call with an excuse. Plus, the four-year-old had tried to speak to me.

Stephen pecked me on the cheek as if I were his maiden aunt. He wasn't smiling, would barely look at me. It was like he wasn't trying to hide that he was about to break up with me. The fact that he looked and smelled as delicious as ever made it hurt that much worse.

"Do you want a corn dog?" I gestured to the nearest food truck.

He twitched his shoulder in the most irritatingly vague way.

He looked claustrophobic, hunching uncomfortably against the onslaught of people from every direction.

"Nachos? Churros?" I pointed out another truck, desperate to steer the date back toward a semblance of normalcy.

He reached back and scratched his neck.

"Guess that's a no then," I mumbled, and proceeded to buy myself one of everything. Stephen bought a beer and slouched behind me as I found a spot on the curb to sit on. I ate, and he sat beside me in silence. It is a special kind of torture to eat in front of someone who's neither eating nor talking. I barely resisted the urge to slap him across the face with my churro.

"Stephen, is there something—" Then a blare of music interrupted me as the parade approached.

"Parade's starting," he said, gruffly and unnecessarily.

People around us clapped and whistled. I tossed my garbage in a nearby bin and looked back at Stephen: he stood staring down at his phone, a pillar of gloom among the colorful parade-goers.

Before today, I had never been dumped. Perhaps I just had a selective memory, or perhaps I was truly an irresistible sex goddess. But the point is, I couldn't remember a time when I'd felt so completely horrible. It felt like my organs had been flattened by a truck tire; breathing felt painful and, frankly, pointless. Everything felt wrong; it was like opposite day, that stupid thing we used to say when we were kids, but everything about *me* was opposite. Instead of flawless, I felt ugly. Instead of quick and funny, I felt stupid and boring. Despite the whirl of color and music happening all around me, I felt like my world had been sucked dry of joy.

I solemnly wished to never, *ever* feel that way again.

We watched the parade side by side, without touching. We were certainly the most grave, least loving people for miles around. Finally, as though he couldn't take it anymore, Stephen turned to me. "Rachel, we need to talk."

I blinked up at him, waiting; there was no need for me to say anything.

He took a deep breath, his dark eyebrows pulling together, his upper lip pouting. I would never forgive him for how handsome he looked in that moment.

"You're a great girl. I've had a lot of fun with you. But I can't see you anymore."

I gazed away from him, my eyes following two Hula-Hoopers in the parade procession.

"Any particular reason?" I asked, my voice flat.

"I—" He hesitated. "I caught feelings for someone else. But it's complicated."

This surprised me. I turned toward him and asked, "What do you mean? How?"

"It...it's complicated because she's..."

"No, not that. I mean, how did you catch feelings for someone else?"

He looked puzzled; splotches of dark red had appeared high on his cheeks. "I mean, she...I..."

My brain felt slow. And then realization dawned, and I took a hasty step back from him, landing on someone else's foot. I ignored their exclamation of pain, staring at Stephen.

"You mean while we've been dating? Did you cheat on me?"

His brow furrowed deeper. "Cheat on you? I didn't realize we were exclusive."

"You what?" I could hear the way my voice grew higher. "We were together. Remember? Boyfriend and girlfriend?"

Stephen looked truly concerned. "Rachel, I thought we were on the same page. We didn't say..."

"No. *I* thought we were on the same page. At the wedding?" I felt dizzy. A dozen women dressed all in feathers skated by in synchronized formation, eliciting a raucous cheer from onlookers. A man on stilts dressed like a wizard lurched past, leering down at members of the crowd. I shrank back when he dipped his face close to mine, baring his teeth.

"Shit, I'm sorry." Stephen sounded miserable.

"And this girl…"

"She doesn't want me to break up with you, but I can't help it. I think I love her."

I flinched. "Wow. Okay."

"Okay?"

"What else can I say? We're done."

"I'm really sorry, Rachel."

I tightened my lips in a grimace, wanting him to leave. He seemed to take the hint. He stooped down and hugged me awkwardly, his chin bumping the top of my head. Hands in his pockets, he shouldered his way through the crowd. I watched him until he disappeared.

I stood there for a long moment, assaulted by all sorts of unwanted thoughts: *There goes the only relationship I'd had in nearly two years; Now I have to start all over again; Perhaps I will never have what Jane has with Owen.*

People around me jostled forward as a marching band made its way past us. I drifted back toward the food trucks and bought myself a beer, drank it down, then bought another. By the time I'd finished them, I felt marginally better. Thinking I would find a bathroom and then go home, I headed back toward the main street just as the naked bike ride began. I stopped to watch and felt a smile spread across my face. It's hard to watch the naked denizens of Seattle, in all shapes, sizes, and colors, tooling along in a never-ending stream of bikes, without smiling. There were people painted gold and rainbow, people painted green wearing crowns of yellow petals, people painted to look like zebras and skeletons. There were big boobs and small ones, body hair and butt cracks. There were people as bare as the day they were born, hair blowing in the wind, smiling as if this was the happiest day of their lives.

My heart lifted. I ran back to Fremont Coffee, where I'd chained my bike, and stripped off my clothes with wild abandon. I was just about to pedal away when a nearby man called me over.

"Paint ya?" He was a fiftysomething hippie wearing a tie-dye shirt and cutoff shorts, holding a paintbrush in one hand and a roller in the other.

I wheeled my bike toward him; it was a curious thing to feel the breeze blow across my nipples and pubes.

"Only got a few colors left." He pointed to them.

"I like the pink."

"Pink it is, then." He happily dipped the roller in the bubble gum–pink paint. I stood with my arms and legs wide as he rolled the paint over my skin. It was cold at first, but the feeling of the smooth roller and silky paint was exquisite. "Goose bumps!" He smiled at me over the rim of his round sunglasses.

"How many people have you painted?" I asked.

"Today? Oh, fifty, sixty. Been doing this for thirty years, ever since the parade started in 1989."

"That's the year I was born!" Somehow I felt like this meant something.

"Imagine that!" He rolled paint down my left arm. "A momentous year. Think you'll live up to its legacy?"

Not knowing exactly what he meant, I nodded. "I'll do my best."

"Good girl." He put down the roller and wiped his hands on his shirt. "All done. Do a few twirls to let it dry, and then fly!"

I obeyed, spinning round and round, naked and pink and joyful. Giggles poured out of me as I thought how amazing it was that twenty minutes before, I'd felt miserable.

"Thank you!" I flung one leg over my bike.

"Fly! Fly!" he called. And off I flew.

CHAPTER 12

FROM NOW ON, I would be prescribing naked bike rides to everyone going through a breakup. It was incredibly effective as a mood booster. A week later, my heart felt as good as new. It was a beautiful summer morning, the sun was shining, and I was on my way to a bridal shop to watch Jane try on dresses. I had cold brews for everyone, ice rattling cheerfully as I walked down the sidewalk.

I arrived at the shop in a delightful mood. I was exactly on time, but Mom and Jane were already there. (They both got this early bird gene—I didn't understand it. It was indecent to show up early anywhere, in my opinion.) They were both cheerful too. Sun, coffee, wedding dresses. What wasn't to be cheerful about?

Jane stood at the front desk and went over the details of her wedding with the shop assistant, who jotted everything down with the utmost seriousness. (As she should! I couldn't believe it: my *sister* was getting *married* and she had *details* like a date and a venue!) I sat on a settee, sipping my coffee and admiring Jane's poise. Even in jeans and a T-shirt—boatneck with Breton stripes, naturally—she looked elegant.

"Big day," I said to Mom. "Are you excited?"

"I'm so proud." Her voice sounded tearful as she dabbed her lower lashes with her pinkie finger. "So very proud."

"Mom, you can't start crying now; she hasn't even tried on a wedding dress yet."

She chortled and dragged a tissue out of her purse.

"I know." She composed herself. "You're right."

"Okay. We're all set." Jane beamed at us. "Let's pick some dresses!"

We dashed around the shop, plucking dresses off the racks and showing them to Jane. She liked lace and silk, not too much tulle, nothing big or poofy. Once she had a dozen or so, the assistant ushered her into the curtained-off dressing room. Mom and I sat just outside on an overstuffed couch. Mom was so excited she couldn't even be bothered to harass me. She just smiled pleasantly, bubbling over with anticipation.

The assistant whipped open the curtain with a flourish. There was a long moment of silence as Mom and I gazed raptly at Jane, and then all three of us burst out laughing.

"Next!" I cried.

Jane's figure is best described as "a beanpole with a bosom." Her boobs are just a tad smaller than mine, and the rest of her is teeny tiny. Somehow the first dress made her look like an ear of corn, straight and shapeless all the way down. She wanted something demure, but it would have to be a little more formfitting than that. Mom, of course, was advocating for something backless, with a slit up the side, that also showed cleavage. I think she secretly wanted everyone to see how hot Jane's bod was because it reflected well on her own genes.

Look, if I'm being honest, my mom still had it. She was ancient, yes, but she was in good shape and understood how to use a push-up bra to her advantage. Also, her curly hair game was on point.

After a few minutes of whispers, laughs, and what sounded like a muffled boxing match behind the curtain, Jane emerged again, this time clipped into a beaded halter-neck gown that made her look like a mermaid. She looked down at herself skeptically.

"Are you going for the mermaid look?" I asked.

"No...and I can hardly walk in this."

"I think it's lovely." Mom's eyes were misty.

Jane looked like she was willing to reconsider her own opinion in light of Mom's.

"Go." I waved my hands. "You've got ten more back there."

The assistant hustled her away again.

"I did like it." Mom had a pout in her voice.

"I know, I know." I patted her hand.

"Rachel. When do I get to meet your boyfriend?"

I was so taken aback I was quite breathless for a moment. I mouthed wordlessly at her; she was doing her stern, unblinking look. And then I was saved by the sound of the curtain being thrown open once more.

"Wow," I breathed, as Mom said, "Oh, Jane."

Jane was beaming, turning this way and that to see her reflection. The gown had a silk bodice with thin straps, delicate tiers of silk-lined tulle flowing down the length of the skirt.

"You look like a princess." I beamed.

"I didn't think I liked tulle." Jane spread her hands over the skirt.

"That happens a lot," the assistant said. "What you think you like can be very different from what you actually like when you're trying the dresses on."

"It's beautiful," Mom said. "Very tasteful neckline."

Jane caught my eye and I smirked. The neckline scooped gently down to show just enough cleavage to satisfy everyone.

"It really is perfect," Jane breathed, admiring herself in the mirror.

"Yes, it is, but you have to try on the rest." It was lucky I was there to take charge, really. What would my family do without my leadership? "There could be an even better one in there."

"Okay, okay." Jane couldn't stop smiling as she closed the curtain behind her.

I felt the smile on my face too as I turned to look at Mom again.

"Wow, that one was—"

"Rachel Renée Weiss." Mom's voice was hard and clipped, completely incongruous with the touching moment we'd all just shared. My heart jumped to my throat. Somehow, even as a fully grown adult, nothing scared me more than my mom's stern voice.

"What?" I'd reverted to the whiny tone that should have been left well back in my teenage years. It was her fault: she did this to me.

"It is inconceivable—*inconceivable*—that you would treat me this way," she hissed.

"What way? What are you talking about?"

"Hiding things from me. Not telling me a single thing about the man in your life. Heaven forbid you should think of introducing him to the family."

"Mom...," I moaned.

Jane reappeared, the assistant crowing, "I think you'll like this one!"

Mom and I snapped to attention. It was a minimalist silk number with some sort of cape hanging down the back.

"Oh, darling." Mom's voice was thick with emotion—I stared at her in disbelief. Was it possible my mother was actually a sociopath? "You could be on the cover of *Vogue*."

Jane flushed with pleasure.

"What do you think, Jane?" I asked.

"It's—it's really nice…," she began hesitantly. As I suspected.

"It is, but it's not really *you*, is it?"

She grasped this statement gratefully. "Maybe not. Not really my style. Really pretty, though."

Looking disappointed, the assistant waved her inside again. As soon as we were alone, Mom pounced, turning her head so fast to glare at me, I'm surprised she didn't crick her neck.

"Tell me why. Why would you keep this from me? You know all I want is for you to be happy—"

"Happily wed," I muttered.

"Speak up; don't grumble!" Mom boomed. Before I could speak out, she barreled on. "What have I done to make you want to *hurt* me?"

"Mom! I don't want to hurt you!"

Jane and the assistant stood before us once more, both staring at us with their mouths open.

"Sorry," I mumbled, my face hot.

"This—um—this one is very flattering, I think." The assistant presented Jane like a game show hostess.

It was a fussy lace concoction with a keyhole neckline.

"No," Mom and I said together. They vanished without another word.

"Mom." I kept my voice low in an attempt to set a good example for her. "Listen, the truth is—"

"The truth is what? That you hate me?" She never was one to follow an example.

"I don't hate you! We broke up!"

Jane whipped the curtain open, the next gown hanging halfway off her, the assistant standing behind her with clips in hand.

"What?" Mom and Jane asked at once.

"We…" I cast an aggrieved eye at the assistant, who was attempting to do up the back of Jane's dress, her face bright red. "Stephen and I broke up. There. Are you happy?"

"No!" Jane looked devastated. "Rachel, I'm so sorry."

Mom's nostrils flared. I had a sudden instinct to bolt for the door. (Why don't I listen to my instincts? Why?)

"It's okay. It…it wasn't right. It just didn't work out."

Mom licked her lips, like a tiger preparing to feast on its prey. (Is that what tigers do? I don't know, but I felt like a trembling antelope preparing to meet my maker.)

"You broke up?" Mom's voice was deadly quiet. "After two months?"

"Um…" I considered telling her we'd been seeing each other since January, and then thought, on the whole, that might make things worse. "Yes?"

And then Mom did possibly the most embarrassing thing she could do: she burst into loud, wet tears.

"Ohhh. Ohhh!" she moaned, as though she'd just lost her entire family on the *Titanic*.

The assistant looked petrified and ran off, mumbling something about tea.

"Mom. Shhh." Jane rushed to her side, rubbing her back.

"You wouldn't have liked him anyway! Look—Jane is getting married! Doesn't that make you happy?"

"What about *you*, Rachel? I want you to get married too!" Mom sobbed.

"I will…someday. But I'm only—" I stopped myself, cursing silently. Why was I turning thirty this year? It nullified all my excuses for not being married/successful/a mom/etc. Getting old was truly very inconvenient.

Mom sobbed all the harder, no doubt realizing that it was only five months to my birthday because I had to go and open my big mouth.

"Rachel will find someone, Mom, don't worry. We know this is coming from a place of love. But you don't have to worry so much."

"Besides, I thought you wanted me to marry Christopher Butkus anyway."

Her eyes flashed and I regretted my words instantly.

"If you can't take a relationship seriously, then you don't deserve Christopher Butkus."

"Ouch, Mom."

Jane stopped rubbing her back, looking affronted. "Isn't that a bit harsh?"

"No." Mom leaned forward, wagging a finger in my face. "Rachel, you need to learn. Everything is a joke to you. Well, some things are serious. Some things can't be laughed off. Ending up old and alone is one of those things. Life is not full of opportunities. If you can't take a chance when it's presented to you, if you can't take one single thing seriously, well then, you don't deserve someone as wonderful as Christopher Butkus."

A ringing silence followed this speech, in which the assistant bustled over with paper cups of grayish tea.

"Weddings can be emotional." She kept her eyes lowered as she handed us the cups. "They bring out so many hopes and dreams, regrets and memories. Very normal, very normal." She hurried away again to the safety of the front desk. I gazed after her, full of stunned admiration. What a professional.

"Mom, I think you're being a little unfair," Jane whispered. "Rachel does try. This guy just wasn't right for her."

"Well, neither is Christopher Butkus. I don't want him hurt," Mom said crisply.

"What?!"

"If this is what you do to men—mess around with their hearts, dump them after mere weeks—I don't want you anywhere near him."

"I..."

"Mom, shouldn't you be more worried about Rachel's feelings?"

"Oh no. No, no. I know what she's like. I was just the same before I married your father. All fun, no commitment. Breaking hearts left and right." She sniffed. "Just know that there is a ticking clock. The good men get snapped up. If you don't play your cards right soon, you'll end up picking through the divorcés in a few years' time."

I exchanged a look with Jane over Mom's head. We both pressed our lips together, trying not to laugh. The assistant seemed to think it was safe to return; she lifted her eyebrows at Jane, gesturing to the dress she had on.

Jane shook her head. "Let's try the next one."

With a relieved sigh, the assistant closed the curtain again.

Mom gazed away from me, out the window. I watched her profile, still fighting back a laugh. Though her flair for the dramatic did, at times, make my life a living hell, I rather liked her opinion of me. Rachel Weiss, Breaker of Hearts, Slayer of Fuckboys.

And on the bright side, my breakup with Stephen seemed to have finally put the whole Christopher Butkus thing out of her mind.

CHAPTER 13

THREE DAYS LATER, I awoke to a mysterious message from Sumira. She had just spent an hour talking to Amy and apparently thought that I needed to reach out to her. So I sent a message to the group chat.

Rachel Weiss 7:37 AM:
Hey Ames, what's up?
Everything OK?

Sumira Khan 7:40 AM:
No, you need to message
her separately. She
muted the group chat
a while ago.

Eva Galvez 7:42 AM:
What? Why would she mute
the chat?

My blood chilled. Amy had muted the group chat? How could she? And why hadn't I noticed?

I called her, and she insisted on meeting for coffee before she would explain what was going on. I agreed to meet her at a Starbucks on my lunch break; she was apparently taking a sick day from work.

She looked...not herself. Her hair was all stringy and she wasn't wearing any makeup. She was already at a table nursing a cup of tea. Nothing makes a person seem unwell in my book more than choosing tea over coffee. She half stood when she saw me, then hastily sat back down, her lips pressed into a miserable line. I thought she was going to tell me she had cancer.

"Hi, Rachel. Thank you for meeting me." Her voice was tight and thin.

"Amy." I sat beside her and grasped her hands. "What is going on? Please tell me you're okay."

Her mouth wobbled and she shook her head.

"Are you sick? Is it Ryan? Is he—"

"Rachel, please stop. Stop being nice to me."

"What are you talking about?"

"I'm so sorry. I did something—" Amy's voice grew choked and she broke off.

I was getting seriously alarmed now. I leaned in close and whispered, "Whatever it is, it'll be okay. I'll help you. I'm very familiar with dealing with felons now, thanks to my mom, so just—"

"I slept with Stephen," she whispered back.

I was so shocked that at first I didn't equate Stephen to *my* Stephen, to Stephen Branson. My first thought was: *So she actually cheated on Ryan but it's okay, people don't burn women at the stake for committing adultery anymore. And maybe if she loves this person, this Stephen, then—wait. Stephen?*

"Stephen *Branson*?" Just to be sure.

"Yes."

"Ah. I see." I drummed my fingers on the table. "But—when?" My brain felt foggy—my married best friend sleeping with my boyfriend: this was uncharted territory for me. I probed my innermost feelings and was surprised to find that I wasn't hurt or jealous, merely concerned for my friend. Apparently I was truly over Stephen.

"That night we went to Havana."

"What? Did you...in the bathroom?" I couldn't see where else they would have done it.

"No." Amy sounded like she was going to cry. "I went home with him."

"You *did*?"

"Remember, he left without saying goodbye, and then...and then I left."

"Oh." The words hit me with shocking force; I remembered that moment clearly, remembered how innocently I'd accepted Amy's words without questioning them. The idea that she was off for a secret rendezvous with Stephen would have been absurd. And yet—I remembered her missing wedding ring, the way she'd gazed at Stephen as if she wanted to devour him, the way he remembered what I'd told him about her being sexually frustrated. The way he'd singled her out for conversation, and how I'd thought it was because he was trying to get to know my friends. I'd thought he was doing that for me.

"I feel stupid. I had no idea."

"Rachel, please don't. I'm the one who should feel bad—and I do feel awful. I cheated on Ryan, I made your boyfriend cheat on you. I haven't been able to sleep, I—"

And then I remembered something Stephen had said when he

broke up with me. That he thought he loved this mystery woman he'd been with.

"Did it happen more than once?"

She nodded, her eyes filling with tears. "Twice."

"Amy."

"I know. But it was so...good. And I'd already done it once. It was easy to do it again."

I know it's wrong, but I almost wanted to laugh. It was so *good*? Was sex with Ryan that mediocre? Or maybe Amy and Stephen had a chemistry that I'd lacked with him. Perhaps that was one of the things that had been wrong with our relationship—if you could even call it that.

"Rachel, I'm so, so sorry."

"Stop. It's over. Stephen was never right for me. I'm glad it's over."

I'd hated it while it was happening, but after the breakup, it was like a weight had been lifted from me. I didn't have to try so hard anymore.

Amy was crying now, sniffling into a paper napkin.

"But Ames, what about you? What about Ryan?"

"I haven't told him...It's not that I want to be with Stephen, because I don't. I never want to see him again. But Ryan...I can't tell him."

"Okay, but your marriage. Are things better now? Now that you..." The image of Amy's pale skin entwined with Stephen's tan limbs dropped into my mind, and I mentally karate-chopped it out of existence. "Now that you tried sleeping with someone else?"

"Not really, no." Amy's tears stopped falling and she sat back in her chair. "I haven't felt attracted to him since."

"Shit."

"Yeah."

I stood and Amy started, looking terrified. "Are you leaving?"

"No. Be right back." I returned a few minutes later with two cappuccinos and a brownie. I cut it in half and slid a piece to her.

She gave me a watery smile. "Thanks."

"I'm your best friend. I can tell when caffeine and sugar are needed."

We spent the next hour discussing Ryan and the possibility she hadn't let herself consider before—the possibility of the D-word. At first the idea of divorce brought on a torrent of fresh tears as she remembered her wedding and thought about how painful it would be to tell their families that it was over. But by the time we reached the dregs of our cappuccinos, Amy's face was suffused with hope as she imagined being single again, moving into an apartment of her own, and getting a cat—Ryan was allergic. No more cleaning up after him, no more being banished from the living room during *Warhammer* sessions, no more fights about sex.

Before we parted, I perched on the edge of her chair and gave her a sideways hug.

"You just have to think about what's right for you."

She was quiet for a long time, and I felt some tears slide into my hair.

Finally she squeezed me tighter and whispered, "A cat."

After I filled the girls in (with Amy's permission), Eva declared an emergency wine and cheese night. We gathered at her place and rehashed how Amy and I were both feeling about everything. We didn't go too far into the sordid details of Amy's escapades with Stephen—I didn't know if I could handle it—or into what Amy

was going to do about Ryan. (Her eyes welled up just at the mention of his name.) In the end, Eva and Sumira entertained us with
gossip about their colleagues, and Amy promised she would never
mute the group chat again.

"Hear, hear." I lifted my glass of white. "To sharing TMI and
memes forever."

"I'll drink to that," Eva agreed.

It just proved the power of friendship: despite having been on
the receiving end of a crushing revelation a few hours earlier, I
still ended the day laughing until I cried, wine drunk on a Tuesday night with my girls.

With everything that had been going on—my employer-
mandated shrink sessions, breaking up with Stephen, Amy sleeping with Stephen, helping Jane with wedding planning, moderat-
ing my mom's insane schemes—I deserved a little pampering. So
I treated myself to some summery highlights, using a 60-percent-
off Groupon I found.

The stylist oohed over my curls, and I sipped free espresso and
read every *Us Weekly* article that mentioned Meghan Markle—a
true American icon. I was engrossed in Meghan's skin-care routine and enjoying myself so heartily I barely noticed when the
stylist checked her watch, swore to herself, and scampered over
to remove the foils from my hair.

I left the salon with pep in my step and stopped to take a few
selfies. The sun glinted off my new caramel highlights; I wanted
to capture this moment for my dating profile. As I walked home,
all felt right with the world. The air was warm and fragrant with

honeysuckle. The group chat was back on track. And I was leaving tomorrow on the annual Weiss family vacation. Rachel Weiss was back, baby.

Almost by muscle memory at this point, I posted a photo of my new hair to Instagram. Just as predictably, Christopher replied to it. It tickled me how he didn't even pretend to wait a few minutes before replying, like people do to avoid seeming overly eager. He just saw my stories and messaged me. Just like that.

> **Christopher Butkus 7:09 PM:**
> Looking fresh.

> **Rachel Weiss 7:10 PM:**
> Why thank you, kind sir.

> **Christopher Butkus 7:11 PM:**
> Any special occasion? Another glamorous party or night out on the town?

I loved that this was his impression of me. Someone whose calendar was chock full of glam.

> **Rachel Weiss 7:12 PM:**
> Going away for the weekend.

I may or may not have left out the part about it being with my family—you know, to add to my mystique. He typed for a moment, then stopped. I felt a strange pang, and then an even stranger swoop in my stomach when he started typing again.

Christopher Butkus 7:15 PM:
Good for you! I'm getting out
of town for the weekend too.
Enjoy it!

I resisted the urge to ask where he was going and who he was
going with—honestly, it was none of my business. I gave his message a thumbs-up and put my phone back in my bag, determined
to enjoy the summer-evening air on my skin.

CHAPTER 14

I WOKE AT THE butt crack of dawn to await the family chariot. Dad had wanted to leave at four a.m., but we'd shouted him down. I swear that man is obsessed with traffic patterns. I sent a quick goodbye to the group chat.

> **Rachel Weiss 7:03 AM:**
> Good morning, friends. If you don't hear from me within three days, please send a search and rescue team to the town of Leavenworth and tell them I may have been clobbered to death by my mother's overwhelmingly misguided love.

Twenty minutes later, my parents were already yelling at me. Something about how it always takes me half an hour to leave my apartment, even when they've given me twenty-four hours' heads-up. I could barely hear them over the sound of the twins sobbing next to me in the back seat because Dad refused to stop for Starbucks until we'd driven at least fifty miles.

It was so unfair that Jane and Owen got to drive themselves. Just because they were engaged. And because they had a car and I didn't. And because Dad's Subaru only fit five people. It was so inconvenient that Mom and Dad decided to have twins after me. As if I were not the perfect reproductive swan song.

We arrived in Leavenworth just after noon, about two hours later than Google Maps had predicted. It was the bane of my dad's existence that the women in his family insisted on stopping at least five times on every road trip: to pee, to buy coffee, to go shopping at every outlet mall we passed, to buy more coffee—you get the idea.

We were staying at the same vacation cabin we'd stayed at nearly every year of my life. It was in a little clustered community of other cabins and had a wraparound porch with a firepit, a grill, and a hot tub. Truth be told, it was quite nice, which was surprising given that Mom and Dad were the ones who had chosen it. Normally they couldn't be trusted to choose toilet paper.

Anyway, we arrived and stumbled out of the Subaru, all of us choking and gasping for air. (The twins had purchased bagfuls of body spray and air fresheners from the Bath & Body Works at the outlet mall and proceeded to test them all at once.) I should clarify: Dad and I were choking and gasping, and Mom was going, "Ooh, nature doesn't smell nearly as nice as the car—girls, spray some of that cotton candy one over here." The twins pranced into the house behind Mom, spraying the air around her like her personal scent fairies as Dad and I schlepped the luggage inside. The twins immediately ran through the upstairs bedrooms screaming, "I get this one! No, this one!"

I ignored them, helping Dad stock the fridge and cabinets with the food we'd brought for the week—enough to feed a frat house for three months. I'd assumed—innocently believing there was still some good in the world—that I would get my usual room, one of the three with a queen bed. When I'd finished in the kitchen and lugged my suitcase up the stairs, however, I found that the twins had each claimed one of the grown-up rooms, leaving only the loft with four twin beds that they usually shared.

"Very funny, you two," I called, pulling one of their bags off my usual queen bed. "Hilarious joke."

I had backed halfway out of the bedroom, dragging Abby's duffel along the wood floor, when I stopped, the hairs on the back of my neck prickling with a sudden presence. Too late I realized that there was one twin on either side of me, each with a finger poised menacingly on the pump of a spray bottle.

And that was how I ended up sitting on a child's bed in the loft, coughing up lungfuls of mingled cotton candy and mango sorbet vapors. Mom joined me briefly to explain that she thought it best to let the twins have the queen beds.

"They're having a difficult summer," she said. "It's hard, working a full-time job."

"I wouldn't know anything about that." I coughed.

"They're working harder at summer camp than they've ever had to work before."

I doubted this very much. From everything I'd heard from the twins—and seen on their social media stories—their job consisted of sunbathing in hammocks and forcing children to row them around in canoes.

When Jane and Owen arrived, they deposited their things on two of the other twin beds without argument. No doubt the scent of my brutal attack still lingered on the air.

The unpleasantness was all but forgotten as the day wore on. We went into town and availed ourselves of everything the Bavarian tourist trap had to offer: sausages and beer for lunch, chocolate and wine tastings, and endless souvenir shops. Mom came away with one bag stuffed with decorative magnets and another of bespoke soaps in festive shapes. For dinner Dad grilled enough burgers for everyone to have six. It's as though once he gets a grill spatula in hand, he can't stop himself. We ate on the porch, gathered around the firepit, as the setting sun washed the whole scene in rosy light. I was reminded that sometimes, my family could be quite fun.

And then Jane and Owen excused themselves, saying they were too stuffed for dessert and were calling it a night.

"Oh, Jane," Mom called after her. "Take your usual room. You two should have a queen bed. And privacy."

Jane and Owen's faces lit up as the twins squawked in outrage. I swallowed back any arguments about (a) Mom not saying the same for me and (b) the fact that I would now have to share the loft with one of the twins. At least Jane would be happy.

"Thanks, Mom. That would be really nice." Jane smiled.

"Of course." Mom waved a hand. "You can't be in the loft. You two should be making whoopee."

The twins' protests turned to shrieks of disgust. Jane's smile fell, color leaching from her cheeks, and Owen turned a horrified face to me, hands flying to his cheeks in a mock scream over Jane's shoulder.

Mom, oblivious to the horror she had evoked, was still talking: "—like rabbits at your age, trust me, I remember." Dad slipped off his chair at these words. "And anyway, I don't want to be kept waiting for grandchildren. Go on, go on, we'll all be out here for a while yet, so you've got plenty of time."

And that was how I ended up sharing the loft with my big sister and her fiancé.

"Good night, Owen!" I said happily as I climbed into my twin bed.

"Night." He had chosen the bed farthest from Jane. I imagine he would have chosen to sleep in the middle of the woods if he'd had a sleeping bag.

"Good night, Jane!"

She pretended to be asleep. I can't say I blamed her.

In the morning, everyone was immersed in their leisure activity of choice (except the twins, who never woke up before noon). Jane and Owen were out on a run. Mom was halfway through her first vacation novel. (The cover was evoking something *torrid* and *steamy* with a muscled pirate clutching a breathless woman to his chest. God, I'd learned so much from Mom's romance novels as a tween. Maybe I would read that one when she finished it.) Dad was outside chopping wood. The last one was a bit of a mystery, since the grill and the firepit both ran on gas, but who was I to ask questions about what men find enjoyable?

I made myself a bowl of cereal and a mug of coffee and settled into a comfy seat on the porch, watching the morning mist hover above the grass and catch on the peaks of distant mountains. All manner of thoughts drifted pleasantly across my mind. The hours and hours of vacation time still ahead of me, the fact that I was still young and there really might be another career for me out there outside of tech support, and the very real possibility that there were dozens of hunky Jewish men in the Seattle area just *waiting* for me to finish creating my Jdate account. That's what I loved about vacations: the real world was on hold, and anything seemed possible.

By bedtime, I felt more refreshed and relaxed than I'd felt in years. All I'd done that day was eat, soak in the hot tub, and read Mom's pirate novel. My family was clearly feeling relaxed as well, because they'd hardly annoyed me at all. (Apart from Abby asking if my highlights were supposed to be that color. I ignored her. But truth be told, they were looking a bit more copper than caramel today. Ah well.) All we had planned for the next day was a leisurely float on the river. I assumed it would be another lovely, peaceful day.

Because I never, ever learn.

CHAPTER 15

THE NEXT MORNING, I woke suddenly to Jane and Owen hissing in what they apparently thought was a quiet fashion. They smelled like cold sweat too, having just returned from a run. I had been having *very* pleasant dreams involving the pirate from the book—I was a cleaning wench on his ship, scrubbing the deck on hands and knees as he approached me from behind to point out a spot that I had missed—when Jane's voice infiltrated my subconscious.

"—no reason to tell her," she whispered.

"Why not? She'll think it's funny," Owen whispered back.

"Owen, no. She's having a nice time. Imagine how annoying my mom will be if she finds out."

"But they will find out."

"Not necessarily. The cabins are far apart. We probably won't see him again."

At this point, goose bumps sprouted on my skin. I shot upright, fully awake.

"Who are you guys talking about?"

Jane jumped and clutched her heart over her pristine white jogging tank top. "I thought you were asleep."

"You guys are the loudest whisperers on the planet. Now tell me the gossip."

"We saw—" Owen began.

"Owen!" Jane said.

"Jane. Let the man talk."

Owen grinned triumphantly and continued in a rush, "We just saw Christopher Butkus."

"What?" I cried, then clapped a hand over my mouth. Jane had been right: we did not need Mom to hear this.

Owen nodded. "Just now, on our way back from our run. He was outside one of the other cabins."

"But—I—" I didn't understand what was happening to me. A cold mixture of dread and excitement was spreading across my skin. I was half-annoyed, half-jubilant. Stirrings of highly inappropriate feelings hadn't yet cleared my system after my lust-fueled pirate dream, and my body was reacting to the idea of Christopher Butkus as it would to the idea of any handsome male in the heat of the moment. I shook out my hands, itching to slap some sense back into myself.

"Ugh."

"I know." Jane shook her head sympathetically. "So annoying. But I doubt we'll run into him again, so don't worry."

"Ha." Jane didn't know about my habit of running into Christopher Butkus anywhere and everywhere. "Who was he with?" A traitorous and slutty voice in my head was hoping against hope that it wasn't an Andrea or a Xio.

"His parents and a few other older people. Looked like a family trip. They were on a nature walk."

"Ew." I stood, suddenly feeling much more myself. I had been half-asleep, that was all. And now the idea of the Butkuses on a brisk early-morning walk, pointing out leaves and squirrel poo with delight, made me feel appropriately bored with the whole idea.

"Don't worry, they didn't see us," Jane said.

"Good. Let's not mention this to Mom?"

"Agreed." She left to take a shower. Owen went downstairs, muttering something about breakfast, but no doubt secretly wanting to be seen by Mom and Dad the whole time Jane was in the shower so no one would have any funny ideas.

After lunch, Jane, Owen, the twins, and I piled into the car and drove to the float place. It was a beautiful day. Perfect weather. We rented life jackets and inner tubes and hopped on the Leavenworth Outdoor Center shuttle. The staff took us to the drop-off point and told us the float would take about four hours and to stay hydrated and not drink alcohol. And off we went. The water was almost painfully cold, but the sun was hot, and floating gently along the river felt heavenly.

There were hordes of people on the river. We were only five, and we'd clipped our tubes together so we wouldn't lose each other, but there were groups of twelve or more with music blaring, causing traffic jams for the tubes behind them. Almost every group had a cooler from which they passed around icy cans of La Croix and beer—the no-alcohol rule was always blatantly ignored. There were a couple people with those novelty floaties instead of heavy-duty tubes—a flamingo and a shark—posing for pictures like the river was one long photo shoot. (We saw them a couple hours later, drenched and shivering on their friends' tubes, dragging their punctured floaties behind them.)

"Beautiful day for it." Owen leaned back with his arms behind his head, aviator sunglasses glinting.

"Mm-hmm." Jane twined one long leg over his, trailing her fingers in the water.

"Yes indeed." The twins stifled laughter as they knocked their Gatorade bottles together in a toast. After they swilled some back, they sucked their teeth and grimaced.

"Something wrong with your Gatorade?" I asked.

"Nope!" They went about unzipping their life jackets and taking videos of each other.

"You're so going to drop those phones in the river." I settled back, sighing as the sun warmed my face and neck.

"Hey!" Jane snapped. "You keep those life jackets on." I looked around to see the twins baring their itty-bitty bikinis, trying to hide the life jackets under their bums.

"But they look dumb—"

"I'm trying to get a tan."

"Keep them on. The river gets choppy, you know that. Safety first," Jane said.

"Yes, Mom," they grumbled, sticking their arms back in the life jackets.

When Ollie's tube knocked against mine, I caught a distinct whiff of alcohol. I cracked one lazy eye open and saw that, sure enough, they were steadily growing sillier and sillier. I closed my eyes again, choosing not to say anything, because Jane was in such a responsible mood, I wouldn't have put it past her to make them dump out the contents of their Gatorade bottles—and I thought I might want some later. Four hours is a long time.

"Hi, Jane!"

We all looked around to see a smiling woman in a Mariners cap waving as she floated away.

"Hi, Ellen!" Jane called after her, waving. "That was Ellen from work," she told us. "Funny how we always see someone we know on the river. Remember last year it was the twins' friends?"

"Thank God this year it was your coworker and not—" I began, and then stopped, the words dying in my throat. There, drifting along not far behind us, was Christopher Butkus. He had his back to us and was chatting animatedly to his mom and another older woman. His hair was wet and tousled, shining bronze in the sunlight, and the back of his neck looked tan, and—*oh my God*, why was I noticing any of this?

"Hide me," I hissed, paddling my hands in the water, trying to steer my tube behind Jane and Owen.

"What—oh." Jane followed my gaze toward the Butkuses. "You don't need to hide, don't be silly. It's fine."

"Um…" Abby raised her brows, giving me a once-over.

"She's right. Look at me!" I was wearing an old one-piece with one of Jane's long-sleeved 5K shirts on top, covered by the mildewy standard-issue life jacket. My hair was piled in a messy bun on top of my head, my makeup-less face was—thankfully—mostly covered by my sunglasses, and the crowning jewel of this ensemble was my pale, unshaven legs sticking straight out in front of me. This thought made me realize that my equally unshaven bikini line was probably also on full display. I struggled with the hem of my wet shirt, tugging it down as far as it would go.

"Spin me, spin me." I reached my hands out to Jane and Owen. They pulled my tube around so I was facing the riverbank, my back toward the middle of the river and anyone who might happen to pass us by. "Thank you," I whispered, feeling safely incognito.

"Hi, Christopher!" the twins shouted, waving their hands above their heads.

"What the hell?!" I hissed.

"Hey, it's the Weisses," said a friendly voice very close behind me.
I gave a tiny nod and wave over my shoulder and then turned

my head back around, feigning great interest in the rocks and tree branches of the riverbank.

There was a general chorus of hellos from the rest of the Butkuses. Out of the corner of my eye, I saw Mr. and Mrs. Butkus float on ahead, and I'd just thought I was home free when I felt a gentle bump against my tube.

"Ride any bikes lately?" Christopher's voice asked softly in my ear.

I jerked around to face him. "Excuse me?"

He had grabbed the handle on the side of my tube. His eyes glinted with laughter; he wasn't wearing sunglasses, and I could see every fleck of green and brown in his eyes, every fold of skin at their corners as he struggled not to laugh.

"You look good in pink." He let go of the handle.

I mouthed angrily, unable to form words as he floated off.

"You know I live in Fremont." He was laughing openly now. "Is it so surprising that I would watch the parade?"

I flipped over and plunged my face into the water. When I sat up again, he had drifted away to join his family, his single tube moving rapidly with the current. My blood seemed to be pounding in my veins, hot with embarrassment. The idea of Christopher on the sidelines, watching as I pedaled my bike with joyful abandon, my breasts flopping in the wind, my face pink and grinning like a deranged Pixar character's...

"Give me some of that Gatorade," I snapped at the twins.

"No! You have your own water."

"GIVE IT TO ME."

I took a swill and smacked my lips. It was more vodka than Gatorade. Ollie held out her hand, expecting to get the drink back, but I waved her off.

"You can share the other one. That alone would be enough

to knock both of you out cold. Where did you even get vodka?"

"Shh." They cast nervous looks at Jane. But she was reclining in her tube, not paying us the slightest attention.

Reader, I should have known. If it was something Jane would have disapproved of, I should have taken a leaf out of her responsible-older-sister handbook. And yet…and yet. They don't call me Rachel Weiss for nothing.

An hour later, I was pleasantly tingly, the thought of Christopher Butkus banished from my mind. (Okay, nearly banished. Every so often I would replay those words—*Ride any bikes lately?*—at which point I'd take a swig.) The twins were a bit past tingly, if I had to guess. They hadn't stopped laughing like hyenas for so long I wondered when they would come up for air. After a solid ten minutes of cackling, Jane and Owen gave them a bemused look but seemed to write it off as teenage twin weirdness—a phenomenon that can explain away most of the twins' personalities.

"—has to be at least forty." *(Deranged giggle.)*

"He can still get it!" *(Snort. Shriek.)*

"I dare you to send him a nude."

"No, I DARE YOU." *(Snicker.)*

"Okay, but I'll just say it's you." *(Scream of mirth.)*

"You know," I said lazily, "just thinking out loud here, but I don't think either of you should send nudes to your history teacher."

"What?" Jane yelled, sitting upright.

At this, the twins fell about laughing so hard I actually thought they might choke on water and die. Don't judge me too harshly because I was content to watch. But their episode was interrupted by shouts from up the river calling back:

"Rocks! Shallow! Look out!"

"Okay, everybody." Owen slipped easily into dad mode. "You know what to do. Looks like the shallow part is up on the left. Everybody paddle to the right."

The landscape of the river is different every year, but a few shallow bits are generally preferable to quick-moving rapids in deep water, which can happen sometimes. Of course, you can also have quick-moving shallow bits…

After a minute or two it became apparent that all the grunting and paddling was happening up front, and that the twins, who were at the back, were still laughing and clutching each other silently. We were approaching the rocks and hadn't moved nearly enough toward the other side of the river.

"What's wrong with them?" Jane asked, an edge of panic growing in her voice.

"They…they may be a little drunk." I paddled with all my might.

"Drunk?!"

"Jane!" Owen pointed at the boulders peeking out of the water ahead. "Focus."

"Oh no." Jane leaned halfway out of her tube to try to steer us. "Girls! Help us paddle away from the rocks."

The twins finally snapped to attention and added their paddles to the water, but too late. Our tubes slowed, catching against the shallow river bottom in front of the big rocks. We laughed with relief: we hadn't crashed violently against the boulders. We would just have to push ourselves free. Owen slipped off his tube and tugged at Jane's.

"Everyone stay on your tube. The current is fast right here." He struggled to keep his footing as he freed Jane's tube.

"Careful, honey," Jane said, and then we were both rocked by a sudden disturbance. We looked around to see that the twins had jumped out to help Owen pull the tubes.

"No!"

"Get back in!"

The water barely covered their skinny ankles, but the rocks were slippery. They tried to heave themselves back into their floats, but their combined weight jolted the connected tubes into motion: the fast current caught us, sending the twins tumbling back into the water as our tubes were carried onward. Owen tried to pull the tubes back to the shallows, but the river was too fast and quickly becoming too deep. He jumped back into his tube while he still had the chance. Jane and I screamed. The twins were bobbing, saved by their life jackets, but I knew we would lose track of them if they got swept off in the current. I jumped into the water and Jane screamed louder.

The cold current caught at my legs; swimming upstream was impossible. I looked around, water pouring into my mouth, and saw that Jane had caught a low-hanging tree branch and had, for the moment, managed to stop the floats from being carried downstream. Every other second, the twins' heads would pop up with a shriek and then be submerged under the water again. I trod water as hard as I could, trying simultaneously to gauge where the twins were headed and not get too far away from Jane. The current sent Ollie crashing into me, and I launched her with all my might toward Jane. I didn't have time to see if she made it, because Abby was rushing away toward the middle of the river. I kicked after her and caught the handle of her life jacket. She thrashed as the life jacket tightened around her neck.

"Stop fighting me!" I yelled, the words garbled by water.

She was gasping, either with sobs or laughter, I wasn't sure. By some good luck, we managed to splash our way over to the tubes. The branch Jane had been holding had snapped, but Owen had grabbed another, smaller one. Jane was holding Ollie by the arms.

"Grab on," I told Abby. She clutched the handle of a tube with cold, white hands. "Stay there."

I inched over to Jane and Ollie and tried to heave her up by the butt. Jane grabbed her under the armpits. We were all slippery and going numb with cold. I caught a bony butt cheek to the face and groaned, my arms shaking as I tried to hold her up.

"Use your upper-body strength!" Jane yelled at her.

"What upper-body strength?!" Ollie shrieked, folding her torso over the edge of Jane's tube. Finally she slithered up and over and lay there in a shivering lump. Jane gingerly climbed over into one of the empty tubes.

"Help me!" Abby cried, her knuckles white around the tube handle.

Jane panted, clutching for her hands, as I slid from one float to the next to try to reach them.

"Jane…," Owen called.

"Just hold on!" she shouted back.

"I can't!" And with a sickening snap, Owen's branch broke. The five tubes were whisked away, towing Abby and me behind them.

Abby wailed, her hands already tired from holding on for so long. I lost track of time as we moved swiftly down the river trying to heave Abby up, Jane reaching down from the tube, scrabbling to hold on to her life jacket, me in the water, holding on to the tube for dear life with one hand and pushing her up with the other hand.

At one point, when Abby's butt was resting precariously atop my head as I squawked and tried not to swallow any more water, and Jane loomed above us screaming, "Rachel! Push!" I realized how utterly ridiculous this must look to our fellow river floaters. And as we drifted in this flattering formation, with the eye that wasn't being flooded with a stream of water from my sister's life jacket, I saw the gobsmacked face of Christopher Butkus. He and his family were floating in a civilized manner on the other side of the river.

While I was momentarily distracted by this mortification, my arms spasmed and Abby tumbled off my shoulders and into the river.

"Abby!"

I scanned the water, trying to pinpoint where she was so I would only have to dive once. My arms felt like overcooked spaghetti. I spotted her trying to stand in a shallow rocky spot near the bank, slipping and sliding as the current rushed around her ankles. I took a deep breath and then paused when I heard someone shouting my name.

"Rachel, stay there! Get in your tube."

A few yards away, Christopher whipped off his white T-shirt. Before I could process what I was seeing, he dived in, his arms slicing through the water as he swam straight across, as though the current didn't exist.

He had a perfect freestyle stroke. He turned his head to take a breath and caught sight of me, still submerged and clutching the side of my tube.

"Get in!" he shouted before plunging his face back in the water.

It took all the strength I had left to hoist myself up. Jane reached over to squeeze my hand as we watched Christopher swim over to Abby.

"Climb on my back," he called to her. She was on her knees in the shallows, her skin red and mottled from the cold water.

"I can't!" she wailed.

"Get on!" I shouted, as Jane yelled, "You can do it, Abby!"

Christopher helped maneuver her onto his back, her arms wrapping around his neck. I stared, feeling my mouth drop open, as his biceps bulged with the strain. Where had those been hiding? He swam slowly and carefully now, but the current was on his side, and they reached us in a matter of seconds.

Christopher put one elbow on my tube as he helped Abby slither off his back; I merely gaped at his slick skin and defined pecs, inches away from me. I was too exhausted to pretend not to notice. Abby clutched Ollie, both of them sobbing. Jane and Owen thanked Christopher profusely. I think I nodded. He was panting and clearly freezing, so he wasted no time before giving a wave and going to catch up with his family. They had stopped to wait for him at a sandy alcove up ahead. They looked scandalized, as did the other people floating nearby. I was too drained, too cold, and too confused to care that my family had become the laughingstock of the Wenatchee River.

None of us spoke on the car ride back to the cabin.

I was huddled in an old college sweatshirt with a towel around my waist, shivering uncontrollably despite the heat blasting in the car. My arms, shoulders, and pecs were so tired and aching, I could barely lift my water bottle. Jane, pale with cold, rested her head against the passenger side window and hadn't looked at any of us since we'd gotten in the car. I'd never seen her so angry. The twins had fallen into a shivering stupor, and I wondered vaguely if they had hypothermia (honestly, they would deserve it). I think Owen was just afraid to break the silence.

Finally, as we pulled up to the house, Abby spoke.

"Rachel...," she began slowly, her voice hoarse. I sat up straighter, prepared to accept her apology with grace. "Your hair... the sun turned it bright orange. I mean, more orange than it was before."

"Get out. Get out of the car!"

They didn't need telling twice. The twins scampered off into the house, Jane and Owen following them without a word. I crawled into the front seat and flipped down the visor mirror. It was true: where yesterday my highlights might have been brassy with possibly a *hint* of orange, now they glowed bright, like I'd painted my hair with Cheeto dust.

While a part of me wanted to break down and cry right there in the car, I was so numb that I knew I had to go inside and get warm.

Mom was on the front porch talking to Jane, her expression stricken. As I approached, Jane slipped inside, leaving me on the porch with Mom.

"You let them drink?" Mom's voice was shrill. "They almost drowned!"

"Um..." I stopped, clutching the towel around my waist. Was she really going to do this right now? "I didn't give them the alcohol. They did that all by themselves."

"Is this funny to you?" Mom's voice rose higher. She folded her arms over her pristine cardigan, her face pinched with distress. I hated that she was warm and dry and clean while I was standing there wet and colder than death, and I hated that she was so upset at me when it was the twins who had put themselves in danger.

"Oh no." I backed away from her. "I wouldn't dare make a joke about your precious twins. I know that's all you care about. Helping them when they screw up. Making sure they're successful even though they don't do shit to deserve it."

She followed me down the steps and onto the lawn.

"You have no idea what it's like, do you?" She was serious and forbidding, almost vulnerable without her usual aura of hysteria. "Raising four girls. I worry about you, all of you, all the time."

"All of us?" A breeze rushed through the trees and caught at my wet and tangled hair. "Funny, I don't remember you helping me get internships or"—I lowered my voice to a hiss, even though there was no one around to hear us—"cheating to help me get into college."

"You can't honestly tell me that you've forgotten everything I did to help push you in the right direction. I would do anything—*anything*—to help my children succeed. Do you think I don't know the girls are silly?" She spoke quickly, the words streaming together. "You're all silly, you're all like me, except Jane, thank God for Jane. Maybe I wouldn't worry about your futures as much if you were boys, maybe then you'd be more focused, less like me."

"Mom! That's a horribly misogynistic thing to say."

"Well, I don't know what it would be like to have boys, do I? Maybe it would be easier. Women have to try so much harder, and when you're not serious about anything, when you're girly and frivolous, how do I know you're going to be successful? I never needed a proper career, did I? I got lucky with your father, I only had to work part-time here and there. But the world is a different place now, and you're all going to have to make your own way..."

"But"—I softened at the genuine fear in her words—"but you don't have to try so hard, do you? The twins would be fine going to any college. Community college, state schools. They'll be okay!"

"We need them to get a *scholarship*. We have no college fund for them. And God knows if those two were saddled with student debt they would sink like stones. There's only so much we can do to help them, and if we can't even pay for their college..."

I felt my mouth drop open.

"Why didn't you think of any of this before you had the twins?"

"The twins were an accident, Rachel!"

"A what?!"

"For God's sake, I was only thirty-eight when I had them... These things happen. Your father and I planned on sending two children to college; we saved up all your lives so we could send you and Jane to whichever schools you wanted. And then life happened, and suddenly we were paying for day care for two at the same time that Jane was going to college. We always meant to start the twins' college funds, but things kept coming up—electrical work on the house, the year your father got laid off, and your college tuition costing more than expected, and now...well, here we are."

I stepped shakily over to the porch steps and sat down. I'd had no idea—*no* idea. I thought of my fancy liberal arts education at Whitman and the hundreds of thousands of dollars my parents had spent so I could study literature and have the time of my life for four years just so I could end up in a dead-end tech job...

"I'm sorry." I looked up at Mom. "I didn't know."

"I know you didn't. We didn't want any of you to know. We just want you to be happy." She brushed past me and paused on her way to the front door. "Please don't tell the twins."

As the door closed behind her, I dropped my face into my hands. I was so dehydrated that no tears would come, but my eyes and throat burned. *We just want you to be happy.* And look at me now: ancient and single, making just enough money to get by in a job I hated, plagued by zits and orange hair and in imminent need of dentures.

Footsteps crunched across the grass and twigs in front of me. I raised my eyes and fought back an incredulous laugh. Someone, somewhere—probably the ghost of my Grandma Pearl—was messing with me for their own entertainment.

Christopher Butkus was walking toward me. He looked like he'd showered, wearing a fresh white T-shirt with preppy pink shorts and white sneakers with tall socks. He smiled, clutching a Tupperware container. I wondered, without really caring very much, how much he'd just heard of my conversation with Mom.

"That was some performance on the river," he said by way of greeting.

I stood, my face so numb I couldn't manage a word in response. I knew I should say something along the lines of "Thank you for saving my sister's life," but I couldn't muster the strength.

Instead I found myself asking, "Is your family stalking my family?"

"Yes," he said seriously. "We actually work for the FBI and have been collecting data on the Weisses for some time now."

I didn't respond, unnerved by the actual possibility that my mom really was under investigation for the SAT scandal. I dropped my eyes to the container in Christopher's hands.

"My aunt baked cookies." He held it out to me. "I thought you might like some."

"Thank you. Very thoughtful."

He looked—and smelled—so good that I wanted to be gone from his presence immediately. Him seeing me in my current state was almost more than I could bear at this point. "Well, I should probably go change; I'm a bit—"

He took a sudden step toward me. "Actually, Rachel, the cookies were just an excuse."

"What?"

"I wanted to talk to you."

I clutched the plastic container to my chest, feeling faint, and nodded for him to continue, hoping it would be quick.

"I..." He looked around. "Could we sit?" He gestured toward the cushioned sofa on the porch.

"Okay." I followed him and settled into the opposite corner of the sofa, keeping as much distance between us as possible.

He flashed a nervous grin at me and then lowered his eyes to his lap, where his fingers were tented. I was filled with a rush of foreboding, though I couldn't fathom what he was about to say.

"What is this about?" I asked. "If it's about Stephen, you two should work that out on your own. Leave me out of it."

"Stephen?" His expression became clouded. "Are you two still...?"

"No. God no."

A radiant smile overtook his face. "Good. That makes this easier. Because, Rachel, I..." He took a deep breath and, with a sense of purpose, raised his eyes to meet mine. "I wanted to tell you that I think you're...I think you're the most incredible woman I've ever met."

The silence after this pronouncement clanged, deafeningly, in my ears. I blinked slowly. Christopher's smooth, freshly shaven cheeks flushed red.

"It's..." He looked down at his hands again and smiled, nervous and yet easily confident in the way only a wealthy, handsome white man can be. "It's the most amazing thing. I haven't been able to stop thinking about you since the first night we met. And then every time I see you, you're doing something so...insane, so startling, it's like...you make me feel more alive than anyone I know. You're not perfect; you're messy, and you don't try to be perfect like most women do these days. You're impulsive. I've

never seen you read a book. Your family is bizarre and embarrassing, but it doesn't matter; in fact, I like it. Everything about you
is funny and..." He broke off, running a hand through his damp
hair. "I'm butchering this. I'm a little nervous. But Rachel..." He
lurched forward and grabbed my cold hands. I was so startled that
I jerked my hands back and sat on them. He let out a strained little
laugh at this and continued. "This is crazy, and I've never done
this before, but Rachel, I think I'm in love with you."

My first thought was: *Did he really have to do this while my cold
bathing suit was riding up my butt and chafing my nipples?*

My second thought was: *Wait...what the fuck just happened?*

And then parts of his speech came back to me in a slow-motion
replay, and fury bubbled up in my chest, warming me better than
anything had in hours.

"Are you finished?"

He still had a pleasantly flustered and expectant look on his
face. I kept my eyes on it without blinking so I would see the
instant it crumbled.

"Um, yes." He encouraged me to speak with an awkwardly
gallant wave of his hand.

"Oh, good. So is now the time when I'm supposed to fall into
your arms? You're the good-looking millionaire and I'm the poor
commoner you've taken a liking to, so that's how it's supposed to
work, right?"

There it was: a spasm moved across his brow, his pupils dilated,
his nostrils flared. Not so confident anymore.

"No, really, what did you think would happen? That I would be
grateful that you're into me despite how embarrassing you think
I am?"

"I don't think you're—"

"Let me stop you right there. You think I'm imperfect,

messy, and—oh yeah—insane. You think my family is bizarre and embarrassing." The color drained from his face as I spit his words back at him. "Well, I'm sorry we're not prim and proper buttoned-up WASPs. No, you know what? I'm not sorry. At least we're interesting. Did you really think insulting my family was going to make me fall in love with you? And just because I don't name-drop books or document everything I read on social media doesn't mean I don't *read*. Are you serious with that? I read fifty books last year."

"I didn't mean—it came out all wrong—"

"I'm not finished." I stood, and it felt good to tower over him despite the towel I still grasped around my waist. "What kind of patriarchal fever dream led you to believe that proclaiming your love for me would work out well for you? When have I ever—*ever*—given the impression that I was into you? You know nothing about me—except where my parents live and what I look like riding a bike naked. You've probably never been with a Jewish girl before and thought, *Hey, here's my chance!*"

"Rachel, wait."

"No, *Christopher*, I will not wait. I haven't been sitting around waiting for a man to swoop in and change my life. And even if I was, there is no way I could ever be with someone like you. People who make millions and billions of dollars from their corporations make me sick. Not to mention the way you date drop-dead gorgeous women like Xio and Andrea for a few weeks, then probably can't even remember their names after you switch them out for someone new. And the way you treated your best friend? Friendship is the most important thing in the world to me. Even if it weren't for all the other things I just listed, I could never be with someone who stole their best friend's idea and cheated him out of money that should have been rightfully his."

Christopher looked stunned now. His normally smiling mouth was slack, his brows lowered. I figured I'd more than gotten my point across.

"So thank you for telling me you love me in the most insulting way possible. You've reaffirmed everything I thought about guys like you. Now if you'll excuse me, I need to get out of these wet clothes and forget this day ever happened."

I took a step toward the door, then doubled back. Christopher looked up, a ray of hope lighting his face.

"I'm taking the cookies." I grabbed the Tupperware, and the ray of hope extinguished itself. "Goodbye, Christopher."

I slammed the front door behind me and stomped up the stairs without acknowledging the various members of my family in the kitchen and living room. I locked myself in the bathroom, filled the tub with the hottest water possible, and finally, *finally* took off those damn wet clothes. Then I sank into the bath and didn't get out until I'd eaten every last cookie.

CHAPTER 16

AFTER I'D CHANGED INTO dry clothes and regained a body temperature suitable to human life, I rinsed out the Tupperware and slunk through the woods in the direction Christopher had come from. There were only a few cabins around here, and the first one I stumbled upon had several cars parked in front of it, including a Tesla, so. Of course he would drive a Tesla. I darted up to the front door and left the empty container on the mat. I didn't want the reminder hanging around our kitchen, and I didn't want to give him any excuse to speak to me again—though I doubted he would ask for it back.

Pleased that I'd put an end to the whole thing, I returned to our cabin and nicked another of Mom's steamy novels—this one featuring a shirtless knight wielding a sword, his cape and curly hair rippling in the wind. I curled up on the couch and lost myself in this tempting fantasy for several hours.

Mom and Dad had gone out for groceries and wine, and when they returned, I heard Mom coo, "Ohh, how lovely! I wonder who left these."

I sat bolt upright. *Surely not.*

"Cookies!" the twins squealed.

Mom bustled into the living room holding the very same container, now packed full of a fresh batch.

"Rachel, did you see who left these? How very thoughtful!"

"No," I grumbled.

"Speak up, speak—"

"*No!*" I shouted so loud that Mom frowned at me. "I didn't see…I have no idea. It's probably a prank. Wouldn't eat them if I were you."

I added this last bit because the oatmeal chocolate chip cookies had been, in fact, delicious, and I wanted them all to myself again.

"Don't be ridiculous." Mom headed into the kitchen. "Must've been a neighbor."

"Ooh, a neighbor," the twins trilled, staring at me with buggy eyes. I drew one finger across my throat, but they ignored the threat and made smooching noises at me as they followed Mom into the kitchen.

For the rest of the evening, that Tupperware drew my eyes as if it were a naughty picture of Christopher Butkus himself. I tried to ignore it, but my gaze drifted toward it as we ate dinner, as I made coffee and washed dishes. *The most incredible woman I've ever met. Think I'm in love with you.*

Bizarre. Embarrassing.

No way I could ever be with someone like you.

If he had refilled the cookie container, what did that mean? Did it mean that my words hadn't burned that bridge as effectively as I'd hoped? Had I really hoped that?

The more time passed, the more I wondered if I had overreacted. Truth be told, I had never actually entertained the idea of

Christopher Butkus as a romantic partner. He was always a joke: first as someone my mom foisted upon me, then as an obnoxious tech bro, then as someone I maybe, sometimes, occasionally enjoyed talking to—and who could swim to a girl's rescue without a second thought. But as a man I could see myself with? As a handsome man with shapely biceps and strong hands, with a smooth jaw and the clean scent of cologne emanating from the warmth of his skin—

What? No!

No, Rachel, absolutely not. I really had to stop reading these romance novels. My mind had sustained a serious shock; it was weak and susceptible to inappropriate fantasizing.

After dessert and coffee, the family went for a nighttime Jacuzzi soak. I chose instead to curl up on the porch sofa with a blanket, having no desire to submerge myself in water again. I only slightly regretted my choice, as the sofa reminded me of the conversation I'd had on it mere hours before.

"I really do wish we knew who had left those delicious cookies so we could repay the favor." Mom's voice carried over the sound of the bubbling jets. Jane, squished between Dad and Owen, glanced over at me. I couldn't read her expression. We'd barely spoken since we'd gotten home from the river. I was itching to tell her everything Christopher had said, but I assumed she was still mad at me.

"How would you repay them? Bake them cookies? Like a never-ending cookie showdown?" Abby laughed.

"I don't think we need any more snark from you two today," I snapped.

Abby glared at me and then turned to Mom. "Maybe it was Christopher Butkus. We saw the Butkuses today."

Mom's squawk of reply was lost in a splash; she seemed to have lost her balance on the edge of the hot tub.

"Christopher—Christopher Butkus?" Mom swiveled her head to look at me.

"Shh." I was unable to stop my eyes from flicking toward the dark woods in the direction of the Butkuses' cabin. I didn't really think Christopher would be lurking nearby to spy on us, but still.

Mom followed my gaze, her face becoming apoplectic.

"They're here? Rachel? You knew? They must think us so rude! We haven't even said hello."

"We didn't ask them to come to Leavenworth. It's okay. They didn't even leave a note on the cookies. Maybe they weren't from them."

"Or maybe," Abby continued, her tone becoming aggressive, "they were. It would make sense, since Christopher was here earlier declaring his love for Rachel."

There was a long silence punctuated with little splashes, during which I contemplated what it would be like to steal Dad's car and take off into the night so I'd never have to speak to Mom or the twins again. This fantasy was a brief distraction from the exponentially mounting tension; we all knew the longer Mom stayed silent, the worse the explosion would be.

Finally, I shouted, "Oh my God, just say something!" right as Mom roared, "RACHEL RENÉE WEISS?"

I half expected the rest of the family to run for shelter, but they stayed put, the twins smirking in a satisfied way, Dad looking nervous, Owen riveted, and Jane concerned.

I pulled the blanket up to my face and began, "It's not...," but Mom cut me off.

"Didn't I tell you not to mess with that poor boy's heart?"

"*Why* do you care so much about his feelings?"

"He's a gem. He's a responsible boy who loves his parents, and it's a wonder he's still single, and I don't want you ruining him for whatever worthy girl comes along for him."

"Rachel *is* worthy," Jane burst out. I gave her a tight smile of thanks.

"The reason your precious gem is still single is because he dates supermodels and tosses them aside when he's bored of them." I crossed my arms.

"Or because he puts all his hopes in the wrong basket." That stung a bit; I didn't know what I had done to make my mother insult my baskethood.

"Don't worry, he won't make that mistake again. At least not with me."

"What did you say to him?"

"I…" I looked away, not wanting to see Mom's or Jane's reaction to my next words. "I told him he was wasting his time; I'm not interested."

Mom stood abruptly, sending Jacuzzi water sloshing as she reached for her fuzzy bathrobe. She stood very close to me, dripping on me, as if she didn't want the others to hear her.

"After everything your father and I have done for you, everything we've sacrificed so you would be successful, I don't understand how—HOW—you can spit in the face of an opportunity like that."

At this injustice, I jumped to my feet so we were face-to-face.

"You *just* said I wasn't good enough for him, that you didn't want me hurting him. Make up your mind!"

"If you can't recognize good luck when it's right in front of you—when a gorgeous and rich man tells you he loves you—then I just don't know where we went wrong with you."

"I wasn't interested! I don't like him!"

"At some point, you have to get over it! You can't afford to be so picky, Rachel, you just—"

"Beth." Dad spoke quietly, still resting his back against the jets in the tub. "That's enough."

"But she—"

"She doesn't like the fellow. What more needs to be said?"

"But it's—" Mom gestured toward the Butkuses' cabin, then grasped her head in both hands as if she couldn't articulate the enormity of the problem.

"Our little girl shouldn't settle for anything—or anyone—less than her heart's desire. None of them should." Dad's voice was low and even. Jane tossed a glowing look at Owen. Some sort of tidal wave surged in my chest, filling my throat with tears.

"But..." Mom trailed off, the wind taken out of her sails.

"Rachel will be successful enough on her own. She certainly doesn't need anyone else's success. In fact, she might not like being overshadowed." Dad looked at me with a glimmer of laughter in his eyes.

I wrapped the blanket tighter around me, suddenly wishing everyone would go inside; I wasn't sure how much longer I could swallow back these tears.

"Bedtime." Jane climbed out of the hot tub and gestured for the others to follow her. She always knows what I need.

I waited a few minutes before heading inside myself. The fire was on in the living room. I settled in front of it, trying to make sense of the whirl of thoughts and feelings inside me. The floor overhead creaked with footsteps as everyone made their way to bed.

"Hey." Jane stood in the dark stairwell.

"Hi." I patted the cushion on the floor beside me. She sat down, and I offered her half of the blanket.

"What happened?" she whispered.

"He…" I stared into the flames, letting my vision blur with the dancing light. "He came and, out of nowhere, said he thought he was in love with me. But he somehow insulted me at the same time." I don't know why, but I didn't want to tell her that he had insulted our family too. "And I told him I could never be with someone like him who just cares about wealth, someone who treats his friends like crap."

"His friends?"

"You know Stephen?" I filled her in on everything Stephen had told me.

"What a scumbag." Jane hugged her knees. Sitting beside my sister, telling her everything and knowing that she agreed with me, made me feel lighter than I had all day.

"I know. And to think Mom loves him."

"I honestly think she would trade all four of us in exchange for him," Jane said, and we started laughing and couldn't stop, our shoulders bumping together, finally doubling over in a breathless heap.

"Are you okay?" Jane asked before we went upstairs.

"Yeah, I'm fine. I just want to be home in my own apartment. Away from Mom and the Butkuses."

"One more day." And on that cheerful note, we headed up to the loft.

Jane stopped me just outside. "By the way, Dad's sleeping in the fourth bed. Mom kicked him out because he should have convinced you to marry Christopher."

It took several long minutes for us to recover from the subsequent silent giggle-fest.

I climbed into my twin bed. "Good night, Jane. Good night, Owen. Good night, Dad."

"Night," they chorused, Dad sounding a little grumpy.

"And Dad...thanks," I whispered.

CHAPTER 17

EVERYONE WAS QUIET AS we packed up to leave the next morning. I assumed the twins were tired after their near-death experience. Mom was being solemn and formal after our blow up—very unlike her, but I didn't ask questions. I just savored the silence.

As I was zipping up my weekender, Jane entered the room. She tapped an envelope against her palm.

"This was on the doormat when Owen and I left for our run earlier."

Puzzled, I took it from her. It had my name written on the front in unfamiliar handwriting. My stomach sank and fluttered all at once. I didn't know anyone else in Leavenworth; this could only be from one person.

Jane's eyes roved across my face, a concerned crease between her brows. "I'll...let you read it." She pulled the door closed behind her.

I perched on the edge of my bed and tore the envelope open. Inside was a formal-looking letter, written in smooth, black ink.

July 14th, 6:00 a.m.

Dear Rachel,

I haven't been able to sleep since our conversation went so badly. I would like to try to explain a few things. I hope you'll do me the courtesy of reading this letter, though you certainly owe me nothing.

First, I want to apologize for the way I sprang all that on you with no warning. It embarrasses me to the point of physical pain when I think about it. It was just as you said. It was arrogance, pure and simple. I'm sorry that I assumed you shared my feelings. I'm sorry I said hurtful things. I can't account for my total lack of emotional intelligence in this instance, except maybe to say I got carried away with an idea...a fantasy.

Second, I feel that a few explanations are necessary. This is not to start an argument or to convince you that you were wrong about anything. I fully expect that you never wish to speak to me again, even after reading this, and I understand that. Sometimes, in a heated moment, words don't come to me as quickly as I'd like. Only afterward can I form coherent thoughts, but I don't think you have the same problem, do you? Consider these explanations to be both an apology and a plea for you not to think of me as a villain. Though I know you can never see me romantically, I hope you can see me as a decent person.

I will tackle the topic with no easy answer first. You view money as a character flaw, and on that we must disagree. I try to do good in the world. My company was born out of a desire to help the planet. That it has made a lot of money is, in my view, something to be optimistic about. Still, I agree with you that one man does not need an obscene collection of wealth, and I plan to think long and hard about what else I can do with mine.

The topic of my business will, of course, make you think of Stephen Branson. I was surprised by what you told me about him, because I had never before heard that version of events. This is a longer story, so I will try to make it short. I don't want to speak ill of anyone, but the truth is not flattering. If you ever wish to see evidence to support my side of the story, I have emails and bank statements to back it up.

Yes, Stephen and I were friends in college, and yes, we thought up the concept of Pageant together. After graduation, we parted ways, and when I decided to try Pageant in the real world, I invited him to join me. He, however, claimed that he had a much more lucrative business opportunity and declined. A year or two later, he contacted me to ask for a large sum of money. Our friendship had ended years before, but he was desperate. He had been conned into a multilevel marketing scheme and was out tens of thousands of dollars. I looked into legal defenses, ways to help him get his money back, but when I couldn't find any, I gave him the money he needed. He had burned a lot of bridges when he was part of the scheme, and he had been my best friend once. He insisted that he would pay me back one day, but I told him the point of me giving him that money was to get him out of debt, and that he could repay me by getting himself a decent job and getting back on his feet. I believe he did that, although I had no evidence one way or another, because I never heard from him again. I have reason to believe he blocked me on everything after I gave him the money. Seeing him at the wedding with you was the first time I'd had any contact with him in years.

Lastly, you accused me of dating women like Xio and then forgetting them. I never dated Xio. I can see why you had this mistaken impression after seeing us together on Valentine's Day, but Xio works at Pageant and we were on our way to a colleague's party

*that night. You mentioned Andrea too. That wedding was our first
and last date. We didn't have much in common. I don't deny that
I have dated gorgeous women. The women in my social circle are
often beautiful, intelligent, charming—sometimes a combination
of the three. I won't speak ill of any of them. But I must stop there,
because I have already told you where you stand in my estimation,
and I won't repeat the hated sentiment.*

*Rachel, please know that I am deeply sorry for everything. If I
could take back everything and continue bumping into you around
town, nothing more than a friendly neighbor, I would. I might never
forgive myself for my idiocy, but I hope you can.*

Respectfully yours,
Christopher W. Butkus

It felt as though hours passed before my mind pieced itself back
together. I gazed out the window as we drove through precari-
ous gray-and-purple mountain roads and then through lush green
countryside dotted with cows. And great thinker that I am, the
first coherent thought that dropped into my mind was: Who was
he to have such lovely handwriting? *Honestly.* And the nerve of
him accurately naming my feelings and...and writing so elo-
quently. *How?* And *why?* And...

Look, if what he'd written about Stephen was true, then Christopher was a good friend, and Stephen was a liar. But that did
not dismiss Christopher's rich-white-man entitlement. Or the fact
that he was arrogant enough to profess his love for me in the most
awkward and unwanted way possible. *No, thank you.*

The letter was shoved inside my backpack, and I nudged my

backpack deeper underneath the seat in front of me, as if it would make me feel better to be two inches farther away from it. The hated letter.

I won't repeat the hated sentiment.

Had he really used the word *love*?

I had to stop thinking about this immediately. For my sanity. I closed my eyes and tried to sleep.

CHAPTER 18

AFTER WORK ON MONDAY, Sumira invited us over to her apartment building's rooftop. We settled onto the sun-warmed settees under a large patio umbrella.

"On the menu tonight"—Sumira waved a hand over the little spread she'd laid out—"chips and dip. And some fresh gossip. Who wants to go first?"

"Well…" Amy wore a secretive smile. "I kind of have an update."

"A good one, I hope?"

"Yeah. Ryan has been putting in some effort. He actually suggested that we try couples therapy. And not only that, he actually did the research and found a therapist for us to try."

"Dang. Good for him!" I scrutinized Amy's face, looking for signs of doubt. "And how are you feeling about…everything? About him?"

"Honestly, it means a lot to me that he's trying so hard. He's making me feel like, I don't know, like our marriage is important to him."

"As he should!" Sumira interjected.

"So I'm happy for the moment. I feel like we're on the right track. We'll see how things go from here, I guess."

We all told her that we were happy for her. And then they immediately turned to me.

"Okay, spill, Rachel." Eva's mouth was full of guacamole.

I'd filled them in on the events of the past weekend in the group chat, but they wanted details. And they wanted to see the letter. Especially Amy, who had a thing for Jane Austen heroes.

"I still can't believe he wrote you an actual letter." She cracked open a La Croix. "How romantic is that?"

"Are we calling it romantic?" Sumira wrinkled her nose. "This was an unwanted advance."

"Right," Eva agreed. "There's nothing swoon-worthy about pursuing a person who's not into you."

"I know, but, like, Rachel said he has nice handwriting." Amy raised her eyebrows like that settled it.

I sighed and extracted the letter from my bag.

"Here. Go nuts." With a shriek, they all dived toward the now somewhat worn piece of paper.

"Stop, don't rip it!" Amy held the letter with both hands as Eva and Sumira read over her shoulders.

There were some exclamations of shock and amusement as they read, followed by an uncharacteristic hush.

After a moment, Sumira broke the silence. "The man knows how to write a letter."

Eva began, "Stephen was in a—" in a tone of glee, but Amy interrupted her. "Can we please not talk about the Stephen part?"

Quiet fell again, and my friends went back to eating their chips and dip, glancing at me to gauge how I was feeling. How was I feeling? It was a fabulous letter—I knew that. Every time I read it I felt myself soften a little. Did a part of me want to continue bumping into him around town? Of course. Was the fiery, angry part of me still there too, righteous as ever? *Of course.* I had been right when I shot him down, and this letter wasn't going to change that.

"Are you gonna sleep with him?" Sumira asked. Always classy, that one. I threw a corn chip at her.

"No." I tried to sound dignified. "I'm not going to sleep with a man just because he puts pen to paper for me."

"You've done it for less," Eva muttered, and Sumira snorted.

"No, actually, this whole debacle has shown me something. It's shown me that...I'm literally flawless."

Amy exchanged a sideways glance with Sumira while Eva stared at me in disbelief.

"I mean, look. A man like Christopher is, objectively, a catch. He's mega successful. He's not hideous...Actually, he's quite— never mind. He makes Jewish mothers lose their minds. And he apparently lost his mind over me. Sure, he used some unflattering descriptions, but he was declaring his *love* to me. And he barely knows me. This just reaffirms what I've always thought: I am a goddess." I punctuated this by crunching into a hummus-laden chip.

There was a long, thoughtful pause.

"A goddess with nacho cheese hair," Sumira said, and the girls cackled like the witches they are.

She had a point, though. As the conversation devolved into silliness, I took out my phone and scheduled an appointment with a new colorist.

The days turned sultry and humid as August neared. My hair was glossy and brown again. I treated myself to a Madewell sundress that made me look like a swarthy season 1 Daenerys Targaryen. And while all of these things injected a sense of fresh hope into my life, they could not protect me from the more nefarious aspects of my existence. Such as Kenneth.

"Um, Rachel—Rachel, hi." Kenneth hovered on the edge of my peripheral vision. This sort of entrance irritated me more than if he had pole-vaulted into my cubicle with jazz hands.

"Hello, Kenneth." I swiveled around to face him.

"Sheryl is on vacation this week, and Cam was covering for her, but now Cam is out sick, so..." He pushed his glasses up his nose and grabbed the stapler from my desk, inspecting it—why? "I'll need you to cover for them. Both."

Several potential responses ran through my mind, including the crucial fact that I was only one person, who worked only forty hours per week. But I swallowed these retorts, reminding myself that I was here for the money. The money that I needed to buy food and sundresses.

"Okay."

"Okay?" He looked up in surprise, and the stapler swung open. Had he thought he might need it for self-defense?

"Of course. I'll do my best."

Visibly relieved, he set down the stapler. "Thank you, Rachel!" As he walked away, he pointed at me as if he were my sports coach and shouted, "Gold star!"

I sighed and turned back to my ever-growing list of customer complaints. If only gold star stickers could be converted to American currency.

On my lunch break, I sat on the steps outside, my legs stretched out in the sun, and swiped on Tinder.

"Ew. No. Double ew." I swiped left again and again. Seattle singles had some explaining to do. Perhaps if I set my distance to one mile I would get some respectable, employed guys swiping near me on their lunch breaks. Hmm. Here was one: blond, fit but not intimidatingly so, and with photographic evidence of normal-looking friends. I scrolled down to his bio: "Brent, 30. My truck identifies as a Prius. Gun grabbers swipe left."

And on that revolting note, I tossed the rest of my sandwich in the trash. Men were all the same: complete wastes of DNA. Anyway, why was I wasting my time? I was destined to be a spinster crone, wasn't I? I should be shopping for a cabin in the woods and some cats, not a man. My phone buzzed, and for once I was relieved to see a text from my mom, as it beat the alternative of a message from any of my so-called matches.

"Everyone is invited to dinner tonight! It's a bit of a celebration!"

A last-minute celebratory dinner invite from my mother? This could not be good.

Mom was in such an exultant mood that she ordered Chinese for dinner. Jane had arrived before me, and when I raised my eyebrows at Mom prancing around scooping chow mein and cashew chicken into serving dishes, Jane gave me a knowing *Wait till you hear it* look.

"Mom, what are we celebrating?" I pinched a chow mein noodle.

"Some very exciting news." She slapped my hand.

I glanced around at the rest of my family for a clue. The twins were sprawled on the living room carpet watching a beauty vlogger, mouths slightly open and eyes glazed. Dad was in his armchair reading—I had to do a double take—a book called *The Mask of Masculinity*. (Honestly, what was it with him?)

"Are you going to tell me?" I asked, following Mom to the dining room with a bowl of hot and sour soup.

She set a dish down on the table and turned to me with her hands clasped under her chin.

"We talked to that wretched man, and everything is fine. It's all over."

What does it say about me that when she said, "wretched man," my first thought was of Christopher Butkus?

"I'm not quite following. What's over?"

"The ridiculous matter of cheating on the SATs." She waved her hand indignantly.

"Mom!" I looked around at the twins. "I thought you didn't want them to know."

"Oh, they know. They had to be questioned by him too."

"By who?"

"The man. The detective." She opened a cupboard and extracted the Shabbat candles.

I clapped my hands to my mouth. "You guys were actually questioned by a detective?"

"Yes, and according to our lawyer, that's the end of it. We might even get some of the settlement money when it's all sorted out. As an innocent party swept up in this illegal scheme."

"But—you—innocent?" I glanced at Jane, who pressed her lips together.

"Yes, dear." Mom stopped her bustling and turned to face me, her large, guileless eyes betraying no hint of anything. Her acting ability—or is it cognitive dissonance?—is shocking, to say the least.

"Well." It took me several moments to adjust to this new version of reality. "Mom, was it really an accident? Did you know what you were doing? Because it's wrong on so many—"

"Rachel," my dad interrupted, his voice low. He shook his head in a bemused sort of way. "She didn't."

"She didn't?"

"She heard about this guy from a friend of a friend who swore he was the best tutor on the West Coast. That he helped so-and-so's son get his SAT scores up by six hundred points. She didn't know it was a scam."

"I wouldn't call it a scam, I would call it *blatantly cheating*! And our current finances aside, we are the definition of privilege, Dad. It just doesn't seem like you all are taking it seriously."

"But if she didn't do it on purpose," Jane added, sounding hesitant.

"It's just..." I wasn't sure what my point was, but I knew that I wanted to make them understand. I swear, it's like parents have never heard the term *privilege* before in their lives.

"Do you *want* your mother to get in legal trouble?" Dad asked.

"What—no! But..."

Mom looked at me balefully. The twins swiped on their phones, not listening to a word.

"What kind of life lessons are you teaching them?" I gestured wildly to my little sisters.

"Oh, they wouldn't pay attention to any type of lesson from me, even if I were to teach it buck naked with a hedgehog on my head." All of us (except the twins) simply stared at her. "Anyway," she continued, "I still have to share the big news!"

"That wasn't the big news?"

Jane shrugged; apparently she was still in the dark about this part as well.

The six of us gathered around the table, Mom did the blessing over the candles, and then, the instant our backsides touched our chairs, she clanged a spoon against her wineglass.

"We have an announcement," she crooned, the pile of curls on her head wobbling with excitement.

"Yes, we know," I said. "Are you pregnant?"

Mom shot me a very dirty look. With a glance at Dad, who was nodding at her encouragingly, she gathered herself and continued.

"The twins have received a scholarship!"

"Wonderful!" Jane clapped.

"Was this scholarship based on the fraudulent SAT scores or...?" Dad shook his head at me firmly, so I changed tack. "How much is it?" If Mom was going to make this big a deal each time the twins received a few hundred dollars from the Jewish Federation or Burger King Scholars, it was going to be hard to keep up the excited facade.

Mom pressed her palms together and took a deep breath.

"Full. Ride."

Still waiting for the punch line, I looked around. Jane's mouth had dropped open. Dad was beaming.

"What?" I was confused. "Full ride to where?"

"The college of their choice! Dear, go get the check."

Dad obliged and returned a moment later with an official-looking letter and a glossy check. Jane and I peered down at them; the letter expressed bland congratulations for some generic achievements and stated that the organization was committed to assisting families with multiples to afford higher education. Jane gasped and shoved the check under my nose. It took my mind several seconds to comprehend the number of zeroes.

"Three hundred thousand dollars?" I shrieked.

Mom was practically weeping with joy. The twins looked up with vague smiles before returning to their phone screens.

"That's incredible!" Jane stood to hug everyone in turn.

"But what—how? Did you write the essay for them?" I shot at Mom suspiciously.

"Oh, who knows. We've applied to so many I can hardly remember anymore."

Dad leaned over the table to take the check back, and I gave it one last sweeping look. (I may never see such a large sum of money again.) My eye fell on the branding: Tempest Scholars.

It was like swallowing ice water. Christopher? Had he heard my conversation with Mom that day outside the cabin? Was it possible—would he do this?

I plan to think long and hard about what else I can do with my wealth. Perhaps he had really meant those words. Perhaps—but was it more than generosity? Was he trying to make amends?

I struggled to make sense of my feelings. I didn't know *what* to feel: I had no experience with such a vast amount of money, nor with any amount of money being given to my family by a man who had professed his love to me. I did have experience with men falling for me and with rejecting those men; but those episodes usually ended with them making drunken phone calls and spiteful tweets and blocking me on Instagram. Never—*never*—with a generous gift that would forever alter the lives of my parents and sisters.

But—I took a gulp of wine—I was probably mistaken. Christopher didn't have a monopoly on the word *tempest*. I would have to look it up later.

"What do you know about the organization?" I kept my voice light as everyone began to serve themselves. "Tempest Scholars?"

"Now, now." Dad chuckled. "When someone gives you a pretty penny you don't ask too many questions."

I looked at Mom, eyebrows raised.

"I googled them. Local company. Nice website," she said, most unhelpfully.

Jane gave me a quizzical look. I mouthed that I would tell her later.

After dinner I took Jane aside and told her my suspicions.

"You know, I bet you're right." She sounded thoughtful. "When I saw that check, I wondered. Somehow I doubt it's usual for scholarship organizations to send three hundred thousand dollars at a time."

"Yes." I let out my breath. "So what do I do? Do I ask him?"

"Ask him? I don't know. Wouldn't he have made it clear if he wanted us to know it was him?"

"But why would he do this?"

"Well, you told me that he heard your conversation with Mom about how they can't pay for college, so maybe...the goodness of his heart?"

I stared at her blankly.

"Generosity?" she supplied.

"Wanting nothing in return?" I asked, just to be clear.

"Since he did it anonymously...looks that way."

I still felt quite out of my depth. On the one hand, I didn't know what I could say, and on the other hand, how could I not say anything?

"Dessert is served!" Mom called. "Rachel, Jane, what are you doing in the powder room?"

I followed Jane to the kitchen and proceeded to numb my confused state of mind with four slices of chocolate cake. The fact that Mom didn't say anything showed just how blissed out three hundred thousand smackeroos made her—although when I reached for the fourth slice, I did catch her eyes drifting down to my waistline.

At home, I lit a vanilla candle and made myself a soothing mug of chamomile tea. I fully intended to watch *Love Island* until I was in a state of advanced relaxation. And yet. My gaze kept drifting toward my phone on the coffee table, until finally I snatched it up and searched for Tempest Scholars.

There was a website. It was sparse, and under "About Us" it read, "Tempest Scholars is run by a group of anonymous benefactors in the Pacific Northwest."

I searched for how to find out when a website was created. Two minutes later, I had confirmed that the domain had been purchased within the last week. So either the organization was brand new, or it was just a cover for whoever had sent the money. And I now had a pretty good idea who that was. But Jane had had a point: He'd done it anonymously. He didn't want anything in return. So I just had to go on as if I didn't know, as if I had no idea that Christopher Butkus—a man who was spontaneous enough to tell me he loved me, thoughtful enough to write me an apology letter—had paid my sisters' college tuition and added a decade to my mother's life in stress reduction.

I would put him out of my mind. I would. But you know how a song will keep playing in your head as your brain tries to figure out the lyrics? My brain, the poor old broad, couldn't puzzle this one out. Christopher Butkus didn't fit into any of my past experiences. As a single twentysomething in this, the twenty-first century, I thought I'd seen it all: the seductive ones who made eyes at you from across a party, the kindred spirits who confided all their secrets that very first night and then ended up having a girlfriend, the ones with piercings that would make a boomer faint. But now it seemed that everything I'd known was on a smaller scale. I'd thought grand gestures only happened in Meg Ryan films. But that was the word for Christopher's actions: *grand*.

But if I were Meg Ryan and he were Tom Hanks, everything would be out in the open and the grand gesture would be the finale. But it wasn't like that at all: he'd had the wrong idea, the feelings were not mutual, and now he was simply apologizing. Hoping that I might forgive him for his idiocy. Would I? Forgive him?

CHAPTER 19

I NEEDED A HAPPY hour. I needed to sip a cold drink at a sunny sidewalk table downtown and feel the alcohol fizz through my veins. I put out an open call in the group chat and Sumira accepted.

It was a picture-perfect Friday afternoon. It was days like today that tricked people into moving to Seattle: the cerulean sky, the tang of sea salt in the air, and the contrast of warm sun with the slight nip of cool in the shade. Sumira and I got our usual table at Mr. West.

"You look hot," she said by way of greeting. I was wearing my Daenerys sundress.

"Back at you." She was wearing linen pants and a silk top, her black hair tumbling over one shoulder.

"Nothing like a drink with a friend to build up the old ego." She grinned. We ordered rosé and a cheese plate, then dived into our latest life updates.

"Anything new with Christopher, since the last thing?" Sumira asked after we'd devoured most of the cheese. I'd already filled the girls in on the Tempest Scholars incident, and I hadn't planned on bringing it up again today. Frankly, I was tired of thinking about him.

"No, nothing. I'm ready to close the book on that whole chapter."

"Yeah. He was never right for you." Sumira didn't sound completely convinced. She fidgeted with the stem of her wineglass. "And we need to hold out for guys that are right for us." Her voice grew stronger and she sat up straighter, giving me a level look. "Like, I could never have settled for any of the guys in my past, right? But Rachel—"

"Oh my God, yeah." I paused to swill down my last gulp of wine. "Remember Ajay at the holiday party and how in love with you he was? Can you imagine if you'd settled for someone like him or Jamal? You are so out of their league." I gestured to the waiter for another glass.

Sumira stared at me for a moment, uncharacteristically silent.

"What, do I have something in my teeth?"

"Uh—no. You're fine." She turned her head away from me, gazing across the street and chewing on her lip.

"Everything okay? Did you want another drink?"

"Nah, I'm good." A beat later, she looked back at me with a typical Sumira quirk of the eyebrows. "Okay, you *have* to tell me where you got that dress."

On the bus home, I was pleasantly bubbly from my two glasses of rosé, and it felt like everyone on the bus was staring at me. Clearly they couldn't help it: I was glowing with summer-Friday energy and all the compliments Sumira had showered on me.

Wait. At least one person on the bus definitely *was* staring at me, and I was kind of feeling his scruffy vibe. Except he reminded me of my ex—oh my God, it was Felix. My ex, Felix. I hadn't seen him since we'd broken up almost three years before. Why did we break up? He was hot.

Oh, right: he had the maturity of a fifteen-year-old and drank a six-pack of beer every night. I would just pretend I didn't see him.

And now he was coming toward me.

I couldn't blame him, really. I was wearing *the* dress.

He looked good, like he'd spent the last few years working out. His biceps were peeking out from his T-shirt in a highly distracting way. He smiled at me—he was a charmingly simple person, simple as a Labrador. And obviously I was feeling good about myself post–happy hour, and I decided it was only right that fate should throw a little flirtation my way.

He called, "Rachel!" as though he couldn't believe his luck, and we caught up in that quick way of exes who find themselves both single. I noticed—and greatly appreciated—that his eyes roved slowly down my body and his smile broadened. I might not have spent the last three years in a gym, but the years had been good to me too: for example, I'd figured out that whole exfoliation thing and how to shape my brows. As we were talking, we came to his stop and he gave me a questioning look, so I followed him off the bus.

As we walked the couple blocks to his apartment, I had the jarring realization that this was a person who could talk more than me. A second realization followed closely on its heels, and that was that he had spent the last ten minutes talking about rock climbing. Now, while rock climbing has its benefits—see exhibits A and B, Felix's biceps—it has many, many downfalls. The first is that everyone who does it becomes utterly obsessed, and the second is that it is skull-crushingly boring. Imagine, if you will, that you had never heard of rock climbing the sport, and some fervent individual began talking your ear off about how they like to hurl themselves onto massive rocks on the weekends. You see what I mean? You would be nodding politely while glancing around to see if there was anyone who could help you in case the individual tried to drag you off to their rock cave.

"Wow, nice place." I was being polite; it wasn't. There were bicycles hanging from the walls and roommates sprawled on the couch eating spaghetti.

"Thanks." He dropped his backpack by the door. "Anyway, I can show you those climbing photos I mentioned...They're in my room."

Unfortunately (and astonishingly), the conversation took an even worse turn. We sat side by side on Felix's bed as he flicked through a small photo album of some exotic mountain climb. He and his friends were all outfitted in what looked like the entirety of REI's merchandise. After a few pictures, I noticed Felix was always standing next to the same pretty girl.

"Who's that?" I pointed to her.

"Natascha." He waited a beat before adding, "My ex."

"Oh. So you're saying I didn't leave you so brokenhearted that you never dated again?"

He shook his head with a miserable attempt at a laugh.

"What's the story?" I softened my voice out of respect for his feelings.

Poor boy, he shook himself out of it and continued in a casual voice, "We dated for almost two years. I was actually going to propose to her, but then she left. She moved to Georgia to go to nursing school."

"Nursing school? Pfft." A sort of nonchalant/deranged noise came out of my mouth while inside my thoughts were scrambling. This small, chic girl climbed mountains and had moved across the country to save lives. She'd broken up with Felix to do something brave and life changing. I'd broken up with Felix because I wanted to sleep with a guy named Antoni. But, I reminded myself, Antoni was a European sex god, a once-in-a-lifetime chance—a chance I got to experience nearly half a dozen times. So, definitely worth it.

Anyway, I was losing my grip: I was supposed to be allowing a man to appreciate my body the way it deserved to be appreciated, not sinking under self-doubt and comparing myself to *Natascha*.

"Interesting." I set the photo album aside. "But you know what I find more interesting? These." (I had been longing to touch his arms the entire time he'd been talking.)

He growled and took control of the situation. Felix always was good at taking control.

But...then I began to question things. All sorts of things. Like, I used to enjoy kissing Felix; had I been so naive and innocent then that I'd thought his slobbery technique was good? Or was there something wrong with me now, that I couldn't appreciate the feeling of an uncomplicated man groping me in his uncomplicated way? Or could it be that my aging body was closing itself off to worldly pleasures now that I had been celibate for over two months? Perhaps, I thought as Felix stuck his tongue in my ear, this was it for me; I'd had my fun and now my time was up and there was a nunnery somewhere waiting for me. Yes: a mystical convent cloistered in the mountains with a magical list of new arrivals—women whose vaginas have given up on the world—where, at this very moment, the name *Rachel Weiss* was appearing in shimmering ink. I must take my place there at once. (I hoped they wouldn't mind a Jewish nun.)

It was then that my mind veered off in an alarming direction. (I must look into modern-day lobotomies. Surely there was a quick laser surgery that would snip out unwanted thoughts?) I wondered—*inexplicably*—what Christopher Butkus would be like in bed. Even in the privacy of my own brain, it was too mortifying to contemplate what sort of lover Christopher Butkus would be. But, say, afterward...would he fall asleep with the speed and expertise of a narcoleptic, the way Felix used to? Would he want to spoon? Would he—I squirmed at the thought, kicking at Felix's grubby sheets—would he pull me onto his chest, into that perfect spot under his arm, and smooth back my hair and kiss my face?

I stood up swiftly. Felix looked dumbfounded. I was filled with an overwhelming desire to leave but said, "Um. I just need to use the bathroom real quick."

"No problem. It's down the hall on the left."

I pulled my dress down and grabbed my bag, muttering that I needed to freshen my lipstick.

"Take your time," he said.

In the bathroom, I catalogued my options: I could either slip past his spaghetti-eating roommates or climb out the tiny window above the toilet. It was an easy decision. I climbed onto the tank and perched myself on the window ledge. As I swung my legs over, I wished there was a tree I could shimmy onto. But there was a sort of sloping roof—the lower floor jutted out past the second floor—so I slid down onto it, the shingles catching at my dress. I had to crab-walk to the edge, where I was confronted with the drop. Felix's building was one of those Seattle houses with an unimaginably steep driveway. I could either scuttle across the roof to the other side of the building or drop down fifteen feet onto the concrete driveway. With a sigh, I got on my knees and turned myself around, then began to lower myself down. The idea was that I would hold on to the roof with both hands to get my feet as close to the ground as possible before letting go. The reality was that the weight of my bum combined with the weakness of my arms made me topple off the roof all at once. A few seconds later, Felix, who must've heard the crash and my piercing shriek, stuck his head out the bathroom window.

"Rachel?"

"Ow."

"Are you okay?"

I pushed myself up and felt my left leg crumple under my weight. My ankle throbbed.

"Why did you jump out the window?"

I pretended not to hear this.

"I think I need to go to the ER." There was a pause as he stared down at me. A very long pause.

"D'you want me to—"

"I'll get an Uber."

"Okay, cool. Well. It was nice, um—"

"See you, Felix." I turned and hobbled away. When I was out of sight of his building, I leaned against a parked car and summoned my Uber.

I thought my troubles were winding down, but they were only beginning. The driver pulled up and opened his window to greet me, and my limbs turned to jelly when I saw that he looked exactly like Adam Driver.

Was I delirious from the pain of my ankle? Was I doing word association—Uber driver, Adam Driver? I might never know, but the evidence was all before me: he had dark, luscious hair and sad eyes, like a kicked puppy. He also had a delicious southern accent.

"ER, huh? How'd you get banged up?"

There was an undeniably sexy rumble to his voice. My ego was so bruised by my embarrassing exit that I wanted Adam Driver to soothe it. I wanted to be impulsive and sensual, not to be shut away in a magical nunnery. I wanted to be driven mad with lust each time he flicked those deep-brown eyes toward me in the rearview mirror.

But I...wasn't. What was wrong with me? First I had forgone ex sex with Felix, and now I couldn't even summon some inappropriate stirrings when Adam Driver was driving my Uber?

"I jumped out a window."

"Why'd you go and do that? You weren't in danger, I hope?"

"No, no. I'm only a danger to myself."

He let out a low *hmm*, and the corner of his mouth curled up as his eyes flicked toward me again. I swear, it felt like the whole evening had been fated, leading me to this point, like the universe knew about my Kylo Ren fantasies. My mind raced ahead: I was meant to sleep with this sexy, southern Kylo Ren. I could see it unfold: The eye contact would get more and more heated at each stoplight, until finally I asked him to pull over, and he would turn around to ask me if everything was okay, and this magnetic attraction would overpower us. We would spring together, unable to stop ourselves from devouring one another and tearing off our clothes.

Yet the more I thought about it, the less appealing it sounded. I gave a tiny, confused whimper.

"Your leg?" he asked. "Hurts, doesn't it?"

The pain in my ankle had, in fact, increased, and I felt like my sense of self was sliding around, unsteady and confused. I asked Adam/Kylo questions about himself so I wouldn't have to think. He told me about his podcast and his hopes of becoming a voice actor—a goal I heartily encouraged—and within a few minutes we were pulling up to the hospital.

"Here we are, Miss Rachel. Need any help getting inside?"

"I'll be okay. Thanks, Ad—er—" I checked the app and saw that his actual name was Matt. "Matt. Good luck with the podcast."

"Hey." He stuck his head out of the driver's-side window as I hauled myself out of the back seat. "I never do this, but how'd you like to get a drink with me sometime?"

I froze. *Yes,* screamed the little slutty Rachel in my head. *Say yes to Adam/Kylo/Matt!* But his words reminded me of someone else's: *I've never done this before, but Rachel, I think I'm in love with you.*

"I'm flattered, but I don't think so." *What? No! Damn you, Christopher!*

"Ah." He gave me a rueful smile and slapped the side of his car. "Can't blame a guy for tryin'. Have a good one."

Completely devoid of breath, I hobbled into the hospital without looking back. I must have looked as pale and shell-shocked as I felt, because the woman at the desk called me over with concern in her voice.

"Can you stand to fill out the paperwork? Here, take a seat and I'll bring it over to you."

I murmured my thanks and fell into a stiff chair. I scribbled my information onto the form she gave me and handed it back without a word. After several minutes of blankness, my mind whirred back to life.

I'd rejected Adam Driver.

I'd ruined my Kylo Ren fantasy forever.

I've never not pursued my wildest fantasies before.

What was happening to me? I didn't even know who I was anymore.

This was all Christopher's fault. Ever since he accosted me, I'd felt discombobulated, unsure of everything. I was always so certain of myself and my opinions, always right about everything. And then this man, this Christopher Butkus, throws himself in my path and makes me question everything I've ever thought about men. Men like him are vile, boring, and selfish. But he... wasn't? I could see that Christopher Butkus was objectively a desirable man. And yet I had felt so sure of myself when I rejected him. I had been cruel at the time, I could see that now. But had I been wrong?

It didn't help that my mother's voice had infiltrated my mind. The woman may be insane, but she was still my mother and her opinion mattered to me, as much as I wished it didn't. Everything that had happened was making me question my judgment, and I didn't *want* to question my judgment. I wanted to go back to my sure footing, my sense of absolute Rachel-ness. But clearly I had been wrong about Christopher in some ways, like his relationship with Stephen. So what if I was wrong about other things?

All this introspection was making me panic. I buried my face in my hands and moaned.

"The nurse will be out shortly, dear," the woman at the desk called to me.

"Thank you," I mumbled. Having a physical injury to mask my inner turmoil was quite convenient.

An hour later, I sent a picture of my ankle boot to the group chat. My ankle was sprained, and I would have to wear the boot for about a month. They responded with alarm and sympathy, and I explained the events of the evening in as few words as possible.

"I suppose this is the universe's way of telling me to take it easy. Lay low. Focus on myself," I concluded.

Eva replied, oh so helpfully, "Or...hear me out...the universe could simply be telling you not to jump off any more rooftops."

CHAPTER 20

THE NEXT MORNING, I awoke in a haze of embarrassment and physical pain. I regretted every choice I had made in the last twenty-four hours, or perhaps...ever?

There was already a message from Amy in the group chat, which I read with one eye squinted shut. It was a link to a *Seattle Times* article. I opened it with a lurch of existential dread.

> PAGEANT CEO LAUNCHES NEW NONPROFIT
>
> A new nonprofit, launched Friday by local CEO
> Christopher Butkus, will aim to improve the
> quality of arts and humanities education in
> Seattle-area public schools. Its first project will be
> to launch after-school programs focused on art
> and music in lower-income communities.

Right. Of course he had. Excellent!
No, really...good for him.
Look, I knew the world didn't revolve around me. I did know that. But this news made me feel like absolute garbage (and I

hadn't thought I could feel worse than when I woke up ten minutes before). Christopher Butkus had just spun up a nonprofit that would change people's lives. And, if I were to indulge myself in one more self-centered thought, I had an inkling that he had only gotten the idea after our conversation. After he'd told me he was going to think hard about how to spend his money. Which would mean that he'd gotten the idea and executed it in two weeks.

Two weeks.

And I'd been sitting like mold on a log for the better part of a decade, content to gather a paycheck from an unfulfilling job. Letting the years slip by.

What was I *doing* with my life?

My best friends were all where they were meant to be in their careers: Amy had five years of teaching under her belt, Sumira was climbing the corporate ladder, and Eva had bounced around for a while before finally deciding to go to library school. Jane had a fabulous and interesting career working for the local news channel. And there was Natascha, Felix's tiny ex, who'd upended her life to go to nursing school.

Meanwhile I was stuck. I spent my days fielding tickets from senior citizens with no concept of modern technology. The week before, there had been the man who couldn't figure out how to work his GPS. (We do not sell GPS technology.) And the week before that was the one who couldn't figure out how to download our app onto his phone—his Nokia flip phone. And in between these support tickets that raised my blood pressure to dangerous levels, there was Kenneth. Lately he'd been avoiding eye contact with me because of that time his gaze slipped down to my cleavage. He'd been so flustered that he stopped talking midsentence and backed away from me like I was the queen of England. He backed all the way down the hall and around the corner.

And Christopher had a successful business, and now this nonprofit...I noted with mild surprise that he'd chosen to focus on the arts instead of STEM. Everyone, even nontech people, thought that focusing on STEM was the right thing to do. But Christopher had chosen the arts. It was almost like he knew that we had to emphasize arts and humanities to flourish as a society. And I hadn't even told him that. He just *knew*.

Right, well, I wasn't going to sit here and mope all weekend. I was going to take steps toward...something. I was going to move *forward*.

I made myself a green smoothie and then typed a list into the group chat.

Rachel Weiss 8:42 AM:
It's time for a new me. My old ways aren't working anymore. I hereby pledge that starting today: I'm going to do yoga (with modifications for my ankle), I'm finally going to read *The Life-Changing Magic of Tidying Up* and *You Are a Badass* (both of which have been sitting on my nightstand for a year), and I'm going to try a vegan lifestyle. It's time for me to stop talking the talk and start walking the walk. Oh, and I'm swearing off men. There's no point in

dating and hooking up when the real work needs to happen within.

Amy McDonald 8:57 AM:
Good for you, Rach. I believe in you.

After a few minutes of reflection I made one update.

Rachel Weiss 9:02 AM:
Before I go plant-based I better finish off all the ice cream in my freezer. Wouldn't want it to go to waste.

After my ice cream breakfast, I got to work. I bought a Groupon for a month of beginner yoga and signed up for that afternoon's class. Then I filled my biggest water bottle with ice water, grabbed a blanket, and hobbled to the park around the corner, where I spent a couple hours lying in the sun reading my inspirational books. After reading a few chapters, I felt pumped. I could do this! I could become the best version of Rachel Weiss.

It turned out that beginner yoga was a lot easier than hot yoga. Especially considering that I got to lie down during half of the poses because of my ankle. On my way home from the studio, I stopped at PCC and loaded a basket with peaches, plums, cherries, greens, almond milk, and nondairy fudge pops.

After yoga, I focused all my energy on tidying up. It was immediately apparent that none of my clothes brought me joy and I was going to have to buy a whole new wardrobe with my nonexistent expendable income. My denim miniskirt? My green wrap dress? They all reminded me of the silly, unserious version of Rachel. I couldn't even look at them. Marie Kondo wanted me to be a nudist.

I would just have to come back to my clothes later. I shoved them back into my closet; it looked like a disaster zone, but at least I could shut the door. The rest of my apartment was easier: I Swiffered and dusted and filled a whole box for charity. By Sunday night, the kitchen gleamed, the counters empty except for a mason jar holding a bouquet of flowers I'd purchased at the farmers market. I sank onto the couch to enjoy my vegan pizza. My little living room glimmered from the twinkle lights draped across the walls. My ankle throbbed faintly, but I felt good, like I'd accomplished something.

The long days of summer rolled on, and I settled into my new routine. I was a paragon of virtue, sticking to my resolutions like nobody's business. (Except the vegan part, which lasted all of two days. Pizza without cheese? Toast without butter? And don't even get me started on the coffee. How had no one ever told me that black coffee was disgusting? Adding almond milk just made it worse. Life was hard enough without forcing myself to enjoy milk squeezed from an almond's breast.)

In a few short weeks, I'd made great progress in my quest for self-improvement, but something was still missing. I'd been focusing on my mental and physical health, but I hadn't done much to help anyone else. I decided to look into volunteering. And okay, perhaps my motives weren't entirely selfless: Jane had just gotten promoted to her dream job as a special correspondent, and it made me think about my own career. I didn't know where I wanted to go, but maybe volunteering would give me some ideas.

When I mentioned this to the girls, Eva told me that the public library was looking for volunteers to help with its seniors-and-technology program. I applied online, and they asked me to start two weeks later.

On the first Monday in September, I took the bus from work to the library. I'd forgotten how cute my neighborhood branch was. It was a quaint old building with wood ceiling beams nestled on a hill above the canal. That alone was like a breath of fresh air after my cold, colorless office building. I introduced myself to the librarian, a lovely woman named Karen, and she ushered me into a study room where three white-haired women awaited me. I was five minutes early; these women were apparently so eager to learn, they'd arrived well before me.

"Here are your pupils," Karen said.

"I thought there would be more of them," I whispered, adjusting my sweater. With the first hint of fall in the air, I'd worn a cardigan with corduroys and boots and felt very bookish, like it was the first day of school.

"Consider yourself lucky," Karen whispered back. "Three is more than enough. Their questions are never-ending." Then she addressed the waiting seniors. "This is Rachel Weiss, our new volunteer. She's here to help you with all your technological needs."

"Hello, everyone." I smiled brightly.

"Let me know if you need anything." Karen waved as she slipped away.

"Now." I settled into a chair at the ladies' table. "How about some introductions?"

"I'm Phyllis." The tallest and, apparently, bossiest of them straightened up. "Former elementary school teacher and vice principal."

"Helen." The second sat with a pencil poised above a notebook.

I could tell I wasn't the only one feeling the first-day-of-school vibes.

"I'm Jin." The third was cupping her iPhone in both hands with a deeply anxious look on her face.

"Wonderful. And as you heard, I'm Rachel. I'm a Seattle native and I work as a—"

"Rachel," Jin interrupted, holding her phone toward me as if afraid it would bite her. "Can you help me see photos of my grandson?"

"Absolutely."

"Do it so I can see." Helen held her pencil at the ready.

"And I need to know how to follow my grandchildren on Insta-gram, and how to start a blog." Phyllis sounded fierce.

"Okay." I blinked in surprise. "Let me start with Jin, and then we'll get to you, Phyllis."

I showed Jin how to find the photos she was looking for—more difficult than one would expect given that I didn't know whether these photos were online, in a private album, or in an email, and Jin had no idea either—and Helen copied out the instructions for her. Then I tackled Phyllis's request, Helen watching and scrib-bling with occasional murmurs of amazement.

"Helen," I said when Phyllis was satisfied. "What questions do you have?"

"I…" She blushed. "I don't know any of it."

I hesitated.

"I see. Do you have a phone or a computer?"

"Yes." She nodded and reached for her bag. She pulled out a brand-new iPhone, iPad, and laptop. "My son Jason bought them for me."

"Bless him. He didn't show you how to use them?" *Oh, Jason*, I thought, *good intentions, poor follow-through.*

Helen shook her head, and Jin gaped at all the gadgets spread on the table. Phyllis ignored us, absorbed in starting her blog.

"What tasks do you think you'll want to do most often?" I asked.

"Search for information and keep up with friends and family on social media." Helen's voice had a practiced air of confidence.

"Great! And do you think you'll be more comfortable generally using your phone, the tablet, or the computer?"

That stumped her. She looked worried as she surveyed her options.

Jin leaned forward and tapped on the iPhone. "Phone. You have to use your phone for the social media."

"And the computer for searching Google," Phyllis added, her eyes still on her screen.

Helen nodded, jotting it all down in her notebook.

"Um, actually. You can use all three of them...for anything. Anything on the internet. Or," I added as an afterthought, "not on the internet."

The three of them looked at me as if I'd just announced that gravity was a myth.

"What do you mean?" Phyllis's sharp voice told me she was not used to being corrected.

"Well...all of these devices can connect to the internet. Social media, Google, and email are all located on the internet. And with..." I paused, then stood and began to pace the room, thinking.

"Do I need to plug the phone into the other ones?" Helen asked. "How do they communicate? If I post on Facebook from my phone, how does my computer know?"

I exhaled, long and slowly, then spotted a marker on the dry-erase board.

"The internet," I began, sketching on the board as I went,

"is a network of peer-to-peer connections. It transmits data via—"

I stopped when I realized Phyllis was glaring at me, Helen had broken the tip of her pencil, and Jin was looking from me to her phone, horrified and transfixed.

I capped the pen and stared up at the board, wondering for the first time if I was actually up to this challenge. I had never taught anyone before. How was I supposed to teach these three women how to use technology? It was like they were highly educated aliens, or time travelers, smart in their own way but completely unfamiliar with life in the twenty-first century. But then I looked back at them, at the hope and fear in their faces, and I almost laughed. I was Rachel Weiss: of course I could do this.

"Okay. Look. We don't have to understand everything. We just have to understand enough for our own purposes. Like, we get that the theory of relativity is important, but who can actually explain it, right?" Phyllis raised her hand. "Just an example, Phyllis! Anyway. Let's just break this down into pieces that are relevant and easy to digest, okay?"

After taking a moment for Helen to sharpen her pencil, I started again, answering their questions with bite-size answers. At the end of the allotted ninety minutes, they were satisfied.

"You're much better than the last volunteer." Helen packed away her pencil and notebook.

"He was a dolt," Phyllis agreed.

"What happened to your leg?" Jin asked.

"Oh, that?" I laughed and then said, deadpan, "I jumped out of my ex's window."

"Jump? Why?" Jin sounded concerned as Phyllis frowned and Helen's face lit up.

"You're single?" Helen beamed. "My Jason is a few years older than you, but—"

"Now, now." I slung my bag over my shoulder. "I've given up on men in order to work on myself. As you can see, I'm volunteering and—and..." I sighed. "Well, I don't know what else yet, but no men for me. Sorry, Helen."

"Ah well. Good for you."

"It is good!" Jin nodded. "My aunt never married. Lived to be one hundred and seven."

"Oh my." I thought privately that my escapades thus far had surely shaved several years off my life already.

"Thank you, Rachel." Phyllis shook my hand. "See you next week."

"Next week? But I thought I answered all of your questions?"

"Yes, of course, but I have to bring my quilting group. They'll love you."

Hearing this from Phyllis kept a smile stuck on my face the whole way home.

CHAPTER 21

ON SUNDAY WE GATHERED for a picnic lunch at Green Lake to celebrate Amy's birthday. As Amy unpacked the food from her basket (because of course Amy would prepare her own birthday lunch), I asked, "Where's Sumira?"

"She bailed last minute." Eva sprawled out on Amy's gingham blanket. "Said something came up."

"That's very vague." I tipped my head back, enjoying the feeling of the sun dappling my face and chest.

Amy looked a little troubled, frowning as she opened a Tupperware container of finger sandwiches. "Hope she's okay."

"Hey." I kept my voice bright, trying to cheer her up. "Want your present?"

She did indeed perk up as I handed her a glittery gift bag. She withdrew a book. "Oh my God, Rachel, what is this?"

"It's Gwyneth Paltrow's sex book. For you and Ryan."

Eva snorted.

Amy thumbed through it uncertainly.

"Jane recommended it."

"Jane used this book with Owen?" Amy and Eva both looked

amused and impressed. "That's a side of her I was not aware of," Eva added.

I nodded and helped myself to a smoked salmon sandwich. "How are things with Ryan, anyway? You've been quiet on the marriage front."

"You know, Ryan is okay." Amy stowed the book back in the gift bag. "Things have been pretty good. Couples therapy is helping. It's been months since I burst into tears when he wasn't in the mood for sex."

"And are you"—Eva paused delicately—"having any?"

"More than before. Still not a lot. But I've made peace with it for now. I do love him." Amy plucked a bunch of grapes from another Tupperware container and popped one in her mouth. "The other day—he knows how much I love *Downton Abbey*, and he asked if I would rewatch it with him so he could get to know my favorite show."

"Okay, that's sweet," Eva said.

"Very," I agreed.

"I'll let you know what he thinks about this sex book." Amy smirked. "Speaking of Jane, how's her new job? She's a special correspondent now?"

"Yes! Special correspondent for women's issues."

"Yikes." Eva cringed.

"No, it'll be cool stuff like women in politics and equal pay."

"And reproductive rights? Domestic violence?"

"Hmm...I guess, maybe. But she's really excited. Do you guys want to watch her TV debut with me? It's next Thursday."

"Definitely!" Amy nodded.

"Great. Who has cable?"

"We have ESPN, Disney, and Netflix." Amy counted off on her fingers.

"And I just share your Netflix account, Rach," Eva said.

"Wait," I said, "I thought I was using your Netflix account."

"Huh. Whose Netflix account are we using?"

There was an awkward pause. "We need to find someone who has cable. I'm so not watching with my mom. I'll ask around and let you guys know."

We polished off the sandwiches and munched on fruit, watching our fellow Seattleites gamboling in the sun like happy kittens. We watched a couple of athletic-looking people balancing on a tightrope slung between two trees.

"That reminds me," I said. "I'm getting my ankle boot off this week. I'll have to do physical therapy, though."

"PT isn't bad," Eva said. "I did it when I had tennis elbow. My therapist was super cute. I actually looked forward to appointments with her."

"Ooh." I feigned excitement that I did not feel in the slightest. "Perhaps this will be the meet-cute I've been waiting for. Maybe I'll have a strapping young physical therapist named Jeremy."

"Now I'm just picturing Jeremy Coltrain," Eva said.

"I miss watching him on TV every week." Amy sighed. "I wonder how he's doing."

A few days later, I sent a message to the group chat.

> **Rachel Weiss 6:44 PM:**
> If anyone was curious, my physical therapist is not a Jeremy. He is a balding, curly-haired man named Howard.

Eva Galvez 6:50 PM:
Enough said.

Rachel Weiss 6:52 PM:
He is not quite old enough to be my father, but old enough to make me wonder if he could be. He does, however, have an exceedingly gentle touch.

Eva Galvez 6:53 PM:
Is this about to get weird?

Rachel Weiss 6:57 PM:
Never say never.

This was my life now: I woke up and fixed myself a sensible breakfast. (Coffee and peanut butter Cap'n Crunch. Sensible for my wallet, not my health.) I worked all day, so diligently that Kenneth made me his deputy sticker-giver-outer. Mondays I volunteered at the library. Wednesdays I did ankle exercises with Howard. I was a saint.

Dear God. The only man to have touched me in the past month was Howard. What had my life become?

It turned out that Jane and Owen were the only people I knew with cable, aside from my parents. So on Thursday night, we headed to their condo to watch Jane's TV debut with Owen.

He greeted us with a huge, excited smile. "I made popcorn!" He ushered us in the door. "Hey, aren't there usually four of you?"

Indeed, Sumira had canceled at the last minute—again. This was starting to seem fishy, but now was not the moment to dwell on that. Owen had, as promised, prepared two huge bowls of popcorn: one sweet, one salty. It was clear that he wished Jane were there to watch with him because it was such a big moment, but of course she was across town recording on live TV. He kept saying, "Jane on live TV!" like he was so proud.

A few minutes in, I realized he kept texting someone, and I wondered if he was blowing up Jane's phone, so I snuck a glance. No. The man was texting my own mother. Clearly they were on equal levels of excitement for their dear Jane.

Finally the dusty old news anchors announced a story about a girls' coding class.

"And here to tell us all about it is our very own Jane Weiss."

The camera panned over to Jane, and she was simply radiant. Hair and makeup had taken her usual beauty and cranked it up to megawattage. It was almost blinding, really. She talked about the story she had researched, and then they showed clips of her interviewing some of the coding girls.

We all took turns cooing, "Ooh, she's doing so well" and shushing each other for talking too loud. Five minutes later, it was over.

We applauded, and then Owen turned the volume down and we fell into comfortable chit-chat. Owen asked Eva about her library studies. Amy was curled in an armchair stroking Linus the cat. I watched them for several minutes without Amy noticing: she had a thoughtful look on her face as she cuddled Linus, and I wondered if she was contemplating the value of a cat compared to that of her husband.

We gathered up our things and thanked Owen for letting us join him. As we were filing out the door, he stopped me.

"Have you given any more thought to Jane's bachelorette party yet?"

"Um. Some. I'm still trying to decide…" I trailed off, hoping that would satisfy him. I hoped he wouldn't realize that I was running out of time: the party had to be in October, before Jane's friend Kailey popped out another baby. But I was completely stuck. I knew exactly how I would plan a bachelorette party for myself or one of my friends. But Jane? It's not that she didn't enjoy a good party—Jane knew how to let loose, just in a very mellow way.

"Look," Owen said, "I think she deserves a really fun night. She's been working so hard, she hasn't taken much time for herself."

"Fun…how?" My mind was already barreling ahead, thinking about which places had the best Jane-friendly dance music.

"Well, when Kailey got married, she had a classic Vegas bachelorette party, and Jane loved it. She raved about it. I know you're not going to take her to Vegas or anything like that, but—"

I cut him off, a smile creeping across my face. "Yes! A classic Seattle bachelorette party. I'm so glad you brought it up. I wasn't sure if that would be right for Jane, but now I know exactly what to do!"

Owen beamed back at me. "I knew I could count on you, Rachel."

We hugged goodbye and I headed for the bus stop, my mind spinning with ideas.

That night I crafted an itinerary consisting of karaoke, small bites, and big dance floors. After Jane gave her approval, I sent out an e-vite to her friends and, of course, my besties. (They had to be there to help me get the party started.) I was going to make sure the world's best sister had the bachelorette party she deserved.

CHAPTER 22

TUESDAY MORNING, SHERYL AND I were chatting in the office kitchen, refilling our coffee mugs. She'd asked how my volunteer gig was going, and Kenneth overheard and got all interested.

"Did I hear you say you're giving lectures?" He bustled over to me like a Chihuahua in glasses.

"Um." I gave Sheryl a look that plainly said: *Men...always interrupting girl talk.* "Not exactly. I volunteer with seniors, and yesterday I taught about twenty of them what Wikipedia is. Some of them were really excited to be able to contribute their knowledge of the Battle of Hastings and paper piece quilting techniques."

"But Rachel, this is amazing news." Kenneth glanced at Sheryl, apparently hoping for a moment of privacy with me, but Sheryl looked blithely on. (She was not one to remove herself from a potentially gossip-worthy situation.) "It's just come down from leadership that we need to train our teams on professionalism, diversity and inclusion, things like that."

I nodded, biting back a groan at the prospect of my privileged male coworkers fumbling their way through a conversation about diversity.

"The thing is," Kenneth continued, "they really want to, you know, do this as cheaply as possible."

"Of course," I said. Hey, our billionaire CEO didn't become a billionaire by throwing money at silly things like diversity and inclusion education.

"So..." Kenneth pushed his glasses up and smiled slightly, his face flushing. My blank expression must have told him that I had no idea what he was getting at. "So, if you think you would be up to the challenge..."

"If *I* think—?" I was growing alarmed.

"We could do a test run of our immediate team, see how it goes. If I were the one to come forward with this idea...and if you were the one to step up...well, this could be great for both of us, Rachel."

"A test run?" I was desperately trying to catch up to his train of thought, but it was chugging away without me.

"If you wrote the curriculum and gave a talk, facilitated the discussion. It would start with, say, a dozen people. You could pick the first topic—say, inclusion. And then if it works, you could lecture to other teams—maybe train other volunteers on how to facilitate as well."

I swallowed. Sheryl was nodding in a *Hey, that's not a bad idea* sort of way. My typical reaction to any of Kenneth's ideas was long-suffering patience, but I was having a different reaction now: lecture ideas were piling up in my mind and a smile was bubbling to the surface as I pictured myself in a tight pencil skirt, strutting at the front of a classroom with a long pointer in hand.

"Okay," I heard myself say.

"You'll do it? You're in?" Kenneth was bouncing on the balls of his feet.

"Sure." Truth be told, the idea of being the one in charge of the discussion—being the one to educate these tech nerds—was highly appealing. "I'll have a draft to you on Friday?"

"Yes!" Kenneth high-fived me. "Awesome, Rachel. Ten gold stars!" He backed toward his cubicle, shooting finger guns at me until he disappeared.

A little while later, I came back from a coffee break to find that he actually had decorated my monitor with ten gold stars. It didn't bother me, though.

The next two weeks flew by in a haze of uncharacteristic productivity. I was finalizing bachelorette party plans, buying penis necklaces and other vital supplies, and crafting my first lesson plan. I managed to squeeze in a brunch date with Jane, where she gushed about her new job. She was thriving in her new role, and I was so happy for her.

It didn't even occur to me that the group chat was extra quiet until one evening when Amy messaged us with a lengthy story.

Amy McDonald 6:16 PM:
We've been using the Gwyneth Paltrow book, and some things have happened. Gwyneth recommends "surprising" each other. So I put on the lingerie you guys bought me, and I "surprised" Ryan in the living room while he was playing *Zelda*. I was nervous that he was going to brush me aside or completely ignore me. You know how he

is when he's playing games.
But I was…um…quite
successful in "surprising" him.

Rachel Weiss 6:21 PM:
Please for the love of God
tell us what you mean by
"surprising" him. I need to
know so I can follow along.
Not in a pervy way, just in an
informational way.

Amy McDonald 6:22 PM:
I was giving him a BJ, okay?

Rachel Weiss 6:22 PM:
Excellent

Amy McDonald 6:27 PM:
It was going so well that
neither of us was paying
attention to anything else. And
then…after a few minutes
I happened to look up. And
I screamed. Our neighbor,
Ed, was standing outside the
window, STARING. So we
both stare back at him, and he
doesn't leave, he just stands
there, frozen. And Ryan zips
up his pants and ANSWERS
THE DOOR.

Rachel Weiss 6:28 PM:
WHAT?!

Amy McDonald 6:27 PM:
I KNOW! I ran to the
bedroom, but I heard the gist.
Ed asked—like everything
was completely normal—if
he could borrow our drill.
And Ryan gave it to him, and
neither of them said anything
about the incident. So then
Ryan came into the bedroom
and just stared at me blankly
for a minute, and then we
both started laughing until
we cried, and we collapsed
into bed and then...well, we
had the most passionate sex
we've ever had. Ever.

Rachel Weiss 6:30 PM:
Ames! I'm so glad that story
had a happy ending. I didn't
have quite that scenario in
mind when I gave you
the book.

Amy McDonald 6:31 PM:
Ryan joked that we should

leave the curtains open from
now on.

Rachel Weiss 6:32 PM:
Kinky.

Amy McDonald 6:36 PM:
Really though, Rachel,
thank you. Tonight felt like
a breakthrough for us. I felt
more connected to Ryan than
I've felt in a really long time.
I think…I'm going to stick
with him. See how things go.
I think we have a chance to
make it work.

Rachel Weiss 6:38 PM:
I'm so happy to hear that! But
what about…you know. Are
you going to tell Ryan what
happened?

Amy McDonald 6:41 PM:
I don't think so. Is that awful?
I just don't think Ryan
knowing about what I did
would help anything. If we're
going to have a real shot, I
think I have to learn from it
and just move past it.

I pondered this for a second. What would I do in the same situation? I wasn't sure. But as Amy said, what good would come from telling Ryan that she'd cheated? If the experience only made her want to commit more fully to Ryan, to try harder with him? In the end, would that be so bad? I'd never expected Amy to be perfect—Lord knows I wasn't—and it wasn't my place to tell her what her relationship needed. My place was to support her, mistakes and all.

> **Rachel Weiss 6:43 PM:**
> Ok. I support your decision,
> Ames.

Eva chimed in with her reactions a while later, but Sumira didn't. Apparently I wasn't the only one who noticed. Eva messaged us asking if we'd heard from Sumira lately. In fact, none of us had heard from her since she bailed on Amy's birthday and Jane's viewing party. We all agreed to call her and leave voicemails, thinking that would get a rise out of her (since Sumira hates voicemails).

She hadn't responded by the next morning, but I had other things to think about. Today was my first educational session at work. I prepared by drinking a venti nitro cold brew. The barista had claimed that they weren't allowed to serve nitro in such a large size due to health risks, but I sweet-talked him into it. As I made the final preparations for my session, my heart beat so fast I could see it when I blinked.

By noon I was still alive, still highly caffeinated, and also a huge success. I was undoubtedly the best teacher those techies ever had. We had a phenomenal discussion. Kenneth was practically floating with joy, it went so well. I couldn't wait for the next one. (Did I really just say that about *work*?)

That night I was eating takeout sushi on my couch to celebrate my success when my phone pinged.

> **Sumira Khan sent a photo at 7:47 PM.**

Sumira! I happily opened the group chat. Wait. Had she just sent us a picture of a handwritten letter? What the...?

Feeling uneasy, I opened the image and zoomed in to read it.

My dear friends,

> *I don't know how to do this.*
> *I don't know what to say.*
> *I just know I have to say it.*
> *I'm writing you this letter because it's gone too far now for me to tell you in person. I wouldn't know how to begin. So I need to get all my thoughts out at once, on paper.*
> *I'll rip the Band-Aid off first and then try to explain. I'm engaged. I'm getting married in two months. I'm marrying Ajay—Rachel met him at my work party. You might remember I went out with him on Valentine's Day. And then we continued seeing each other. And we got engaged in July. Our imam chose December 13th as our lucky date. And so, here we are.*
> *I've thought long and hard about why I've hidden all of this from you. You're my best friends. At first, I think I was just embarrassed because Rachel made fun of Ajay for being so young (and he is—he's twenty-four). I didn't know if anything was going to come of it, so I*

didn't mention it. And then when things started getting more serious, I couldn't see how to bring it up, since I'd hidden it from you in the beginning.

And there was part of me that was defiant, that wanted to have secrets. Secrets that I didn't share in the group chat or on social media. It felt good, after a while, to have a secret that I could hold, intact, something big and important that hadn't been picked over and analyzed to death. I don't mean anything against you when I say this. I've loved overanalyzing everything that's happened to us in the last decade. It's just that I never expected to feel so free when I finally kept something to myself. So that is why I kept this from you, in the end. It started with a few omissions and with a secret that kept getting bigger and bigger. And then it turned into something that made me feel somehow both selfish and superior, and more than a little satisfied. But I don't want—I never wanted—this to come between us, and I don't want it to ruin our friendship. I need you all in my life. I want you in my wedding. It just became harder and harder to tell you.

I don't know how I would feel if one of you kept a secret like this from me. I don't know if it will even be possible for you to forgive me. I just know I had to tell you.

With love,
Sumira

> **Sumira Khan has left the chat.**

My salmon nigiri turned to dust in my mouth. My best friend was engaged? To a man I hadn't even known she was dating? How could she keep this from us?

My phone rang with a FaceTime call from Eva. I answered it to see both Eva and Amy already on the call.

"Guys?" Eva said. "Will you say something?"

"I don't know what to say." Amy sounded hollow. "Did you know?"

We both shook our heads.

"I tell her everything." I felt numb. "I tell you all everything."

"We don't even know him." Amy looked close to tears.

"We should have been there for her through all of it," I said. "We should have heard all about their first date, and their second date. We should have screamed with her after he proposed. Does she have a ring? We don't even know."

"But that's the thing," Eva said, "she didn't want any of that. She wanted to keep all the details to herself."

We were quiet for a minute, and then I asked the question that was starting to plague me more than any other.

"What did we do wrong? How could we have thought we were as close as ever, when Sumira felt the opposite? How did we push her away and not even realize it?" I didn't add my last thought, which was ringing in my head: *This is my fault.* I was so self-absorbed that my friend didn't want to confide in me. How could I not have noticed? Did I ever ask her about herself...ever? Did we always just talk about me? Had she actually, secretly, just not wanted to be friends anymore?

"She was hiding it from us, Rachel," Eva said gently. "We couldn't have known she felt that way."

"Do you guys feel that way? Amy? You shut us out earlier this summer."

Amy shook her head. "I was going through something. I was at rock bottom with the Stephen thing. I know how it feels to want some privacy. I can understand that."

"But…" I took a deep breath. Something big was welling up inside me. Of course I'd had friendships that fizzled out over my lifetime. But it had never occurred to me that I might not have my three best-friends-forever…forever.

"I love our group chat," Eva said. "I'd be lost without you guys."

"Sumira did say that she doesn't want our friendship to end over this," Amy added.

"But if she can't tell us about one of the most important things in her life," I said slowly, "does that mean it's already over?"

CHAPTER 23

ON THE OUTSIDE, MY life seemed amazing. It was like what I'd imagined a few weeks before when I'd said I was going to work on myself. I was leading these discussions at work two or three times a week, and it was actually challenging and interesting and I was good at it. The seniors at the library had basically formed a Rachel Weiss fan club: I had my regulars who showed up every week whether they had a technology question or not. And I was doing Howard's exercises every day. It had been ages since I'd gotten in a fight with my mom or drunk a whole bottle of wine by myself.

But inside I felt bruised and weepy. I felt like my heart was broken. All those songs people wrote about heartbreak? I got it now. They weren't talking about romantic heartbreak. They were talking about losing a friend.

Through everything that had ever happened to me—job drama, family insanity, men—I had never questioned that my friends would be there. They had always been the constants in my life. I could take risks, I could be an idiot in other areas of my life, because I always had my friends to back me up, to bail me out, to lean on. And now it was like the pillars that held me up weren't as sturdy as I'd always thought.

Why was I so much more hurt about Sumira keeping this secret from us than I had been about Amy sleeping with Stephen? Was it because I could understand Amy's thinking—because I could understand what it felt like to act impulsively, even when it was wrong? What Sumira had done was different. She had purposely shut out her best friends, kept us in the dark about something huge and important. I had never shut out my friends before. I shared everything with them. I was an oversharer. I needed them in my life. I needed them to weigh in on the important things, to help make sense of life with me. The idea that Sumira could navigate a big life change without us...it made me think she didn't need us anymore. Maybe didn't even want us anymore? And that scared me.

Eva and Amy had both emailed Sumira, saying that they loved her and they were happy for her. But I couldn't. I was angry at her, yes. But I also felt raw and exposed. Like her choosing to shut me out said something about me. Something I had been blind to. Something I didn't want to see.

I'd never thought Ajay was someone Sumira would really like. If I'd thought that, I wouldn't have said what I did about him. I felt horrible, looking back. I'd basically called him a joke, hadn't I? That day at Mr. West, was it possible that she had been about to tell me something about Ajay? I could barely remember now, but surely we'd just been talking all about me and my problems. As usual.

The thing with Amy had been completely different, but I couldn't help noticing a similarity: the fact that I had been too self-absorbed to notice anything amiss. The night that Amy met Stephen, I hadn't noticed a thing. But they must have shared some glances, some conversation, something. And Sumira— who knew how many times she had tried to tell me about Ajay?

Who knew how clear the signs had been, right in front of my face?

Thinking about all of this, it made me wonder why anyone would want to be my friend in the first place. I wasn't prone to negative self-talk like this, and I didn't like it. But I didn't know what else I was supposed to think.

I was tired of feeling sorry for myself, so I got back on Tinder. It wasn't like I was trying to replace Sumira with a guy. Or maybe I was. And maybe I was trying to find the old version of me. I didn't know who I was without my friends, without a string of dates every week, without my usual upbeat attitude. Going on a date felt like a concrete action I could take to feel normal again.

Ten minutes after I started swiping, I had three conversations going. One of the guys asked if I was free tonight, so I said sure.

We met up at a bar in Belltown. I wore a slinky black dress with my curls all wrapped up in a polka-dot scarf. I'd also painted my nails blood red, because it was almost Halloween and I was going out in the night to meet a strange man like a hot-blooded dowager.

He was short but vaguely handsome, and he pecked my cheek in greeting.

"Rachel," he said, and I could tell he was trying to make his voice sound lower than it was, "how thrilling to meet you." This gave me pause. I wondered if he practiced saying different words in the mirror: *how stunning to meet you, how fortuitous, how scrumptious*. A little snort of laughter escaped me at this thought, and he—Connor—quirked an eyebrow at me.

"Oh, I'm not laughing at you, I was just remembering

something funny..." I trailed off at the nonplussed look on his face. "It's really charming to meet you too, Connor. Shall we?" I motioned toward the bar, and he led the way to a couple of stools at the far end.

He dived into what I assumed was normal internet date preamble: how long we'd both lived in Seattle, what we did for work. He told me all about his job in the "music tech" industry, and after two French 75's I was finding him quite interesting. His face had a pleasing, impish quality, and he was a good storyteller, though he talked about himself a fair amount.

And then, somehow, we pivoted to a topic I had naively assumed was not an appropriate part of the first-date repertoire.

"...and that's why I don't understand all the hubbub about next year's election," he was saying, gesturing to the bartender for another martini. "If everyone just focused on their own careers and investments, we'd all be fine, no matter who sits in the White House. And anyway, it's not like they take our votes seriously. That's why I don't even bother."

At that moment, the bartender plunked down Connor's fresh drink, and I met his eyes with a look of horror. He was your typical Seattle lumberjack bartender, and he gave me a look of pity, then walked away with a sad shake of his head.

"Excuse me," I said sweetly to Connor. "Did I hear you correctly? You don't vote?"

"Of course not. I'm a busy man." He twirled his martini glass, not even looking at me, in love with the sound of his own voice. "Politics is a rigged game. There's no point trying to participate in it. Voting is an empty concept, Rachel. Like feminism."

A tequila shot landed in front of me. I looked up to see the bartender backing away, narrowing his eyes pointedly from me to Connor. I felt, suddenly, like we were on a secret mission together—to destroy the small, pompous man beside me. I downed the tequila shot, smacked my lips, and turned, slowly and dangerously, toward Connor.

Five minutes later I was out on the sidewalk, reapplying my lipstick in the cold night air. I had left Connor with the sound of my voice ringing in his ears—and with the bill. The bartender had blown me a kiss on my way out.

I made my way down the street toward my bus stop, swinging my hips with a sense of purpose, like a J.Lo character who's just left a man for dead in an alleyway without breaking a sweat.

"Rachel, wait." I swung around—I thought it might be the bartender come to sweep me off my feet (but I'm pretty sure he was gay). Alas, it was Connor, rushing after me with a strange look on his face.

"What?" I towered over him in my heels, my arms crossed.

"You—" He broke off, looking sort of constipated and desperate. "You're right. I need to think outside my own worldview."

"Oh. Okay." I relaxed my stance. "Well, I'm glad you—"

He cut me off, reaching for my hand. "You taught me something. And you looked damn good doing it." He tugged me toward him and, before I knew what was happening, his tongue was in my mouth.

"Annngh!" I tried to scream, but it's surprisingly difficult when your Tinder date is jamming his tongue down your throat. I settled on kicking and shoving until I managed to dislodge him. He shot his impish grin at me. I smacked his face with my clutch and straightened my jacket. "That was very rude."

As I ran across the street to the shelter of my bus stop, he called after me, "Nice ass!"

Unfortunately, my profanity-laden reply was drowned out by the roar of the approaching bus. I took a seat by a window and peered into the dark street for a minute to be sure Connor wasn't following me. And then I deleted Tinder.

On autopilot, my thumb flicked through my phone—no messages—and opened Instagram. Without consciously deciding to do so, I found myself staring at Christopher Butkus's profile. His smile made him look warm and somehow comforting. Or was I projecting that, based on conversations we'd had? I couldn't bear to think about the last time we'd talked, and so my mind settled on the memory of the sustainability dinner. His flushed face as he explained the name Pageant. His gentle ribbing. The photo he had taken of me—I wanted to be that Rachel. The sparkly-eyed, mischievous one.

Oh God, what was I doing? How pathetic was I, fantasizing about some guy I didn't even like? It was just a bad-date hangover. It was the way Christopher compared favorably to Connor. I knew with inexplicable certainty that Christopher would never shove his tongue down my throat like that. And Christopher Butkus absolutely, definitely voted.

The world was crashing down around my ears. I was estranged from my best friend. I'd been sexually accosted by a Lilliputian libertarian. And now? Now the internet was blowing up with the news that Jeremy Coltrain, our collective *Bachelor* soulmate, had been accused of sexual misconduct.

Once I'd recovered from the shock of seeing the headlines, I skimmed a few of the articles. A former coworker of Jeremy's had come forward, inspired by the #MeToo movement, to denounce the way Jeremy had treated her in the office. He had wolf-whistled at her more than once and called her "hotcakes." Then an anonymous PA from ABC had added her own story: she too had been called "hotcakes" by our beloved Jeremy. And, worse, he had grabbed her rear end.

Her rear end! *Grabbed it.*

I'd seen enough. I closed my laptop and put my phone on airplane mode, then sank back on my bed, where I stayed for fourteen hours. I only got up the next afternoon because it was time to start preparing for Jane's bachelorette party.

I'd rallied for parties before—when I was hungover, heartbroken, or just crazy busy. But pulling myself out of my current state to the heights required for my dear sister's bachelorette party felt like an impossible task. But it was one I'd have to achieve. I couldn't let Jane down.

CHAPTER 24

THE EVENING STARTED OFF with a bang. Literally, unfortunately.

I was all dolled up in a tiny black dress, velvet block heels, and red lipstick. I had a giant novelty balloon in the shape of a diamond ring, a bride-to-be sash, and a bag full of penis necklaces. I was ready.

I entered the karaoke bar with my arms full of bachelorette paraphernalia, and before I could wrestle the balloon through the door, the door slammed on it and it popped so loudly that half the bar patrons dived under their tables, thinking it was a gunshot.

So I did a curtsy, holding my now flaccid balloon, and then I sort of shimmied and said, "Who's ready for a bachelorette party?" but none of our group was there yet, so everyone just stared at me. A few people actually got up and left.

Ego bruised, I skulked to a table in the corner and checked my phone. Eva's Uber was almost here. Amy had declined with the (in my opinion, feeble) excuse that it was her mother-in-law's birthday. I decided to throw the popped balloon in the trash before Jane could see it, in case it was bad luck or something. (Deflated novelty balloon at the bachelorette party was surely up there with the groom seeing the wedding dress, right?)

Jane and Kailey arrived, drawing the attention of pretty much everyone in the bar. Kailey's belly stuck out like she was smuggling a pumpkin, and Jane—well, Jane was Jane. She looked extra bridal: she wore a flowy white dress with long sleeves and a slit up the side and her hair slicked back in a ponytail. Her skin was glowing almost as bright as the rock on her finger. A few of her work friends trooped in after them. A lot of squealing ensued as we all greeted each other, and I draped the bride-to-be sash over Jane's shoulder.

An hour later, the only ones to sing anything had been me, Eva, and one of Jane's coworkers, who had a spectacular voice. (Those people had no place in a karaoke bar; it was just disrespectful.) I was getting nervous that the party was a dud. Jane had been sipping her single vodka cranberry the whole time, and Kailey was being a pathetic pregnant sourpuss. She refused to wear a penis necklace. Jane laughed it off, but I could tell she was hurt. Her own best friend, not willing to wear phallic jewelry for her. She wasn't fooling anyone—we all knew she was extremely familiar with the penis, in theory and in practice: just look at her giant belly.

The karaoke portion of the evening concluded with the entire bar singing along to the bartender's rendition of "Sweet Caroline." Our spirits thus raised, we headed to Nue for nourishment. We feasted on spicy wings, garlic fried rice, and smothered fries, our conversation growing giddier with each fancy cocktail we consumed.

To Jane's disappointment and my glee, Kailey went home after dinner. She claimed she didn't have the energy for dancing.

"Don't worry." I wrapped an arm around Jane's shoulders and waved goodbye to Kailey. "I'll take care of her."

Our next stop was a nearby bar that was having a nineties pop music night. I immediately ordered a round of tequila shots, which Jane loved. She was so exhilarated she called for another round.

The night began to blur in a whirl of flashing lights and sweaty, nostalgia-fueled dancing. It turned out Jane's work friends were pretty fun. They each bought everyone a round of drinks. Once the conversation devolved into her friends shouting questions about Owen's penis size, I pulled a face at Eva. Even when she was very drunk at her own bachelorette party, Jane was too sensitive to field questions about her beloved's private parts. Eva took the hint and loudly suggested that we should let the bride-to-be get home for some beauty rest. The other girls were so blotto that they merely squinted and nodded and followed her out the door.

We didn't, though.

"Jane." I caught her hand before she could follow the others. "Sister dance party?"

I've always had a magical connection with DJs, and that moment was no different: as soon as the words left my mouth, a remix of Destiny's Child's "Jumpin', Jumpin'" blared. Jane and I screamed with delight, and together we jumped into the center of the dance floor.

I was happy with the way the party had turned out. If only we'd gone home after that Destiny's Child song. If only we'd left it at that. If only I hadn't ruined everything.

CHAPTER 25

I SWEAR ON MY first-edition copy of *Harry Potter and the Deathly Hallows*: I don't remember saying it.

I have almost no memory of what happened after our friends went home. I remember whirling around with Jane under the pretty lights, and I remember laughing the way we used to do when we were kids. It was the kind of uncontrollable laughter where you want to keep talking, to keep the joke going, but you can barely get the words out, and you're doubled over, slapping your thighs and trying to breathe. That's what I remember: being in the sister zone. It gets rarer the older you get, and I wanted to keep it going all night, to soak it all in. Just me and Jane.

Like I said, I don't remember saying it. But once we got going like that, I would've said anything to keep Jane laughing.

I awoke the next day around noon, and the first thing I noticed was the number of notifications on my phone. Blearily I typed a feeble joke to the group chat: "Why do I have so many messages? Did I win something? Has Johnny Depp chosen me for his next child bride?"

But their replies were swift and serious.

> **Eva Galvez 12:19 PM:**
> Wait. Before you open any
> of them, you should know,
> there's a video of you and
> Jane that went viral.
> It's not good.

> **Amy McDonald 12:20 PM:**
> It's really not good, Rachel.
> Prepare yourself.

My first thought was that they must've been overreacting. It was probably like a hot-sisters video, but we didn't do anything scandalous. We kept our clothes on and certainly didn't do any kissing-sisters crap. But Eva had sent the link to the video, and I watched it, and then I ran to the bathroom and threw up.

I'd meant to give Jane a memorable party, and instead I'd ruined her life. If only I could go back and undo those last tequila shots, un-go in that bathroom, never have that conversation. I kept going over and over my memories from the night before, and I could sort of remember it now.

But the video showed it all in unforgiving detail.

"Local News Anchor Makes Light of Accusations."

I had no idea what the headline meant, and I saw that the video was less than a minute long, so I thought, *How bad could it be?* So I played it. And there were Jane and I, in the bathroom of that club—and as soon as I saw the shaky iPhone footage I got a clench of dread in my stomach. People only pulled out their phones to record complete strangers if it was a real train wreck. We were cackling with laughter—accurate. We were repeating something, but it was hard to decipher through the laughter. I watched as I sank to my knees and wailed (voice still shaking with mirth), "Jeremyyyyy!" Jane raised her arms to the heavens (or to the stained bathroom ceiling) and crowed, "Why did you do it, Jeremy?" And then I lurched forward and grasped Jane's hands and gasped, as though I were saying something very secret and very clever, "Hashtag me too please!" And Jane screamed and covered her face and laughed until her mascara pooled, and we were chanting it together, clutching our stomachs at the hilarity of it: "Hashtag me too please! Me too, Jeremy!" And then I was prancing around the bathroom smacking my own ass and crooning, "Please call me hotcakes!" And Jane was slumped against a sink, exhausted from laughing, and that's when the video stopped.

Hashtag me too please. My skin crawled with horror.

When the video ended, I could feel the absence of oxygen in my body, and my vision was clouded with gray. I dimly registered the impossibly high number of views on the video, but I closed it before reading any of the comments. I didn't need to read them; nothing anyone wrote could be worse than what I felt. I was despicable. I'd never hated myself—you know me—but after I watched that video, a feeling of loathing clawed up my throat, so strong I wanted to scream. What was wrong with me? How could I be such a complete, vicious idiot? How could I bring poor Jane into something like *this*?

In the minutes that followed, this entire year replayed in my mind: my idiocy at work and with men, every mean and selfish thing I'd ever said. Remembering it all, I called myself names I wouldn't call anyone else. But I deserved it all, because I never learned. I never took anything seriously. Apparently I would never grow up.

If only I hadn't dragged my beloved sister down with me.

When I went to her condo, Owen answered the door. He told me Jane was in bed, and his face told me everything. He despised me, even if Jane was too kind to do so.

Jane looked sick with regret and misery.

"Jane." I perched on the bed beside her. But she cut me off, silently holding out her phone. I thought she was going to show me the video again, so it took me a minute to comprehend the email on her screen. She'd been demoted back to her researcher position. She would no longer be appearing on air.

"No! How can they do this?" The idea of her employer seeing the video hadn't even occurred to me, I'd been so lost in my own guilt.

"They can't have a women's issues reporter who jokes about sexual assault," she said.

"It wasn't *assault*, it was just Jeremy Coltrain, he—"

"Are you really going to defend yourself right now?" Her voice was soft but clipped, and the sight of her sitting up against her pillows, her face drawn and pale with misery I'd caused—it was more than I could take.

"They can't fire you because of this. It'll blow over. Everyone will forget about it in a day or two."

"They haven't fired me. They just don't want me on TV. And I agree with them. Actually, I think they should have fired me."

"How can you agree with them? You deserve that job. It's what you've been working toward."

"Yes." She looked at me, then dropped her eyes to her lap. "It was."

"I can help you. I can help you get the TV position back."

"No, you can't."

"Jane, please just let me try. Look, how about this?" I was thinking furiously on the spot. "You could propose a news story about women and the #MeToo movement. And make a public apology on the air. Tell them it'll help their ratings. Viewers love a scandal, right?"

Her face hardened. I shouldn't have uttered the word *scandal*.

"I'm not going to propose that. They'll think I'm crazy."

"But it might be worth a shot, couldn't it? If it works?"

She raised her eyes to something behind me; I looked around to see Owen standing in the doorway.

"I just want to be alone, Rachel. There's nothing more to say about any of this."

"Jane, I'm so sorry. I'm so, so sorry. Please let me—"

"Rachel." Owen hadn't moved, but his voice held a note of authority I couldn't ignore. "It's time to go."

And so I was home, alone, at the deepest rock bottom I'd ever known. I'd ruined everything. Oh, and I hadn't heard a peep from my mother, which meant either that she was more upset than she'd ever been in her life or that she hadn't realized anything was amiss.

By nighttime, the notifications had stopped coming. No doubt everyone who knew me was either disgusted or unsurprised, or both.

The silence was worse than the constant pinging of my phone, but I knew I deserved it. I deserved nothing but silence.

CHAPTER 26

I STAYED UP UNTIL two in the morning, digging into Jane's LinkedIn connections and drafting messages to her boss, her boss's boss, her colleagues. But I didn't send any of them. I couldn't see how a random message from the other guilty party in the video would help the situation.

Jane hadn't replied to any of my apology texts. In my nearly thirty years as her pesky little sister, she had never iced me out before. Even when I was seventeen and spilled nail polish on the passenger seat of her car. Or when I was nine and dropped her library copy of *Ella Enchanted* in the toilet—she'd always had a terror of getting in trouble with the librarian, but she didn't take it out on me. Or the previous year, when I'd borrowed her Naked eye shadow palette and it fell out of my bike basket and shattered all over the street. "These things happen." That's what she'd said. Jane had the patience of a saint. And how did I reward her? By constantly pushing things one step too far. And now...

I just couldn't believe I'd lost Jane her dream job. And also her reputation. Would she forever be known as the news anchor who had joked about the #MeToo movement?

As I soldiered on with this heavy black cloud over my head, it was not lost on me that Sumira hadn't reached out to me at all. She had to have seen the video. She was probably relieved that she'd ended our friendship before it happened. It was ironic that I'd been feeling so sorry for myself a few days earlier after the Sumira debacle, totally unaware that I would soon be sinking so much further into the depths of absolute shit.

Two weeks before Halloween, I polished off a bottle of bottom-shelf pinot noir on my couch while sobbing over old photos of Jane and me in Paris. That trip, the summer after my freshman year of college and her senior year, had been a highlight of my life. Had our relationship been on a downhill trajectory ever since, and I just hadn't noticed? Did Jane simply tolerate my existence? Was I destined to career through life like a wayward boulder, crushing everyone in my path?

The next morning, I was rewarded with the worst hangover of my life. Clearly I was no longer cut out for drinking a bottle of wine on my own. Inconvenient, since I had never needed wine more.

One week before Halloween, I got back on Tinder and matched with a guy who appeared to be mostly brawn, not much brain. He asked me to meet up at a mojito bar where an apparently "dope jam band" called Space Owl was playing. I told him I'd meet him there at eight. And then, as the time ticked nearer, I found that I didn't have it in me. Absolutely zero percent of my being wanted to meet up with some random guy. So I stayed on my couch and sent him a quick message saying I wasn't feeling well. I felt guilty for bailing on him but glad that I wasn't out there trying to shout-flirt with a stranger over live music.

The next day at noon, my phone pinged.

It was Amy: "It's gone. The video is gone."

I typed back quickly, "What? But that's impossible."

Amy McDonald 12:08 PM:
Go try to watch it. It's been
removed.

Rachel Weiss 12:09 PM:
But videos don't just
disappear from the internet.
How can it be gone?

Amy McDonald 12:10 PM:
I have no idea. Could it have
been Jane's employer?

Rachel Weiss 12:11 PM:
Maybe, but I doubt it.

Amy McDonald 12:12 PM:
Well, you lucked out, I guess.
Maybe someone's looking out
for you.

I spent the rest of my lunch break looking up all the articles
about the video. They were still there, so it wasn't as if it had
never happened. But they all showed a black box saying, "This
video has been removed." Shaking, I texted Jane to tell her that it
was gone. She didn't reply.

CHAPTER 27

IT WAS BOUND TO happen eventually. I was bound to snap. No better day of the year to do it than Halloween, I suppose. I'd felt it coming on for a while. Heartbreak and loneliness didn't suit me; it was like trying to squeeze my voluptuous body into a pencil skirt. It just didn't work.

I knew my friends were enjoying the hallowed day with their significant others. Amy and Ryan were cozily ensconced in their home, handing out candy to tiny devils and sprites. Eva and Jasmine were off winning best couple's costume at a gorgeous costume party downtown. (Eva had sent us a photo. They were sexy Gandalf and sexy Bilbo Baggins. Simply superb.) And how was I spending this Samhain?

I went to work. I wore the same dress, tights, and boots that you might see me in any day of the season. No fairy makeup this year; no gag fangs. The year before last, I'd hidden a pellet of fake blood in my mouth and punctured it while talking to Kenneth. I have reason to believe that I made that man pee his pants at the sight of blood pouring out of my mouth. At the very least, he cried. Anyway, there were no hijinks or costumes for me today. I just wasn't feeling it.

Kenneth snuck around the side of my cubicle, an expectant look on his face, his hands balled in front of his mouth like he was preparing to scream.

"Oh." He let his hands drop. "Rachel, it's Halloween."

I swiveled around to face him, sighing. "Yes, Kenneth, I know."

"You—you didn't dress up." He had on a pair of glasses with spring-loaded bloody eyeballs. They bobbed dejectedly at me.

"Nah. Not this year. I thought I should look professional, you know, for the lecture this afternoon."

Unfortunately, I realized once I arrived in the classroom that Kenneth must have given the participants a heads-up about my proclivity for Halloween shenanigans, because they were all in varying states of costume: there were bunny ears, zombie makeup, a witch's hat, and one fully inflated T-rex who barely fit into her chair. I had to run out of the room and steal Sheryl's bowl of Halloween candy to hand out to my students.

I stayed late at work—shocking, I know—and then ambled over to Mr. West for a drink. I didn't relish the idea of going home alone while everyone else in the city was reveling with friends and loved ones. Why I chose Mr. West, the one place sure to remind me of Sumira, well, that would be for the anthropologists to decide. The old me would have ordered a whole bottle of rosé and started a one-woman party, making best friends with the staff and other patrons. Instead what I did was drink a solitary gimlet, hunched over a table in the back of the café, and try not to think about the last time I was there with Sumira. Finally I threw in the towel on the worst Halloween of my life and caught the bus home.

Well, if I thought waiting until after dark meant Fremont's revelers would all be safely indoors, I was wrong. I stepped off the bus into a mad swirl of humanity. Parents and children in costume scampered down the street, holding hands and shriek-ing with joy. Teenagers and twentysomethings trooped this way and that, kicking up a ruckus. I stood in the middle of it all, alone with people pressing in on all sides. Alone on one of my favorite days of the year. Alone, feeling like someone had taken a chisel directly to my heart: *crack*.

It sounds terribly dramatic, but the ache in my chest was such that my limbs felt heavy; walking felt like a trial. But I forced myself to move, and I headed down a quieter street. It wasn't my usual route home, but I needed to escape the crush of people. The street was lined with sweet houses, their windows glowing jewel bright. Some of them were decorated with skeletons and plastic gravestones. As I walked, my heart rate slowed and I took deep, calming breaths. One of the houses on my left was so beautiful that I stopped to look at it. It was one of those old Colonials that have been lovingly maintained for the last hundred years. The deep front porch and steeply gabled roof were soothing to the eye, and the warm yellow light in the windows made me think it must be comfortable inside. I noticed that the magnolia tree in the yard had little handmade ghosts hanging from its branches, the kind we used to make in school with tissues and Tootsie Pops. For the first time in hours, I felt myself smile, wondering what kind of family lived here, wondering if the parents had taught the kids how to make the little ghosts.

As I was about to walk on, a knot of trick-or-treaters bobbed down the path toward the pretty house. They were so cute—small and chubby—that I paused to watch them collect their candy.

"Trick or treat!" their little voices chorused when the door opened.

"Wow! A mummy! A flower! And is that...an otter? Incred-ible!" The man knelt down to let the kids choose from his candy bowl, and my blood froze. I couldn't breathe. I could only stand and stare as Christopher Butkus let the children take fistfuls of candy, a huge smile on his face as though he was having the time of his life. "Happy Halloween! Have fun out there," he called after them. And my heart—oh, my heart was having a strange day. It seemed to be swelling, or melting, or—I don't know. All I knew was that when Christopher Butkus closed the door of his beautiful house, I wished he would come back out. My entire being longed for him to open the door again, to see me, and to call out my name with that big smile on his face. And this was a confusing sentiment, since the last time I'd seen him I had been yelling about how much I despised him.

And so I stood there for several long minutes, blood rushing around in my veins, heart aching in that strange new way, thinking.

A little while later, I took a steadying breath, raised my hand to the door before me, and knocked. After what felt like a very long time but must have been only a few seconds, the door opened.

"Rachel?" Sumira's voice held a multitude of feelings that I couldn't pick apart, but I knew I was feeling them too. "What are you doing here?"

I thought about words I could say, but nothing felt right. So I threw my arms around her neck and hugged her for a very long time—too long, probably. And then I handed her a bag of Reese's cups.

"My favorite," she whispered. I nodded.

"Was it trick-or-treaters?" came a man's voice.

Sumira met my eyes with a wary look. "Ajay's here," she told me, unnecessarily. "We were about to start watching *Hocus Pocus*."

I nodded briskly, took off my coat, and led the way to her living room.

"Hi, Ajay," I said. "Scoot over."

And that is how I spent the rest of my Halloween: wedged in between Sumira and her fiancé, watching *Hocus Pocus*.

(In case you're wondering: Ajay laughed at all the right parts.)

At home that night, I curled under a blanket on the couch with nothing but a few flickering candles for light. I felt strangely calm and content. It had taken me long enough, but I'd finally made up with Sumira, and she'd apparently forgiven me for my overreaction and my general self-absorbedness. And now that I was alone again, there was only one person that I—inexplicably—wanted to talk to.

I opened Instagram and started typing a message to Christopher.

"Hey. Happy Halloween. How are you?" No, that was stupid… I deleted it and tried again. "Hey, see any good otters lately?" No, that was too stalkerish. "Boo! [Ghost emoji.] Haha, scared you." Ugh. This was pointless.

I closed the app. He didn't want to hear from me. I was being ridiculous. And yet I couldn't stop thinking about him. His house was yet another example of how I'd misjudged him. Sure, you couldn't judge a person by the look of their house, apartment, shack, whatever. But I really had pegged him as a modern-town-house kind of guy, the type of house with aggressive angles

and floor-to-ceiling glass windows. And clearly—as usual—I'd
been wrong. His house was classic. Historical. *Beautiful.*

It was the type of house I imagined myself buying one day.
You know, after I had a few glasses of wine and conveniently forgot about the fact that I'd never be able to afford a house in this
market.

And it occurred to me, not for the first time lately, that I might
be a complete moron. I could barely remember my initial objections to Christopher Butkus. All I wanted to do now was think
about him, to remember the way he'd beamed at those trick-or-
treaters. I wondered if he'd been hosting a Halloween party or if
he'd been home alone, eagerly waiting for the doorbell to ring. I
wanted to learn more about him.

Okay, I would allow myself to google him for ten minutes.
I would obsess over him to my heart's content until the timer
went off, and then I would carry on with my life in a sane and
responsible manner. Perhaps, in a way, this temporary Christopher obsession was protecting me from the Jane-related guilt spi-
ral I'd been living in.

Forty minutes later, I had learned that he was a Virgo, that he
had grown up in Miami, and that he had studied abroad in Zurich.
Truly, this had not been one of my best ideas. Now my head was
full of things I wanted to ask him about but never would, because
then I would have to admit to googling him and also I was never
speaking to him again anyway.

Still, he was in my head now. It was like I had a little Christopher sitting on my shoulder, commenting on everything I did.

As I pulled some pajamas out of a pile of rumpled, clean laun-
dry: "You should try folding it when it's warm from the dryer.
That's what I do." *I bet he does.*

As I spread peanut butter and jelly on bread: "Nice, a PB&J for supper. Classic."

"Did you just say supper?" I muttered to my empty apartment.

When I checked my phone for the billionth time, hoping for a word from Jane: "You could fix it, you know."

At first I ignored this, as one should when hearing strange voices in one's head. But then I thought, *I could?* And little Christopher nodded and said, "You have to think bigger."

But since he was a figment of my imagination and not a fully formed human, he did not expand on this point. What *would* Christopher do, I wondered. He was a grand-gesture type of person. Would he skywrite an apology to Jane? Or storm into the newsroom demanding they put her back on TV? No, probably something with less bravado and more brain. Like...

I sat up straighter and set my empty PB&J plate on the coffee table. *Write.* Not a letter like some Jane Austen hero, but a news story. I could write a story for Jane to present to her boss. I'd already written a lesson plan about the #MeToo movement for one of my educational sessions. (That had been Kenneth's idea. I could only assume that he'd seen the cursed video, but he hadn't mentioned it. He'd just suggested in a soothing and gentle way that I might choose #MeToo as a future topic. That man might have some class after all.) So I could use some of my research as a starting point and go from there. The piece would have to be poignant and powerful. It could be about how #MeToo affects women psychologically—hearing about it all the time and losing trust in men they thought were safe. And different ways to cope with the psychological stress and trauma.

I grabbed my laptop, opened a blank document, and began to write.

CHAPTER 28

I WROTE AND RESEARCHED and fact-checked until the wee hours of the morning. Until the dark autumn sky outside my window became bleached around the edges, a heavy gray streaked with silver. Until my alarm went off at seven o'clock, and I emailed Kenneth to say that I needed a sick day, crawled into bed, and fell asleep.

Around noon, I dragged myself out of bed and into the shower. I had to pitch this story to Jane in person. I wasn't going to risk another email or text that she could just ignore.

But first I had to walk a couple blocks to the print shop. I wanted to print the story to make it more official. And then I stopped in the coffee shop next door to grab a large coffee with a splash of cream, because it was thirty degrees and rainy and I was running on fumes.

When I got to Jane's condo, I knocked confidently, trying to ignore the way my hands shook. I just wanted my sister back. *Please, let this work*, I thought, holding my breath as I heard footsteps approaching the door from inside.

"Hi." Jane looked slightly puzzled but not angry.

"Hi. I have something I want to talk to you about. An idea." I paused. "Please."

She didn't hesitate before opening the door wider and ushering me in. Even if she hated me, Jane wasn't the type of person to leave someone out in the cold. I sat on the couch, clutching my coffee cup with one hand and my bag with the other, glad I'd brought the coffee so Jane didn't have to unwillingly go through the motions of offering me one. She perched warily on the armchair across from me. Linus jumped into her lap at once and glared at me.

I decided to jump right in. Clearly there would be no small talk happening right now. "Remember I had that idea the other day about you pitching a story to your work? About #MeToo?"

Jane sighed, looking frustrated. "Rachel, I told you, I don't feel comfortable doing that."

"Hear me out, please. I wrote it. It's thoroughly fact-checked. I even referenced one of your network's previous stories."

Jane didn't interrupt me this time. She looked bemused.

"It's about sisterhood and trauma and trust," I continued. "It's about how women are feeling heard and seen but also scared, wary, and tired. It's about how, whether the crimes are big or small, whether we know the person or not, each #MeToo story is a blow to our psyche."

"I don't know. I'll read it, but..." Jane frowned as though she was tired of thinking about all this, and I didn't blame her. "I doubt it'll work. They'll have moved on. It's not like they're lacking in special correspondents."

"But not everyone has as many years of experience in their newsroom as you, not everyone is as beautiful as you, as smart as you, as..."

She smiled weakly. "I get it."

"And you could offer to start employer-mandated therapy." The words came out in a rush, without asking my brain for permission.

"What?" Jane half laughed.

"No...nothing. It was just an idea. That maybe they'd be willing to hire you back if you went to therapy. It might help to show that you're really sorry about the video and help the public forgive you or..." I trailed off. "Honestly, I kind of just thought of it because my employer sent me to therapy."

"*What?*" A broad grin spread across her face. I smiled back just seeing it.

"Yeah. It's nothing. It's fine."

"Because of the video?"

"Oh, um...no. It was something different. That I did. Stupid..." I trailed off on a whisper.

After staring at me for a beat, eyes wide and mouth open in a grin, Jane lost it. She laughed harder than I'd seen her laugh since...well, probably since the night that video was taken.

"Okay," she gasped after she'd gathered herself, wiping her eyes with the heel of her hand. "Okay. I'll read the story."

I tried not to look too eager as I handed her the pages. She glanced down at them and then looked back at me, her eyes still shining with laughter.

"Rachel, it actually means a lot to me that you did this. I can tell you put a lot of work into it."

"I'm just trying to make things right. If this doesn't work out and you decide you need a new job, I'll do all the applications, I'll even interview for you if you want."

She pressed her lips together and smirked. Probably imagining how badly I'd butcher a job interview pretending to be Jane.

"Let's hope it doesn't come to that."

CHAPTER 29

TWO DAYS LATER, I returned to my desk after my lunch break and checked my phone. (Yes, shocking, isn't it? I was trying this new thing where I read a book during lunch to get a bit of distance from my phone. After all, I wasn't using dating apps anymore, and I was trying to gently wean myself off sending constant group chat updates.) I fumbled and almost dropped it in surprise when I saw three messages from Jane.

Jane Weiss 12:46 PM:
Your story was great. It gave me the courage to call my boss.

Jane Weiss 12:47 PM:
They thought it was great too. I got my special correspondent job back!

> **Jane Weiss 12:48 PM:**
> Thank you. ☺

I let out a silent scream and punched the air with both fists. It worked! Jane got her job back! Punching the air wasn't sufficient to let out this elated energy: I did a few body rolls and shimmies and—

"Rachel?" Kenneth poked his nose around the corner of my cubicle.

I froze midtwerk. Kenneth was bright pink and appeared to be struggling between the desire to ask what was going on and the desire to slip away like nothing had happened. The latter won: he slowly reversed so that his face disappeared a centimeter at a time.

"Kenneth, wait." I dug around inside my desk drawer until I found what I was looking for. And then I peeled off a gold star from the sticker sheet and pressed it gently onto Kenneth's forehead. "You deserve this. Thanks for telling me to write that #MeToo lesson."

He turned even redder, muttered something incoherent, and went back to his cubicle.

My phone buzzed with a fourth message from Jane: "BTW, offering to go to therapy was the clincher. They loved that idea."

I burst out laughing. When I'd calmed down, I sat back in my swivel chair and spun around, gazing up at the fluorescent lights. Who would've thought I would round out the year having landed not only myself in employer-mandated therapy, but my sister too?

My November therapy session began routinely enough. My therapist asked me how I was doing with that tiny, concerned crease between her brows. (If that crease could talk, it would scream I AM A KIND AND EMPATHETIC LISTENER.)

I told her that I'd made up with Sumira and caught her up on the Jane drama. And after we'd talked about those things, something else occurred to me, and I acquired my own eyebrow crease as I thought about it. I didn't want to bring it up, really, but therapy had this way of forcing thoughts out of my mouth.

"Is there something else on your mind?" she asked.

No, is what I wanted to say. Instead I blurted out, "I saw Christopher Butkus on Halloween. I saw his beautiful house and it's not a modern monstrosity and he made lollipop ghosts and he liked the otter costume the best and I wanted him—I wanted him to see me."

Long, *long* pause.

"But he didn't see you?"

"No. It was dark. I was walking home. I wasn't stalking him or anything."

"Of course not." She smiled gently, like she would never mistake me for someone crazy enough to be a stalker (which, given some of the things I've said in therapy, could not possibly be true. But I appreciated the kind sentiment nonetheless).

I straightened my shoulders with the dignity befitting a non-stalker and thought for a moment.

"It was weird. Seeing him. Almost like my subconscious had been working on the problem of Christopher Butkus for months and I hadn't realized it."

She waited, and I filled in her silence in my mind: *How very fascinating, Rachel. And what did your subconscious tell you, Rachel? I'm dying to hear how it all turned out.*

"Yes," I answered myself, "my subconscious. When I saw him, I felt like I'd been working on all these calculations and the answer was that I didn't hate him. I don't hate him."

The crease deepened: I could tell she was on the edge of her seat with this revelation.

"And that feeling—I can't stop thinking about that feeling."

"Which feeling?" she prompted.

"The feeling of wishing he had seen me and invited me in, and that we had sat together in front of his fire, talking and ribbing each other and sipping hot cider and—" I trailed off, because my imagination was spinning ahead, picturing us inching closer on his sofa, our hands brushing in the candy bowl, and Christopher telling me that his feelings hadn't changed. I could picture the way the firelight would dance across his face. I felt faintly sick with the speed at which my mind was working, and at the whole idea of it.

"Help me. You're supposed to help me, right? So explain why this is happening. I'm not interested in Christopher Butkus. Is this just months of loneliness making me go off the rails? Is it because I feel like he's my last chance at finding someone? Is it because my mom likes him? Why am I fixating on him?"

At this she set down her pen and folded her hands in her lap, her eyes never leaving my face. Her expression was clear, the crease had gone. She simply stared at me, waiting.

Out of habit, I mentally filled in her silence: *Why do you think you are fixating on him, Rachel? Him, of all people? What sets him apart from the other men in your life? Christopher Butkus. What kind of person is he? What kind of man is he? How do you really feel about him?*

"No." I shook my head. "No, you're wrong."

She blinked.

"I don't—I could never—"

She tilted her head, and the corner of her mouth lifted almost imperceptibly. There was no arguing with that.

"Okay, well, if I do...if I *do* have feelings for Christopher Butkus, it will pass. Like a cold. I caught it somehow, and maybe I'll never know how, but it will pass."

"Rachel," she said gently. I leaned in, eager for advice. "Our time is up for today."

If I ignored the unsettling, Christopher Butkus–shaped elephant in the room—the room being my brain—life was good again. I'd unruined my sister's life. The gang was back together now that I had repaired my friendship with Sumira. And we were mere days away from my favorite holiday after Halloween. (How can one not love a holiday centered on mashed potatoes and pie?)

Sumira had asked us all to come over to help her address thank-you cards for the gifts that had already started pouring in. We'd all immediately accepted, grateful for the excuse to see each other in person. With the holidays and Sumira's wedding approaching, everyone was crazy busy.

Sumira's already posh and sleek apartment looked extra minimalistic now, because it was half-packed, with boxes lined against the wall. She was planning to move in with Ajay right after the honeymoon.

"Ladies," Sumira said. We were sitting at her kitchen table, sorting through stacks of envelopes and thank-you cards. "I actually asked you here for a reason. A reason other than licking stamps, I mean."

She stood up and retrieved a basket from the living room. It was full of what appeared to be gift bags. Amy squealed before Sumira even uttered another word.

"Will you be my bridesmaids? I understand if you don't want to, after everything that happened, but I—" Our deafening squeals cut her off.

"Of course!"

"Yes!"

"I thought you'd never ask!"

We tore open the gift bags to find delicate charm bracelets and little boxes of chocolate truffles.

"Sumira, this is the sweetest. You didn't have to do this!"

"I did." She sat down again and looked at all of us. "I'm really, really glad we're okay. I wasn't sure we would still be friends after...what I did."

There was a pause. We'd all patched things up with Sumira in our own ways, but there was no denying that our friendships felt somehow changed. Like we weren't 100 percent on the same page at all times. I guessed this was what growing up felt like, or something.

I tried to defuse the tension. "You can't get rid of us that easily."

Sumira flushed slightly but looked relieved. We turned our attention to the stamps and envelopes at hand.

"Oh, by the way," Sumira said casually, "my cousin will reach out about rehearsal dates for the choreographed bridesmaid dance."

"Excuse me?"

"Choreographed *what*?!"

I burst into laughter. "Well played, my friend, well played."

"Don't worry, guys, there are more gift bags where these came from."

"Well, in that case, sign me up." Eva took a gulp of wine.

"I'll embarrass myself in front of two hundred guests for some swag."

After our laughter died down, we dived into general gossip. Not seeing each other weekly (and not messaging each other 24/7) meant that there was a lot to catch up on. After Eva filled us in on her plans to invite Jasmine to her family's Thanksgiving and Sumira detailed her future mother-in-law's over-the-top requests (such as her own personal videographer to follow her around for the entire wedding), Amy told us she had an announcement.

We all froze with pens in hand. Given recent events, we might always be wary of any surprise announcements in our friend group.

"Ryan and I are getting a hairless cat!"

I let out a relieved sigh. "I thought you were pregnant." Sumira glared at me. "What? Sorry!"

"That's a great compromise," Eva said.

"I'm happy for you, Ames," I agreed.

"Thanks." She beamed. "I'm getting a cat and keeping my husband!"

As Sumira fetched a fresh bottle of rosé from the fridge, I told them I had an announcement too.

I did a little drumroll on the table. "I got Jane her reporter job back! Wait, no—Jane did it herself, really. But I helped."

"How did it happen?" Sumira refilled our glasses.

"You're just telling us now?" Eva sounded indignant.

"I thought it might be nice to tell you in person." I took a small, dignified sip of wine. In truth, it had felt awkward not to spill the beans to the group chat immediately. But I was trying for some growth and independence here.

"Okay, so tell us!" Amy prompted.

I told them about the story I'd written and how Jane got up the nerve to pitch it to her boss. And then I paused, choosing my next words carefully. "I kind of got the idea by thinking about what Christopher would do." The words came out softly. I felt myself flush, and I grabbed another envelope and started scribbling an address on it.

"Christopher Butkus?" Sumira said blankly.

"Yeah." I looked up, confused by her confusion. "I mean, I just thought about how he—he wrote me that letter and he likes grand gestures. And it inspired me to write the story for Jane."

"Aw." Amy tilted her head, as though I'd said something mildly amusing but somewhat pitiable.

"So, just to be clear"—Eva raised her eyebrows—"you've been thinking about Christopher and that letter he wrote you?"

"Yeah, it was—" I shook my head, regretting telling them about this at all. "It was just, like, a thought that I had. Not really important. The main thing is that Jane got her TV job back."

I stuck a stamp on the envelope and grabbed another blank one. I could feel Eva's eyes on me; I flicked my eyes upward and then looked back down to scrawl another address, my face burning now. Without looking, I could tell the three of them were sharing some kind of look, communicating without saying a word.

Stupid. It was pointless to mention Christopher. My friends had no idea I'd been thinking about him at all. Why did I have to bring him up again? They probably didn't want to hear about him ever again after all the drama of a few months ago. And they were right! I shouldn't bother them with my vague, unformed crush that wasn't going to amount to anything. For once in my life, I needed to focus on my friends and not on myself. Especially Sumira: she was getting married, and I'd almost lost her friend-ship. All of my attention and energy needed to be on her now. I'd thought about myself enough for a lifetime. Several lifetimes.

I blinked, stamped the envelope I was holding, and glanced back at the three of them. They were all focused on the task at hand, though Sumira wore a trace of a smile. Probably just laughing at how boy crazy I was.

"Anyway." I wanted to sound robustly sane. "Do we need to bring anything to your *mehndi* party besides our saris? Can we bring food or anything?"

"Nope, my mom is getting it catered, so don't worry about a thing."

"Great! I can't wait. I've always wanted henna. In, you know, a non-cultural-appropriation-type way."

Sumira rolled her eyes with a smile.

"I can't believe it's only three weeks away!" Amy said.

"I know. Actually, can you guys help me decide on my outfit for the *mehndi*? I have a couple options."

"Absolutely. Whatever you need." I meant it. Sumira was the star of the show now, and I was going to be there for her.

CHAPTER 30

ON THIS DAY OF the Turkey, I gave thanks to all the Rachels of my past. The conga-line Rachel. The naked biker Rachel. The Rachel who had a threesome with those two Canadians in Cancún, spring break 2011. (Ah, memories.) Because if it hadn't been for all the Rachels who came before, I wouldn't be the mature adult I was today.

It felt good, really. I felt calm. The air was crisp, and red and orange leaves crackled underfoot. The neighborhood was quiet: everyone was snuggled inside with their families. I wore a sensible and seasonal burnt-sienna dress with tights and high-heeled booties topped with a peacoat, hat, and scarf, the picture of a sophisticated woman on her way to a Thanksgiving dinner. Yesterday had been our first bridesmaid dance rehearsal, and my muscles ached in a satisfying way. (We still had *a lot* of work to do on the dance routine. But I felt like I'd gotten a decent workout, and I'd laughed more than I had in weeks.) I was ensconced in this feeling of acceptance. Like I'd grown up, and nothing was exactly the way I'd thought it would be, and that was okay.

I arrived exactly on time, with a bottle of prosecco for the adults and one of Martinelli's for the twins. Jane and I had agreed not to tell Mom and Dad about the video and Jane getting demoted and undemoted. I expected a peaceful Weiss Thanksgiving. There was, for once, no ongoing family drama.

Dad greeted me with a hearty hug, saying, "My favorite daughter named Rachel!" (His favorite joke.) He was wearing an argyle sweater that stretched a bit noticeably over his paunch, and he had the dewy-eyed, cinnamon-scented aura of one who's been indulging in hard cider and holiday cookies all day.

He took the bottles from me as I hung up my coat. I followed him into the kitchen as he crooned, "We've got bubbles!"

Jane and Owen sat at the kitchen counter, nibbling from a cheese plate. Jane's eyes kept darting toward Mom, who was dashing around the kitchen, muttering to herself and stirring various pots.

"She won't let me help," Jane said morosely as I kissed her hello.

"Smells great, Mom." Mom shot me a look of furious suspicion, as though she thought I was being sarcastic.

Dad popped open the prosecco, and I seated myself next to Jane, helping myself to cheese as Dad poured us each a glass.

"Where are the twins?" I asked. Jane pointed to the dining room, where the twins were quietly engaged in some activity.

"They're making the chocolate turkeys." This gave me a genuine shock—the twins were doing something sweet and productive. Without shrieking. It was like they were little girls again—actually, I can't remember a time from any age when they weren't shrieking.

"Oh yes, aren't they angels?" Mom paused, looking over at them fondly. Jane beamed; Jane loved it when everyone was quiet and content.

Dad sat on the other side of Owen, sipping his drink. "My dear, are you sure I can't help you at all?"

"No, no," Mom said lightly. "Please enjoy yourselves. Everything is almost finished here." And then, inexplicably, she shot me a mutinous look. Some of my sparkling wine dribbled out of my mouth.

"Um. Can *I* help at all?"

"You can toss the salad!" Her voice was thick with some emotion I couldn't put my finger on. "And then take the stuffing out of the oven." She added something under her breath, too quietly to hear.

"What was that?" I asked, salad tongs in hand.

In response she simply glared at me for a moment before turning back to her stirring. I cast a bewildered look at Jane, who shrugged in response.

Does she know? I mouthed to Jane. Dad and Owen had slipped off to the other room, from which sports sounds were now emanating.

"I don't know," Jane said. The twins, who had apparently been watching our whispered conversation, appeared at Jane's side.

"You mean...about this?" Ollie held out her phone, where the infamous video was playing.

"Stop it, stop it," I hissed. "How did you—? I thought it was gone!"

"We saved it, of course." They truly were evil.

"Did you show it to Mom?" Jane had panic in her eyes.

The twins shared a look and then said, with no trace of malice, "Of course not. We would never show that to Mom." And then, with malice returned in full force: "It's just for our own entertainment. And blackmail purposes."

"May I see your phone for a second?" I held out my hand sweetly.

Ollie raised a sardonic eyebrow. "Feel free to delete it. Everything on here is backed up in the cloud."

I spluttered, covering up my confusion with a display of frustration. Honestly, these Gen Z-ers! The cloud, I ask you.

"Well, just…keep it to yourselves."

"Of course." Ollie pocketed her phone.

"I watch it every night to fall asleep," Abby added, straight-faced.

Jane and I exchanged our patented *Why has the Lord burdened us with little sisters?* look, a silent communication we'd perfected over the years.

"Fine. If she hasn't seen the video, then why does Mom hate me?" I hissed, just as Mom called, "Rachel! The stuffing?"

My question went unanswered all through dinner. We sat down to enjoy our repast as much as we were able—in her heightened emotion, Mom had accidentally put raw onions on the yams and marshmallows in the brussels sprouts.

"Delicious, dear," Dad said. (He was, as always, a sport.) "Shall we give thanks?" He paused; the twins were sucking the marshmallow off each sprout, leaving the vegetables soggy and uneaten on their plates, and Mom was (alarmingly) glaring at me from down the table with tears in her eyes.

"I'll start." Dad stood up. "I'm grateful for my beautiful family and the impending nuptials of my eldest daughter."

Jane glowed. "Thank you, Dad. And I'm so—" But she was interrupted by a loud snort from our mother.

"Yes, Mom?" I was getting tired of her histrionics—little did I know they had barely begun.

She seemed to be on the verge of speech, and then she abruptly stood and disappeared into the kitchen, from whence we heard vigorous clanging. Around the table, each member of my family, including Owen, touched a finger to their nose.

"Hey!" I said.

"Nose goes," the twins said.

"Fine." I pushed back from the table. "Apparently I am the most mature adult here."

I found Mom banging a wooden spoon against the bottom of a pot.

"This pot is all"—*clang, clang*—"crusted over. Impossible to clean."

"And you thought whacking it would do the trick?" I approached cautiously and reached for the spoon.

She turned on me so quickly I stumbled backward with my hands in the air.

"You." She shook the spoon at me. "Why, Rachel? Why?"

"Why what, Mom? What have I done this time?"

"Why haven't you found *anyone*? Jane's wedding is five weeks away. Do you know how humiliated I'll be if you don't even bring a date to your sister's wedding?"

I dropped my hands. I didn't know what I'd expected, but it wasn't this. Surely a sane mother shouldn't care this much about her daughter's love life? Is this some kind of mental illness, I wondered?

Not wanting to antagonize her further by suggesting she was mentally ill, I opted to appease her.

"Five weeks, though." I tried to keep my voice calm and upbeat. "That's plenty of time. I could definitely still find a date."

"A date. A date!" The scathing tone of her voice suggested she was not, in fact, appeased. "I don't want you to find a date in five

weeks, Rachel. You had a year! I told you about Christopher Butkus on January first. And you couldn't make it work!" She gripped
the wooden spoon in both hands, a tortured expression on her
face. "And now? Now I would be happy with anyone. Because
now I fear there's no one who will ever take you, and all of the
guests at Jane's wedding will know!"

"They'll know what, exactly? That I'm destined to be single
forever? You know, a lot of successful women never got married.
Susan B. Anthony. Mindy Kaling. Oprah!"

At this Mom let out a theatrical scream. I returned to the dining room without another word. Everyone stared as I took my
seat. Dad and the twins were still eating.

Mom followed me, and Jane asked, "Mom, what's wrong?"

"Your sister refuses to date! She won't even try."

"That's not true!" Jane cast me a sympathetic look. "She does
try."

"Just not very successfully," Abby added.

And then everyone began to voice their own opinion of why I
was still single:

"She's focused on her career," Dad said.

"Have you tried dating apps?" Owen asked.

"—just hasn't found the right person," Jane said.

"—stubborn and doing this just to hurt me, I just can't
understand—" Mom said, not listening to anyone else.

"Perhaps she's been dating the wrong gender," Abby suggested
loudly, as Ollie concluded, "—could always use a sperm donor."

The more they talked, the louder they became, everyone
shouting to be sure their opinion was heard.

I slipped out of my seat and walked out the front door. I considered leaving, but there was still pie. So I sat on the front steps and

groaned, burying my face in my hands. It felt sort of cathartic, so I groaned again, louder, shaking my head with my tongue hanging out like they taught us in yoga. And then, really getting into it, I stood up and threw my arms wide in a Megan Rapinoe stance and shouted to the heavens, "THERE'S NOTHING WRONG WITH BEING SINGLE."

And then the shrubbery rustled and a voice said, "Um. Hello."

My arms shot down to cover my breasts—a sensible reaction when confronted with an unknown assailant, second only to covering something useful, like my organs.

"Who's there?"

Even as I was asking the question, a tall and (damn it all) handsome figure emerged.

"It's me," said Christopher Butkus.

"What were you doing in the bushes?"

"I heard a growling noise and I thought maybe there was a lost dog around somewhere."

"You went looking for a potentially feral animal?"

He shrugged, hands in the pockets of his khakis. "It might have been hurt."

I paused; I was not about to admit that the rabid dog he thought he'd heard was actually me. "It probably ran off."

"Probably." An awkward moment bloomed in the silence, in which I imagined we were both wondering what to say about me shouting into the darkness about being single.

"Happy Thanksgiving," I said quickly.

"You too. I was just leaving." He patted his (flat) stomach and added, "Stuffed. Are you heading home too?"

"No. I was just getting some air. Away from...well." I didn't feel like reminding him that my mom was insufferable.

"Ah." He nodded. "Is everything okay? With you and Jane and…you know."

Oh God. He had seen the video—I knew it. It was ridiculous to have even an inkling of hope that he still had feelings for me. In the dim light of the porch lamp and the crescent moon, I was glad he couldn't see the hot flush coloring my cheeks.

"Yes, that. Well." I tipped my head back, feigning deep thought. "Aside from the eternal humiliation and guilt I'll feel for the rest of my life, yes, we're okay."

"I hoped that after the video disappeared, things would be all right." He said it lightly, but his gaze never left my face.

"You hoped? What do you…" I stopped, my face heating up again, this time from the intensity of his eyes. I couldn't look away. "Christopher?"

"I…I had to help. I had to at least try to help."

"What did you do?"

"I called in a favor."

This extraordinary admission had the same effect as if he had just reached out and grazed my cheek with his fingertips. I wondered. I *wondered*.

It couldn't be easy to make a video disappear; I knew it hadn't been a simple favor. And yet he had done this. And he'd paid for the twins' college. And he'd started a charity—but no, that hadn't been for me, surely; I had simply given him the idea to do something with his money. But the other things. How could they not have been for me? And if he'd still wanted to help me, even after seeing that heinous video…

I didn't know what to say, so I said, "I mean, Jane did lose her reporter job."

"Did she really?"

"Yes. But I helped her get it back. So." I swung my arms and turned toward the dark front yard; I couldn't look at him any longer.

"You did. Of course you did." There was a knowing smile in his voice, and I looked sharply back at him. His expression had gone all soft; he looked—oh God, I don't know how he looked; it was becoming increasingly difficult for me to process anything.

"Anyway." I shivered dramatically. "Cold out here. Not as cold as Zurich, though, eh? Ha. Ha." *Why? Why did I say it?!*

Christopher's eyebrows shot up in surprise. Now he knew I had googled him—I was a walking, talking fiasco.

"Just kidding!" I said heartily. *Why?* "Gotta go, bye."

I had started toward the door when I felt his hand on my elbow and heard him say softly, "Rachel—"

I stopped, unable to face him. Still turned away from him, I said, "Yes?"

He dropped his hand. "You must know that I did it all for you." His voice was gentle enough that I might have imagined it.

My heart thudded. "Because...because of..." I couldn't think of a single possible reason, anything that might explain all the things he'd done.

"I couldn't live knowing that you thought I was some horrible person."

"Right." I looked down at my boots. "So it was because of that. Because of the things I said about you in July."

"Yes, it was—" He stopped, sounding frustrated, and then his hand was on my arm again. "Will you look at me?"

I whirled around. He had moved closer. His face was a mere foot away from mine.

"I might have overstated...some things." I didn't know what I was saying, but it felt like I had to say something. I didn't want to take back the things I'd said about him, because I had truly believed those things at the time. But now? Now it was like he was a different person—or I was.

"No, you were right. I was pushy and arrogant and—"

"Stop. I didn't even know you." My gaze fell to his hands, which were swinging at his sides now. He noticed and flexed his fingers self-consciously. Right: on top of everything else, Christopher Butkus had extremely attractive hands. That wasn't something I needed to know.

"Maybe not. But you saw me." He ducked his head slightly, trying to catch my eye. But I knew what kind of intense eye contact he was apt to make, so I turned my head away. I wasn't sure what would happen if I looked straight at him.

"Maybe. I don't know." I tried to think of the right words to say, to make him feel released from the judgments I'd made about him. To make him feel at peace with the kind of person he was. Without giving away the way I felt now. "Look, Christopher." I chanced a look up at his face and felt myself inhale sharply. His light blue gaze under those furrowed brows sent a shock wave through me. "Consider yourself—you know—absolved. We both said some things that day that were...not fully thought out. I don't think you're a horrible person, okay? Perhaps the opposite, actually." I bit my lip. Was that enough? Had I said too much?

He paused for several long seconds.

"Okay. Thank you. That means a lot, coming from you."

"Coming from me, because I rarely have anything good to say about anybody?" I let out a nervous laugh.

"Yep. Exactly." He half smiled, reflecting my awkwardness back at me. "Rachel Weiss, confidence slayer."

"Well, here, you can have some of that confidence back. Not

too much, though! Wouldn't want you to get cocky." I mimed giving him something with both hands.

He laughed and pretended to take the nothing I was offering him. We both flinched when our hands touched, which led to us doing a little shuffle, each of us trying to maintain a respectable distance.

This isn't awkward at all. I tried to look unconcerned, but really I was a little disturbed by the awkward jig we'd just performed. We were being weirdos. I had to end this on a sane note.

"All right, so, I think we've...reached an agreement. We can put all that silliness behind us. Right?"

"Absolutely." He gave a short nod. "I'll have my people fax your people the documents tomorrow. Pleasure doing business with you."

I stared at him. "You are such a nerd."

A real, genuine laugh escaped him, and I felt myself grin at the sound of it. He held out his hand to shake mine. "Friends?"

I gave his hand a firm squeeze. It was just as large, warm, and dry as I remembered from our first meeting. Honestly, my heart went out to the poor souls living in the world with chilly, moist hands—they didn't stand a chance. I let go of Christopher's before any inappropriate stirrings could make themselves known.

"Friends," I agreed.

"Excellent." He held my gaze for a long beat, the way only he could do. It seemed like he was considering his next words carefully.

And then, behind him, my mother's face appeared in the window of the front door—well, the top half of her face. She must have been standing on tiptoe to see out.

"Go!" I waved Christopher away. "She'll eat you alive if she sees you."

Without stopping to ask what that was supposed to mean, he slipped off toward the street. As Mom flung the door open to demand that I come back inside, I heard him drive away.

And, sappy as it may be, nothing Mom said for the rest of the night fazed me, because I was floating above it all, replaying that conversation with Christopher Butkus again and again. It warmed me better than pie.

CHAPTER 31

"I CAN'T STOP LOOKING at my hand."

"You're drunk."

"Just tipsy on champagne and romance." I sat on Sumira's bedroom floor, my back against her bed. I held my hands up in front of my face. "I love my henna."

Sumira, Amy, and Eva tumbled down around me in a heap of colorful fabric. I picked up Sumira's hands and gazed at them.

"You are going to make the most beautiful bride." These words brought out a chorus of fervent agreement from Amy and Eva. "Remember to thank your mom for agreeing to let us have champagne at the *mehndi* party."

"Pfft. My mom loves champagne; don't even worry about it." She flopped backward onto a throw pillow.

"Was it just me or was your cousin Maira glaring at you all evening?" Amy dug through her clutch for her ChapStick.

"Yeah, she's a teensy bit bitter that I'm getting married first. She's been dating her boyfriend for five years."

"Jesus." Amy swiped on some ChapStick and then fished a bottle of Advil from her clutch and started handing out pills. "Here, everyone take some. We can't have any hangovers tomorrow."

"Big day." Eva tossed a cheeky smirk in Sumira's direction.

"The biggest." I felt my eyes tearing up as I smiled at my gorgeous bridal bestie.

After we'd all swallowed our Advil, Eva said, "Okay, but seriously? The way Ajay was looking at you tonight?"

"And the way you were looking at him!" Amy squealed. "You guys are so in love."

Sumira looked uncharacteristically bashful, her long lashes sweeping her cheeks as she gazed down at her lap. "Yeah. We are."

This elicited a chorus of *aww*s. And then Amy started reminiscing about how nervous she and Ryan had been the night before their own wedding. I straightened up and examined my reflection in the full-length mirror that still hung in Sumira's half-packed bedroom. My hair was falling loose from its chignon, and my face glimmered with the remnants of tonight's festive gold eyeshadow and luminous pink blush. I touched my cheek. In my hot-pink sari, I looked like a confection. And as my best friends discussed the most romantic evenings of their lives, my mind wandered to...well.

I dug my phone out of the pocket of my sari and held it at arm's length, tilting it to find the most flattering angle. I snapped a selfie with a coy, closed-lipped smile.

"Excuse me, what are you doing?" I gave a guilty jolt as Eva spoke over my shoulder. "Shouldn't we be in that selfie?"

"Oh, right, of course!" I took another one with the three of them posing behind me. And then, as they returned to their conversation and started pulling out pajamas and toothbrushes, I opened a new Instagram message and attached the first photo.

"What are you doing?" Eva screeched again, her hand whipping out and stealing my phone.

"Hey!"

"Girl." Sumira was in my face now, her expression severe. "Spill. Now."

"I was just…" I held up my hands innocently. And then, inhibitions softened by all the champagne from earlier, I spilled. "I was going to send that to Christopher."

"What?!"

"No."

"Rachel!"

"Come on! I'm in a hot-pink dress, covered in glitter, drunk on romance. Is it so wrong to want to share that?"

"With him? Yes." Eva zipped my phone in the pocket of her backpack.

"Because he…" I trailed off, trying to remember all the objections I'd had about Christopher before.

"Mm-hmm. Yep." Eva nodded.

"Right. Okay." I trailed off. Eva eyed me beadily. It was fine. I could always send him the photo tomorrow if I still wanted to.

Sumira stopped at her closet on her way to the bathroom; she opened it and fingered the exquisitely detailed red-and-gold gown she was going to wear the next day. She looked almost afraid to touch it. And all thought of Christopher Butkus went *poof.* All I could see at that moment was the look on my friend's face, half-elated and half-terrified. I stood and hugged her from behind, laying my head on her shoulder.

"I'm getting married," she whispered.

"You're getting married." We took a deep breath together.

"Time for bed, ladies!" Amy waved her toothbrush like a conductor's baton. We trooped into the bathroom behind her to wash off the night's festivities to make room for the next day's.

The day passed in a beautiful blur. I didn't have time to think about anything other than what was happening in the moment: hair and makeup, my emerald-green sari, Sumira and Ajay exchanging vows underneath a tent of flowers. There was one dizzy, surreal moment when I realized my best friend was getting married (married!) to a guy I hardly knew. But it passed. Her life was not about me, I knew that. Plus, Ajay looked damn good. If I had to guess, I'd say he'd been lifting weights every day since Sumira's work party, which told me he knew he'd snagged a woman way out of his league and was trying hard to deserve her. He'd better keep that up.

And then it was time for the dreaded moment—no offense to Sumira's cousin Souma, but she had some nutty ideas about the bridesmaid dance. We'd had to talk her out of an interpretive rendition of Sumira's life from birth to death. Her second idea was to act out the history of mankind, culminating in the marriage of Sumira and Ajay. Very into the idea of setting the circle of life to song and dance, that one. We finally settled on the simple idea of—well, okay, it was still a bit complicated.

The music began, and I ran out ahead of the other girls with a tambourine to warm up the crowd. I skipped around the stage like a court jester, for such was my artistic instruction from Souma, who had deemed that I had the "right presence" for it—whatever that meant. (Nothing good, surely.) As I was jangling the tambourine above my head, I thought I glimpsed a certain face in the crowd, but I shook it off, sure I was imagining it. I focused instead on Sumira and Ajay, sitting in the seats of honor before me like the king and queen. And then the other girls joined me, and I swapped the tambourine for a handheld mask of Ajay's face. The girls swarmed around me, feigning swooning fits as I flexed imaginary muscles and blew them kisses. Then we launched into our dance number, which for me (as Ajay) involved a lot of masculine foot stomping as the girls shimmied and twirled.

As I spun around with one of the girls, I glimpsed the face in the crowd again, and with a whooshing feeling as though the stage had dropped out from under me, I realized I wasn't imagining anything: Christopher Butkus was out there, his face alight with laughter as he watched me. The beat of the Bollywood music carried me on, and I went through the motions that Souma had drilled into us: sprinkle the pepper, push the roof away, sneeze in your elbow. It was all I could do to focus on the beat; I couldn't let myself look back at Christopher, though a voice in my head was screaming at the top of her lungs, *What is he doing here?*

Then the music changed and I tossed the Ajay mask to Sumira, who caught it, and the groomsmen stomped onto the stage to tumultuous applause. We paired off, dancing our way through the throes of romance and then, as the melody swelled, we fell into each other's arms to gasps and sighs from the crowd. My dance partner, Ajay's brother, was so dedicated to his performance that he grasped my buttocks quite firmly. When he dipped me, I let my gaze find Christopher: he shook his head and mimed cracking his knuckles, glaring at my partner, and I let out a surprised caw of laughter. Souma shot me a furious look from under her sweaty hair—though this was more comical than threatening, given that we were both hunched over, performing a sort of Cossack dance move. I took her glare to heart, however, and didn't look at Christopher again for the rest of the performance.

When it was over, it took a while for the crowd to settle down, and then it was time for the bride and groom's first dance. The song was sweet and slow. I hid myself in a far corner near the stage, ostensibly watching them dance, but, in truth, I wasn't processing what I was seeing. I was frozen. A small part of me thought I should probably go talk to Christopher. But that seemed impossible. My mind stuttered over the question of why and how he had come to be here. I was grateful for the two hundred wedding guests—surely he wouldn't be able to find me. It wasn't that I didn't want to see him; it was only that it felt too important and too confusing for me to contemplate. That moment, the night of Thanksgiving, came back to me: the feeling of his hand in mine, the unsaid words that had been forming on his lips...What would he have said if my mom hadn't interrupted?

The song ended and another more lively one started. The crowd around me thinned as people joined the dance floor. I allowed myself to scan the room, but I didn't see him, and I thought maybe he'd left. Maybe he had been invited for some work reason; maybe he knew Ajay. That was it. If he had left after seeing me, then that had to be the end—he had no interest in me any longer. Probably he'd left to avoid having to talk to me. At this thought, it was like the music dimmed, like my lungs deflated. I thought of finding Eva and Amy, but they would be dancing with their partners, a thought that paralyzed me with something close to sadness. *Dance, Rachel*, I told myself sternly. *This is Sumira's wedding. Snap out of it and dance, Rachel.*

"Rachel."

He was there. He was at my side, and he was wearing a suit but no tie, top button undone, and I was at eye level with a tuft of dark chest hair, and this acted as a potent reminder that underneath his suit was his naked body, and my blood zinged through my veins as I looked up at Christopher Butkus's face.

"What the hell are you doing here?" I said, because I am that smooth.

"Sumira invited me." He wore a familiar little smirk, and he spoke in a low, amused voice as though we were continuing a conversation we'd just been having.

"Why?" This caught me off guard. I'd never liked surprises, and this felt like someone was playing a prank on me. The strip of midriff showing under my sari prickled with goose bumps.

Christopher hesitated; he didn't seem to know how to answer.

"She..." He trailed off and looked over to the center of the dance floor. I followed his gaze and saw Sumira dancing exuberantly with her new husband. Then she spotted us and threw her arms in the air, pointing at us and whooping.

"Jesus." I turned back to Christopher.

He laughed and stepped closer to me. "She said you would like to see me."

My mind jammed, caught between the urge to call Sumira names and the question Why? *Why did she say that? Why did you agree to come?*

He watched my face closely, in a moment that seemed endless. His searching gaze made me feel shy; it was all too intimate, given that we were standing a foot apart and had barely so much as touched one another. Unless you counted the touch on the elbow...the briefest of handshakes...

I looked up, poised to ask him what he'd wanted to say that night, when the song changed to something slow, and Christopher held out a hand.

"Dance with me?" There was no hint of embarrassment in his voice. He was the same confident, cocky man he'd been back in July, but this time it was doing *everything* for me. A three-alarm fire couldn't have stopped me from taking his hand and following him onto the dance floor.

His palms grazed the bare skin of my midriff before settling around my waist. My body erupted with chills as I twined my arms around his neck. It was hard to look at him—and it was hard not to. His jaw was glazed with stubble, and his eyes were crinkled in a smile. He'd gotten a haircut; his light brown hair was neat and tidy on the sides but messy up top. I wondered if he'd styled it that way on purpose or if he had run his hands through it absentmindedly. I guessed the latter.

And his cologne—I'd never been able to resist a good man scent. It was my fatal weakness. Standing this close to him, with my face inches from the crook of his neck, it was all I could do not to lean in and take a big whiff.

After a few slow revolutions on the spot, he spoke.

"Rachel." Now his voice was husky, a little unsure. He cleared his throat and tried again. "These last six months, I've thought about you more than I care to say. More than was appropriate, I'm sure."

A bushfire erupted in my drawers. If the next words out of his mouth were that he'd wallpapered his house with images of my face with the eyes cut out, I still would want to jump him. But I bottled my lust up inside and gazed at him with polite puzzlement. Like a lady.

"Everything I've done the last few months has been with you in mind," he continued. "You've been my conscience. The angel on my shoulder."

A snort escaped me—I couldn't help it. Me, an angel, honestly. His fingers tightened convulsively around my waist and a smoldering look crossed his face before he let out a little laugh.

"I know." His voice was rough as he leaned closer. "You, an angel?" His breath ruffled my hair, and all laughter ceased immediately as the breath caught in my throat. "But it's true. I consulted you—the Rachel in my mind—for every decision. You made me try harder. To be a good person."

Something in his voice had broken; it quavered, whether with lust or emotion I didn't know. My mouth worked, trying unsuccessfully to form a response.

Finally I managed a small "I'm glad."

"And," I added, suddenly fearing I'd been very rude, "thank you. For everything you've done for my family. Thank you so—"

"Don't thank me. It was selfish, all of it. I did it because I—"

The slow song ended; the music blared suddenly, and colorful lights flashed. Some sort of group dance was starting, and I couldn't have cared less.

"What?" I shouted over the deafening noise.

"Because I—" he shouted back, and people were dancing around us, and there was a sudden fear in his eyes.

"Say it, Christopher Butkus." Flashing lights played across his face. "I dare you."

There was a crescendo in the music and he let out a sort of groan and buried his face in my neck.

He picked me up and spun me around, not caring that half of the wedding guests were staring at us. "I love you, Rachel Weiss. And if there's anything I can ever do to—"

I launched myself toward him, only vaguely aware of the whistles and cheers that surrounded us as I finally, *finally* kissed Christopher Butkus. We were in the center of a dancing circle, and all of a sudden flower petals were raining down on us. We looked up and laughed, pink and white petals sprinkling onto our cheeks and hair. Everyone oohed and aahed, twirling around and raising their arms to the gentle downpour. I felt, as I brushed a petal from Christopher's smooth cheek, like my face might split in half from smiling so wide. He tugged my hand and spun me in against his chest and then out again, and I knew in my bones that I would remember this moment for the rest of my life.

"Welcome to my humble abode."

We were back in my apartment. It was very late, and we'd been sent home with a box of leftover wedding cake.

"I've always wondered where exactly you lived." Christopher took off his jacket and hung it on the hook by the door.

"Did I ever tell you I saw your house on Halloween?" Damn. Of course I'd never told him that. I was just tipsy. Not as tipsy as I should have been after my friend's wedding—but after that kiss, I'd been too distracted to keep drinking.

"You did?" He tilted his head, surprised.

"Please don't run away, I'm not a stalker, I swear. I was walking home and I saw you giving candy to trick-or-treaters."

"Why didn't you say hello?" He sounded so innocent, and it reminded me of one of the things I liked about him: he was genuine, not snarky or jaded.

"Because." I laughed like it was obvious. "We sort of hated each other until tonight. Or until Thanksgiving, I guess."

"*Hate* is a strong word, Rachel." He took a few steps closer and slipped my shawl gently off my shoulders.

"Well. You know what I mean. I couldn't just casually stop by. But you have a nice house. I liked the ghosts."

"Oh yeah, those are fun. I meant for the kids to take them, but I don't think they realized…"

I didn't respond. He clutched my shawl in both hands. I didn't want to talk about Tootsie Pop ghosts anymore.

"Anyway, you're more than welcome to stop by now. I mean, next time you're…in the vicinity."

We both grew quiet. I could tell that he didn't know what to say next any more than I did. Neither of us wanted to discuss the future, to try to put a label on this yet. And neither of us could stop gazing at the other. Without a word, I headed for the kitchen and returned with two forks. We settled on the couch and I handed him one.

"Straight from the box?" he said.

"I'm a rebel."

"I know." His voice was husky. I looked at him quickly and then away again; the tension between us was almost unbearable. But I didn't want to act on it just yet, because I wanted to let it linger: the anticipation, the cake and champagne, the getting-to-know-you conversation with this gorgeous man.

"Tell me everything about yourself," I said, just as he asked, "How's work going?" We laughed, and I told him I'd had this idea about maybe starting a consultancy for teaching tech workers about important social topics, and he didn't make fun of me or say I didn't have enough experience but listened and offered up ideas. We talked about my volunteer work, and his charity and his business, and I found myself drinking up every word, even about work stuff that I would've considered boring a few months before.

We had moved closer on the couch, the cake abandoned on the coffee table. His arm was along the back of the cushions, close enough that I could feel his warmth, though he wasn't touching me.

"Rachel." He hesitated, and I got the feeling that he wanted to say something he'd been thinking about for a while. "You were honest with me in a way no one else has ever been. You made me think about myself, the type of person I wanted to be. You couldn't have been with me back then, this summer, not when you were repulsed by me. Knowing that you once felt that way about me and that I've, somehow, managed to make you..."

He trailed off, and we gazed at each other, the moment sticky with promise.

"That I've managed to make you," he continued, his voice a low rumble, "not hate me...that you've seen the worst of me and now, maybe, seen the best of me..."

I moved closer, close enough to smell his aftershave and see a crumb of chocolate cake on his bottom lip.

"I don't think I've seen the best of you quite yet, Christopher."

His arm shifted behind me, and I startled to feel the warm touch of his fingers on the back of my neck. He moved in and I braced for his kiss, but instead he lifted my hair and kissed the nape of my neck, his fingers toying with the wispy curls there. He lingered, kissing down to the top of my shoulder and back up behind my ear, and the warmth of his breath sent fiery waves through me.

"I've wanted to do that since the night I first met you at your parents' house, when you turned your back on me mid conversation." He spoke without lifting his mouth from my skin. "Incredibly rude."

"If that's the reaction you had, then maybe I should be rude to you more often." I swung one leg over him, straddling his lap.

"Don't you dare." He stood and carried me to the bedroom, where we spent the next two hours making up for a year's worth of rudeness, miscommunications, and sexual tension.

Reader, I know you will understand what I mean when I say that in those two hours I didn't have a single spare moment to think about nuns.

Afterward, as I nestled against his chest, I said, "You know, my birthday is next week, if you want to do that one thing again. As a gift to me, I mean."

He stroked my hair and said, "I would be happy to do that one thing again. And the other things. Birthday or not." I almost purred with happiness.

A moment later, he said thoughtfully, "You know what would be funny?"

"What?" I was always eager for a good joke, even at three in the morning after the best night of my life.

"If you took me to Jane's wedding as your date." He paused, and I sat up to look at him, intrigued. "Just imagine the look on your mom's face."

And with a burst of laughter, I kissed him.

DON'T MISS LAUREN'S NEXT

SCINTILLATING NOVEL!

Coming Fall 2025

ACKNOWLEDGMENTS

Thank you to my agent, Kimberly Whalen. You are the agent a writer's dreams are made of: fierce, fast, funny, and fantastic. Thank you for seeing the potential in my little book. Thank you for making my lifelong dream come true. I am so lucky to be one of your clients.

Thank you to my editor, Sabrina Flemming. Speaking of making dreams come true! The gushing words you wrote back in response to my manuscript are forever imprinted on my heart. I'm still in awe that someone as intelligent and articulate as you fell in love with my story. Your edits helped take it to the next level. Your passion helped turn it into a real, live book. Thank you, thank you, thank you!

Thank you to Tareth Mitch, S. B. Kleinman, Diane Miller-Espada, Marie Mundaca, Caroline Green, Alli Rosenthal, Carolina Martin, and the rest of the people who made this publication possible at Hachette and Forever.

There are so many incredibly kind and helpful writers on the internet, people who take the time to help aspiring writers by offering advice, critiques, query feedback, and commiseration. So many of you have helped me over the years. Thank you to all of those writers from Reddit, QueryManager, Hannah Orenstein's Facebook group, and more. Especially, thanks to the 2024 debut authors I've connected with. And a special shoutout to two podcasts that gave me the motivation to rewrite this book after the pandemic: *Bad on Paper* and *The Shit No One Tells You About Writing*.

And thanks to the IRL writing friends I've made along the way. Tara Nieuwesteeg, my accountability buddy and one of my first readers, I still can't believe I was lucky enough to meet you and Meghan at the Historical Novel Society Conference. You've been there through multiple books and through more of life's highs and lows than I could've imagined all those years ago. I'm grateful to call you a friend.

Meghan Masterson, a joyful spark of a person and a wonderful writer, the first person I told about the idea for this book: I still can't believe you're gone. I miss you.

So much love goes out to my girlfriends. First, to the members of my original group chat, Tania Asim and Jenna Tollefson. Our endless chats got me through so many boring workdays. Thank you to all the other friends I've had throughout my life, especially Maida Suljevic, Callie Nettles, Sophia Margolis, and Sue Jeong. Female friendships are sacred. I love you so much! And to the mom friends I've made since becoming a parent, thank you for the laughter and support. I'll have to write a book about toddler moms someday.

To my mom: thank you for loving us all so fiercely (with only a hint of Mrs. Bennet's trademark anxiety). You raised me to believe anything is possible with enough stubbornness and a refusal to hear the word "no." Thank you for caring about the nitty-gritty of my writing life and being my biggest cheerleader every step of the way. You're always the first person I want to share good news with. And thanks for convincing me to read my first Jane Austen when I was too young to understand half the words, and for being my go-to movie buddy for every Jane Austen adaptation.

Dad, thank you for all the dinner table conversations about literature, history, politics, science, and sump pumps. I like to believe I inherited my curiosity, sense of humor, and general awesomeness from you.

Emily and Summer, what would my life even be without sisters? Thank you for being my sidekicks, for letting me boss you around, for telling me about your lives so I can pilfer your anecdotes for my fiction. And mostly, thanks for all the laughs.

Dave, on our first date, you bought me oysters and laughed at my jokes. I've been hooked on you ever since. Thank you for being an amazing cook, for being a goofball, and for being an incredible dad. I love how excited you get about trick-or-treaters. I'm so glad I get to do life with you. And to our kids: I thought I knew what it felt like to love before I met you, but I had no idea. My life is a thousand times richer thanks to you.

A quick word of thanks to Jdate, the premier dating site for Jewish singles. I poked fun at you in this book, but I actually owe you a lot. Thanks for helping me find my Mr. Darcy, 21st-century style.

Finally, this book was born out of a lifelong love of *Pride and Prejudice* by Jane Austen, *Bridget Jones's Diary* by Helen Fielding, and the Confessions of Georgia Nicolson series by Louise Rennison. For better or for worse, I wouldn't be the writer I am today without these stories.

ABOUT THE AUTHOR

LAUREN APPELBAUM works as a technical editor and has been writing fiction since she could hold a pencil (usually when she's supposed to be doing other things). She lives in Seattle with her family.

You can find out more at:
LaurenAppelbaumBooks.com
Instagram @LaurenAppelbaum